NO ESCAPE

Linda heads up in the elevator. She leans against the back wall, watching the little red numbers tick upward. 8, 9, 10, 11, 12 . . .

And then the elevator jerks and stops.

"What the—" Linda says, pressing her floor number, 18, again. The elevator doesn't budge.

She punches her floor number again once, then twice, then a frantic machine-gun assault.

And the elevator door suddenly slides open.

Linda screams.

It's a raging inferno. Her building's on fire. She can see nothing but flames, and their heat singes her face. The fire makes a roaring sound, and it appears ready to lunge at her, cooking her instantly within the oven of the elevator. In desperation she reaches out and hits the close-door button. The elevator doors mercifully slide shut.

She hears the gears shudder back to life. But instead of beginning to climb again, the elevator starts to drop. *Good,* she thinks instinctively. *Get me down to the ground so I can get out. Away from the fire!*

But the elevator isn't descending floor by floor. It's going far faster than it should be.

"No," Linda gasps. "Oh, dear God, no!"

The elevator drops and begins to plunge . . .

Books by Robert Ross

WHERE DARKNESS LIVES

DON'T CLOSE YOUR EYES

CAUSE OF FEAR

Published by Pinnacle Books

CAUSE
OF
FEAR

ROBERT ROSS

PINNACLE BOOKS
Kensington Publishing Corp.
http://www.kensingtonbooks.com

For Diana

PROLOGUE

Linda Leigh suddenly knows what it feels like to be burned alive.

She awakes to flames. Her room is already consumed, the acrid stink of burning rubber and synthetic fabrics assaulting her more savagely than even the blazing heat. Linda screams for her life, but knows no one will hear her. The fire's roar is like that of a living creature, an angry beast intent on death, louder than any cry for help she could try to make.

Only her bed remains untouched by the flames. She pulls her sheets up around her as if they could protect her from the encroaching cataclysm. She watches in horror as her bureau collapses into white-hot embers, her television set melts like butter, her curtains catch fire and explode.

Linda screams again. Only this time her scream feels artificial, as if she weren't really screaming at all. She stares out into the flames that dance in seemingly sadistic glee, teasing her with their plumage of orange and gold.

There's something out there, she thinks. *Something in the flames.*

Even in her terror, she tries to see what it is.

The shape is dark and shifting, but it is there. Is it a person—the person who set this fire?

Linda pulls back further behind her sheets as the fire begins to lick her bedposts. She struggles to see. What is out there?

Something large. Something enormous. Something dark, lurking behind the flames.

Come, it says.

Linda gasps. It's speaking to her, but not with words. With thoughts. Whatever it is, it is communicating with her through her mind.

Come join me, it calls.

"Who—who are you?"

The heat is stronger now, bearing in on her. The fire seems emboldened, invigorated, by the exchange of words. It surges forward, and Linda shrieks.

Feel the warmth of the flames.

"Help me!" Linda screams.

Feel the warmth, the inviting heat . . .

"Who are you?" she shouts again.

Come join me, Linda.

Linda begins to cry.

Join me in the flames.

"No," she whimpers.

It is only painful for a moment, and then there is bliss. Such bliss . . .

"No," Linda says again.

The fire roars in anger now, furious at her refusal. Malevolent sparks hop onto her blankets like little imps, determined to take her. She swats at them, trying to put them out, as if such action mattered when her room was already a living hell.

She feels the presence in the flames more strongly

now. It looms in toward her, a giant shape—not human. No, not human at all. Some kind of creature. Enormous—with arms, or tentacles, or wings—spreading out as if to claim her. It is so close now she can hear its breathing. A shadow passes over her bed.

You cannot fight me, it tells her. *Go ahead. Touch the beauty of my flames. See how they dance? Aren't they exquisite?*

Her sheets have caught fire now. The conflagration is upon her.

Linda screams.

Join me, the thing in the flames says again.

And just before the fire devours her, Linda sees its face: huge and overpowering, awesome and terrible, with burning eyes and a forked tongue.

Linda screams again.

CHAPTER 1

"What a dream I had last night," she tells Megan. "I woke up in the morning and my sheets were drenched."

Linda reaches for a towel to wrap around herself as they step into the sauna. The heat momentarily troubles her, taking her back to the dream.

"I dreamed I was burning to death. It was hideous. Worst dream I've ever had in my life."

"I told you to go slow on those margaritas at the party," Megan chides. "Birthday or not, sweetie, you ought to know your limit."

"I only had two," Linda tells her. She leans back against the cedar wall, letting the dry heat fill her lungs. "I would never drink too much in front of Geoff. I need to prove I'm a fit mother, after all."

"Were you surprised when he gave you the ring?" Megan grabs her hand. "Let me see it again. What a rock!"

"You bet I was surprised," Linda says, the diamond sparkling on her ring finger. "What a birthday present, huh? I can't believe how lucky I am!"

Little Linda Leigh. That's what everyone's always called her, and not only because she's short. Linda has had one of those lives that just lends itself to the term "little." Nothing very glamorous ever happens to her. Born on a farm in the Midwest, moving to Boston for college, she'd graduated and found a routine job at an insurance company. Until Geoff, she's never dated anyone spectacular. All the other guys in her life had been average joes, working the same kind of nondescript jobs she has. They haven't been unattractive, but neither have they really been handsome—which Linda figured was the best she could get, since, after all, she's hardly Jennifer Aniston herself. Her hair is mousy brown, her face is small, she gets too many freckles if she stays out in the sun too long. Her figure is okay but nothing great, which is why she's here at the gym, toning her thighs, sweating off those extra pounds. Ever since meeting Geoff she's been trying to remake herself into something more worthy of him, because Geoff—well, Geoff could be a movie star.

And he practically is, striding across the Coatsworth College campus with all those students following him around. Dr. Geoffrey Manwaring, tall and broad shouldered, with his cleft chin and iron jaw, is the darling of his department, an eminent scholar of ancient history. It seems incongruous in some ways: Geoff is only thirty-seven, yet he's a leading authority on vanished civilizations and forgotten religions. Linda always smiles when she hears him speak at symposiums, going on about the pharaohs of Egypt or the hanging gardens of Babylon, because he looks so young, younger even than his years, with only a slight frosting of gray at his temples lending him an air of distinguished seniority.

And now he's asked her to marry him. As soon

as his divorce is final, they'll be wed in his home-town of Sunderland, in the rolling hills of western Massachusetts, in a white chapel where all his an-cestors have been married, dating back to the seven-teenth century. It is a dream come true for Linda. Everything is perfect.

Everything except—

"What's the kid gonna say?"

Linda withdraws her hand from Megan's grip. "Oh, I dread telling him. Geoff thinks we ought to do it together. I suppose he's right. Josh is going to have to get used to me sooner or later."

"I don't get it, Linda," Megan says. "You are a likable girl. You are sweet. You are kind. You have practically gotten down on your knees to beg the brat to like you. You have bought him gifts, you have taken him to the circus, you have done every-thing you can. You have been wonderful to him!"

"But I'm not his mother." The heat is getting a bit too intense in the sauna for Linda. She stands, making sure her towel is tucked securely around her. "I'm going to shower, Megan. Can I give you a lift home?"

"No, sweetie, Randy's meeting me. You going out to Sunderland with Geoff this weekend?"

Linda nods. "Yeah. We thought we'd tell Josh when we're out in the country. He's always in a better mood out there."

"Good luck."

"Thanks."

She heads out of the sauna and hangs her towel on a hook. She steps into the shower stall, adjust-ing the water. Her nightmare still troubles her. If she believed in the symbolism of dreams, she'd say it has less to do with too many margaritas than her constant anxiety about Josh. The one glitch in her happiness is that Geoff's eight-year-old son despises her.

His eight-year-old son—for whom the sun rises and sets! Geoff completely adores the boy, and the feeling is mutual. They're forever wrestling on the floor or tossing balls in the park, or laughing at this joke or that comedian, or making goo-goo eyes at each other through the rearview mirror in the car. Josh is Geoff's "best buddy," and the boy looks at his dad with stars in his eyes.

Except when he sits next to Linda, and then it's daggers.

Oh, Josh is polite to her if his father is around—but behind Geoff's back, the boy will stick his tongue out or call her names like "shrimpy" or "munchkin." He knows she won't say a word because a scolding from Geoff would only further drive a wedge between Linda and the boy.

"You'll see," Josh has told her on more than one occasion. "My mother is going to come back, and my father will forget all about you."

It's terribly sad. Josh's mother left them nearly four years ago. The boy's memory of her is dim but beatific. He doesn't remember the scenes Geoff has described for Linda: Gabrielle throwing tantrums, mood-swinging from ice princess to manic monster, threatening to kill Geoff with a kitchen knife. Once he'd come home from class to find her in bed with the paperboy, a sixteen-year-old kid with acne, and it took a great deal of negotiation to keep the boy's parents from bringing a charge of statutory rape against Gabrielle. Josh doesn't know about any of that. He just remembers his mother as a beautiful angel, which Linda supposes is a good thing. But that means he'll forever see Linda as a she-devil intent on taking his mother's place.

She towels herself dry and gets dressed. She's meeting Geoff for dinner at a fancy restaurant downtown with two of his colleagues. She's met them before: Jim and Lucy Oleson, nice enough people, but both are professors and very smart, and around them Linda's always felt a little self-conscious. They use words like "paradigm" and "egregious" and "deconstructing." They write books and give lectures on theory for a living. Linda enters claims for auto accidents, and punches a time clock at the end of her workday.

Gabrielle was brilliant, she thinks, looking at herself in the mirror as she applies her lipstick. She would have become a great scholar and author herself. She was a student of Geoff's when he first came to the college, and he thought she was the most fascinating woman he'd ever met. Absolutely brilliant. She knew as much about ancient Babylon as he did. Sometimes more.

And she was beautiful. Linda has seen the photographs. The ones of her wedding to Geoff are burned into her brain. Blonde and ethereal, Gabrielle was statuesque, elegant, and assured in her white satin wedding dress. Who knew what demons lurked behind that stunning façade?

Josh looks like her, Linda thinks as she hurries out of the gym to her car. More like her than Geoff, to be honest. Blond, already tall for his age, with Gabrielle's same crystal blue eyes.

"He'll come to love me," Linda tries to convince herself as she starts her ignition. "He's got to."

* * *

"You've always been good with children," her mother had told her over the phone. "You were the favorite baby-sitter of all the kids in the neighborhood when you were in high school."

"That's because I was their only baby-sitter, Mom, since I never had any dates."

"That is not true, Linda. What about Andy Hecker?"

"Yeah," Linda had replied, laughing. "What about him?"

Andy Hecker wasn't exactly boyfriend material. He was a gangly, pimply kid who preferred building monster models to practically anything else. Geek with a capital G. And all the rest of the letters in caps, too.

Still, her mother had a point. The kids in the neighborhood *had* liked her. She did fun things with them when she baby-sat. They played Twister. They made pizza from scratch, putting everything from peanuts to marshmallows on top. They stayed up late watching slasher videos.

"The boy will come to love you," Mom said, "once he realizes his mother isn't coming home."

"I hope so."

"I know so. If his father loves you as much as you say he does, the boy will come around."

Linda heard the rooster crow on her parents' farm and felt a little homesick. "If he gives me a ring as I think he will, you will come out here to Massachusetts for the wedding, won't you? You and Daddy both?"

"Of course we will, Linda, honey. Would we miss our baby girl's trip down the aisle? And to a man as successful as Geoff?"

They thought I'd never get married, Linda thought. *They thought I'd be their old maid daughter. Hadn't I al-*

ways been the plain one, "little Linda"? Oh, won't Mom and Dad be impressed with Geoff's house, his car, his four published books?

Geoff was even more successful than Dennis Gunderson, the man Linda's sister Karen had married. Dennis owned the largest chicken-feed supply business in their home state, and Karen had thought she'd made quite the catch when she snared him. Karen hadn't gone on to college like Linda had; she'd never even left the state for so much as a day trip. But she was the beauty in the family, dark and sultry, busty and hippy. Everyone predicted she'd do better than Linda, and until Geoff had come along, Linda had believed them.

Linda remembered that day at the lake when she and Karen had been teenagers, both in high school. She would never forget it.

How could she? It was burned onto her brain.

Karen was one of the popular girls, with her dark hair and small features and delicate hands. "Cute as a button," everyone called her. Linda was just small and blunt. Nobody called her anything.

"Oh, come now, Linda, don't be a spoilsport," Karen insisted.

But Linda didn't want to go out with Karen and her friends to the lake. She knew what it would be like—Karen and the girls giggling over boys, Linda lagging behind, no one paying her even the slightest notice.

"Mary Ann and Jessica asked for you especially," Karen pleaded.

"Right," Linda said. "So I could lug the cooler."

"They enjoy your company," Karen said.

Her mother piped in, scolding Linda for being a "stick in the mud." So Linda relented, heading upstairs to change into her bathing suit.

"You're not wearing that, are you?" Karen asked.

Linda had slipped into a striped red-and-blue one-piece. "Why not?"

"Never wear horizontal stripes," her sister told her. "Especially not across your butt. They make you look fat."

Linda crossed her arms across her chest. "I am not changing."

"Have it your way."

Of course, at the lake, she did feel like a fat troll. She sat with her towel wrapped around her waist, a big floppy hat on her head, her eyes hidden behind large sunglasses. Karen and the girls laughed and chatted, practically ignoring her. When Jake Gandolfini—the hottest boy in the senior class, dark hair and cleft chin and muscles—stopped by their blanket, he kept his back to Linda the whole time, flirting with Karen and her friends.

"I don't want you girls to burn out here in the hot sun," he teased.

Silly little Mary Ann dissolved into giggles. Behind her sunglasses, Linda rolled her eyes.

Jake was grinning now with a devilish idea. "Maybe I ought to put some more lotion on all of you," he said.

The girls squealed. Linda knew "all of you" didn't include her. To Jake, she was just some maiden aunt. Worse: she didn't even exist.

So, one by one, the three of them—Mary Ann, Jessica, and finally Karen—peeled down their shoulder straps so that Jake could slather their backs and shoulders and arms with Number 15 sunblock. Just before it was her turn, Karen looked over at Linda and seethed, "Not a word of this to Mom."

Linda watched from behind her dark glasses, and the image has never left her. It summed up, perfectly symbolized, completely illustrated her life before meeting Geoff: the one outside, watching as the pretty girls exposed their skin, lined up for the handsome jock to touch them, each worthy in a way Linda would never be.

Until now.

"Congratulations, Linda," Lucy Oleson tells her, clasping her hand in greeting.

"Thank you so much."

"I thought ol' Geoff here would never again take that matrimonial plunge, but you must have worked your charm," Jim says, laughing.

Geoff kisses her warmly. How good it feels to be in his arms. He smells great, as usual: that heady scent of aftershave and man sweat.

"Hello, darling," he says to her.

"Sorry I'm late. Traffic—"

"No problem," he says, holding out her chair for her as she sits down. "We were just talking a little shop."

"I just don't see Ronnie Simms getting the position," Lucy says, continuing whatever conversation they had been having before Linda's arrival. "Not with his views of historical revisionism."

"Well, he doesn't view the construct in that way, Lucy," her husband tells her. "He's a revisionist with a proclivity for obduracy. Really, I would think that . . ."

Linda feels Geoff reach under the table and take her hand. They exchange small smiles. Is it any wonder she fell in love with him?

They met cute, as they say in the movies. She was getting into a taxi from one side, he was getting in from the other.

"Uh, I was here first," she insisted.

"I flagged him down," Geoff replied.

"No, you didn't. I flagged him." She leaned in toward the driver. "Who did you stop for?"

"Me, I don' know, I just pull over." The Pakistani cabdriver just shrugged his shoulders.

"Look, miss, I distinctly held up my hand and—"

She hated being called "miss." She folded her arms across her chest. Linda guesses now she was showing, in that moment, a "proclivity for obduracy." She wasn't going to budge.

"I have a flight to catch," she told him in no uncertain terms.

A broad smile spread across Geoff's face, revealing dimples that made her melt. "Well, as it happens, so do I," he said. "Since we're both going to the airport, maybe we can share the ride?"

Funny how fate works. They learned, sitting in traffic outside Logan, that they were both going to Chicago, Linda to rent a car to drive to her hometown of Dowagiac, Michigan, to attend Karen's wedding, Geoff to deliver a talk on ancient religious practices at some seminar. Though Geoff was in first class and Linda was in coach, they managed to find an empty row somewhere over central Connecticut and sat together, finishing their conversation. They agreed to meet for a drink in Chicago on their way back.

But when Linda showed up at his hotel, eager to get away from Karen's reception and all her aunts asking her when she—Linda—was going to tie the knot, Geoff was no where to be found. *What an idiot I've been,* Linda told herself. *To think a smart, successful college professor is going to be interested in me. What a fool.*

"I'm sorry, but is this seat taken?"

She looked up. It was Geoff.

"Did you think I was standing you up?" he asked. "I apologize for being late. Some dreary academic types insisted on challenging my analysis of Zoroastrianism."

"Well," she said, laughing, "I hope you told *them.*"

He ordered a scotch and water. Linda was drinking white wine. She learned he was married—*of course*, she thought at first—but then found out his wife had left him over two years ago and he hadn't heard from her since.

"I can't say I was surprised," Geoff admitted. "Gabrielle was ill. I think she has some kind of mental illness."

"Oh, I'm sorry," Linda said.

"Well, she began acting strangely. . . ." He seemed unwilling to talk about that time. Linda suspected it had been very painful for him. Her heart melted for this handsome, gallant stranger.

"So of course, I've been concerned for her safety. I've hired private detectives to try to find her, and the police have combed dozens of states for some clue to her whereabouts. But no luck."

"I'm so sorry," she said again.

"Well, things hadn't been good between us." Geoff smiled wanly at her over his glass. "Of course, that made the police suspect foul play. When a wife disappears, there's something like a 85 percent chance the husband knows something about it."

Is this man a murderer? Linda suddenly thought. *Is he playing with me?*

"It's true," Geoff said. "So I was hauled down to the police station for a long interrogation and one detective kept giving me the evil eye. But eventually they came around to concluding that I was as clueless as they were."

Linda studied him, just to make sure.

"I have a young son," Geoff told her, and immediately Linda saw the anguish in his eyes. She saw he was no murderer. Even if he'd stopped loving his wife, his son meant the world to him. That was obvious from the look on his face when he spoke of him. "He misses his mother terribly. She wasn't a particularly attentive mother, but since she's been gone, he's kind of romanticized her."

"I suppose that's only natural," Linda said. "Every child wants a mother."

Geoff shook his head and sighed. "You know, as sick as she was, I just can't imagine how she could walk out on her own son."

"What's his name?" Linda asked.

"Joshua. He's a good kid." His eyes grew sad. "But he needs a mother."

"So what's Josh going to say about the wedding plans?"

Linda is startled back to the present. Lucy is grinning at her across the table, having asked a perfectly appropriate question, but one that rattles Linda every time she hears it.

"We're going to tell him this weekend," Geoff answers for her. "Out at the house in Sunderland."

"Well, I'm sure he'll handle it well," Lucy says. "After all, I'm sure he adores Linda."

Linda says nothing.

"Will you get married in Sunderland, too?" Lucy asks. "I remember so well your marriage to Gabrielle out there—"

"We haven't decided yet," Geoff says, looking over at Linda.

"Oh, but you *must,*" Lucy says, reaching across the table to tap Linda's hand. "The chapel out there is so quaint. Get married in the spring, when the forsythia is in bloom. That's what Geoff and Gabrielle did. Oh, my, it was so lovely. The church was decorated with daffodils and white lilacs . . ."

"Well," Linda says, finally speaking up, "it might be nice to do something original to us."

"And a date?" Lucy's asking, not listening. "Have you set a date?"

"Well, the divorce won't be final until the fall," Geoff says.

Jim leans in to rest his chin in his palm. "Why'd you wait so long, buddy? Gabrielle's been gone for a long time, and you can file for divorce one year after desertion."

Linda looks over at Geoff to see how he'll answer. She believes him when he says he fell out of love with Gabrielle long before she left. Still, she *had* been brilliant and beautiful, two things Linda finds difficult believing about herself.

"She's the mother of my son," Geoff says simply. "And he's never stopped talking about her since the day she left."

They all nod.

"Besides," Geoff adds, smiling and reaching over to squeeze Linda's hand. "There was no great motivator until this little lady came along."

She smiles. She feels her cheeks start to burn. At first she assumes she's blushing. She often blushes when Geoff pays her a compliment. It's something that goes back to grammar school, when she'd turn beet red when the teacher called on in her in class. But then she realizes it's more than mere blushing: her face actually begins to hurt. It feels the way it does when she occasionally holds the hair dryer too close to her skin. It feels the way—

—the way it did in her dream last night.

She looks up. The restaurant is suddenly in flames.

Her companions at the table are engulfed in a ferocious conflagration, their skin melting. She sees first Jim, then Lucy, wither and crumple under the flames, as if they were nothing more than cardboard. Then Geoff, too: the man she loves, the man she thought she'd never find, with his handsome face caught on fire.

That's how it is, the thing in the flames tells her. *That's how it will be.*

Linda screams.

CHAPTER 2

"Darling!" Geoff shouts. "What's wrong?"

Her hands are covering her face against the approach of the flames.

"Linda! Are you all right?"

The heat . . . It's gone.

She peers between her fingers. There's no fire. Geoff is fine. Jim and Lucy stare at her as if she were a madwoman.

And might possibly she be?

"I—I felt—fire," she stammers.

"Fire?" Lucy asks.

The waiter has approached their table, fluttering his hands and looking anxious. "Is everything all right?"

"Yes," Geoff says, waving him away. "Bring my fiancée some water, please."

Linda realizes patrons at the other tables are looking at her oddly.

"I thought—I felt this heat—I thought there was a fire—"

"It's okay, darling. There's no fire."

"I thought I saw it," she says, breaking into a sweat now. "It was like a dream I had last night—"

"Maybe we ought to order some food," Jim suggests. "When Lucy's light-headed she gets hot flashes, too."

"Oh, Jim," Lucy says, smirking.

"Are you all right, Linda?" Geoff asks. "Do you want to go for a walk outside?"

"Maybe." She touches her brow and feels the sweat there. "I'll just go to the ladies' room for a moment."

"Do you want me to go with you?" Lucy asks.

"No, no, I'll be fine."

Linda stands, hurrying across the room, avoiding the strange looks from the other guests. She pushes open the door of the ladies' room and stands over the sink, splashing water on her face. She's frightened by the vision. Her heart is racing. But she's embarrassed, too. What must Jim and Lucy think? *Geoff's little girlfriend . . . What a flake.*

But what did it mean? Had her dream so traumatized her she was now having flashbacks? What did they call it? Post-traumatic stress disorder? She'd seen it on Oprah, she thinks.

It had felt so real. Her cheeks were still hot. Maybe she ought to make an appointment with a doctor.

When she returns to the table they're back to discussing historical theory, debating whether Ronnie Simms, whoever he is, should get the chair of some committee or another. Linda tunes out, concentrating on her salad. Geoff holds her hand under the table. She gets through the dinner with some forced smiles and again apologizes for her outburst when they're all saying goodbye. Jim and Lucy assure her it was nothing, but she knows they're going home shaking their heads over Geoff's choice for a bride.

"Do you want me to stay?" Geoff asks when they're back at her apartment.

"No, I'll be okay."

"You sure? Darling, I'm not going to leave until I know you're okay."

God, she loves him. She encircles his neck with her arms. Actually, she'd love for him to stay. To feel his strong, hard body next to hers all night. There's nothing she likes more than waking up beside him, leaning up on her elbow to stare down at him, running her fingers through the nest of black hair on his chest. Geoff is the most exquisite lover she's ever known. Not that she's had all that many: in her twenty-five years, she can count all her men on one hand. But now that she's found Geoff, she doesn't feel the need to ever sample anybody else, ever again.

Yet as much as she might like him to stay, Josh is waiting for Geoff, and the boy always gets very upset when his father doesn't come home. It's a mood only encouraged and made worse by his nanny's obvious disapproval of his father's extracurricular behavior. Julia is an old crone who had been Gabrielle's devoted companion, and who insists that Geoff is still a married man and shouldn't be setting a bad example for his son. Linda can't imagine Julia staying on with them after they're married; she makes no secret of her disdain for Geoff's intended new wife. But Josh is attached to the old woman, and has been ever since his mother walked out on him.

So it's best that Geoff not spend the night. He tells Linda she needs a good night's sleep and that if she still feels jittery in the morning, maybe she ought to give her doctor a call. She insists she'll be fine. Still, Geoff says he'll call her once he's home just to say goodnight one more time.

She calls Megan once he's gone.

"Did I wake you?"

"No, we're just watching Letterman. What's up?"

"Remember the dream I told you about?"

"Yeah. How could I forget?"

"Well, tonight, at the restaurant, I had it again. Except it was a daydream. We were all burning alive."

"Sweetie, what have you been smoking?"

"Nothing. Megan, what's going on with me?"

"You were anxious about having dinner with them, weren't you? Geoff's friends from the college."

"Yes, but—"

"You ought to get your doctor to give you some Xanax. Sweetie, those little pills have done wonders for my well being."

Linda sighs. "Maybe I *have* been overanxious ever since we started planning the wedding."

"That's all it is, sweetie. Nerves can do all sorts of weird things."

Nerves. After she hangs up, Linda heads into the bathroom to study her face in the mirror. There are definitely lines creeping in around her eyes. Worry lines. She manages a small smile. If she tells Megan about those, next she'll be suggesting Botox.

The phone rings. It's Geoff.

"Imagine I'm there beside you tonight," he whispers.

"Oh, I will. I always do."

"Are you looking forward to this weekend, darling?"

She doesn't want to lie but to admit how anx-

ious she is about telling Josh their wedding plans
wouldn't do right now. She wants to prove to Geoff
she's strong, grounded, solid. "Of course I am,"
she says. "I love the Sunderland house."

"It should be beautiful. We'll take a boat out on
the lake."

She purrs, smiling.

"I love you, Linda," he tells her.

She feels as if she'll cry.

"I love you, too, Geoff."

She sleeps like an angel. No dreams. Just blissful
rest, with Geoff's words echoing in her mind all
night.

Friday afternoon comes around, sunny and glorious. Linda's arranged to get out of work early,
and Geoff has no Friday classes. So as soon as Josh
is out of school for the day, Geoff swings by Linda's
apartment in his black Range Rover. Josh is in the
back seat, already watching a video.

"Is that *Spider-Man?*" Linda asks. "Wasn't that a
great movie?"

They'd seen it together at the theater, she and
Geoff and Josh. It was clear that the boy had loved
the movie as he watched it. He was jumping up and
down in his seat, laughing and calling out "Watch it!"
whenever the Green Goblin would appear. But af-
terward, when Linda had asked him if he'd liked
it, he just shrugged.

He does the same thing now, not making eye
contact with Linda as she slides into the front seat.
She sighs, looking over at Julia, who sits primly beside him, her gnarled hands folded in the black cloth
of her lap.

"Hello, Julia," Linda says.

"Miss Leigh." The old woman nods.

"Well, the weather's cooperating anyway," Geoff says as he maneuvers his way into traffic, heading for the Massachusetts Turnpike. "It's gonna be a spectacular weekend."

"Sure looks that way," Linda says, the irony not lost on her.

She lifts an eye to study the pair in the backseat through the rearview mirror. Josh is a pretty little boy, with long black eyelashes over big, round, intense blue eyes. He's as blond as his father is dark, a constant reminder to all of them of his absent mother. He's wearing a yellow-and-green striped shirt and red cargo pants, a colorful contrast to the old woman seated beside him. Julia is in her late sixties, a dour-faced woman with a maze of wrinkles lining her face, her dyed black hair pulled back severely in a bun. She wears a black dress and a white blouse. On her feet pink Nike sneakers seem incongruous, but she needs them to keep up with Josh.

The ride out to western Massachusetts is uneventful, the concrete of the city quickly giving way to green rolling hills. Josh is intent on his video, and Julia comes alive only to occasionally offer him a drink box of orange juice or a handful of granola. Up front, Linda and Geoff make small talk.

"You feeling better?" he asks.

"Much. Guess all I needed was a good night's rest."

"Jim called this morning to ask how you were."

"Oh, Geoff, they must think I'm a total dingbat."

"No, not at all. They were just worried."

She shakes her head, looking out the window as they pass cornfields and cows grazing peacefully in the midmorning sun. "It just seemed so real," she says. "The fire."

"The fire?"

The voice startles her. It's Josh, from the backseat.

"Did you see a fire?" the boy asks her.

It's unusual for him to address anything to her, so she turns around to look at him kindly.

"It was just a dream, Josh. A silly dream."

"I dreamed about fire, too," he says.

"Hush, now, Joshua," Julia tells him.

But the boy is persistent. "It was really hot. Fire everywhere. It was burning me up."

Linda looks over at Geoff, who seems troubled. "Josh, why didn't you tell me about this dream?" he asks.

"Dr. Manwaring," Julia says, "it was just a child's nightmare. I saw no reason to trouble you."

"Did it frighten you, Josh?" Linda asks.

He doesn't answer. He's apparently decided that he'll go no further in sharing any of his thoughts with Linda. He just settles back into watching *Spider-Man*.

"I had a similar dream," Linda tells Julia. "Isn't that peculiar?"

The old woman just shrugs. Linda turns around and faces front again.

"Here we are," Geoff announces, and they pull into the driveway of their destination.

The Manwaring family is an old one in these parts. There's a family tree etched onto the wall in the study, dating all the way back to Rafe de Mesnil Waring, a companion of William the Conqueror in the eleventh century. Geoff's great, great-grandfather built this house in Sunderland in 1872. It's been enlarged and remodeled many times since, but the exterior looks pretty much the same as it did more than a hundred years ago. It's an early Victorian with three floors, two gables, and a central fireplace. Fifteen acres of wood and farmland stretch behind it, most of it overgrown and wild now. A flat, pristine lake, surrounded by pine trees, reflects the afternoon sun. Geoff, being an only child, inherited the estate when his father died, but now uses it only on the occasional weekend or during summer vacations.

"First thing we need to do is air the place out," Julia says, walking around the living room and den, throwing open the windows.

Linda stifles a little surge of resentment. *She acts as if she's the wife here, as if she's the mistress of the house.* Julia has been with the family since soon after Josh was born, so she's opened and closed this house numerous times, while Linda still feels like a guest.

"Then we need to pick some lilacs," Julia announces, tousling Josh's hair as the boy lugs in his backpack. "Oh, how your mother loved the scent of lilacs in this house."

"I'll go pick them!" Josh offers, suddenly alert at the mention of his mother.

The nanny looks over toward her employer. "Is that all right, Dr. Manwaring? The bushes are all in bloom."

Geoff is carrying in folders of student papers he needs to work on over the weekend. "Sure. Maybe you could help him, Linda. Don't let him pick too many."

They exchange a look. It's one of those moments

they try to find where Linda can spend some quality "alone time" with Josh. She smiles.

"Not the white ones," Julia tells her. "Only pick the purple lilacs."

"Why not the white ones?" Linda asks. "I love white lilacs."

The old woman stiffens. "Well, it's just that—well, we only ever have purple—"

Linda smiles. "Then maybe it's time for a change." She watches Julia's face darken.

"Josh!" Linda calls. "Wait up!"

She follows the boy out the door.

They *are* beautiful. Dozens of lilac bushes line the driveway and the side of the house. Their fragrance is so strong it reminds Linda of the perfume counter at Macy's. She sees several varieties of purple, some dark, some barely lavender. And scattered among them, here and there, are several lacy whites.

"Josh!" Linda calls.

The boy has disappeared into the yard somewhere. Linda walks into the cluster of bushes, almost dizzy from the aroma. She begins snapping clumps of the flowers from the branches, choosing two whites for every purple.

She breathes in the fresh air, so exhilarating after weeks in the city. She glances off toward the trees that ring the property. What a beautiful day. Simply glorious. So full of sunlight. She hears a rustle in the trees and then spots the most magnificent bird she has ever seen, red and gold with an enormous wingspan. It swoops out from a tall branch and circles gracefully over her head before disappearing once again in the woods.

She spots Josh between the leaves, on the other side of the bush.

"Are you playing hide-and-seek, Josh? Because I can see you. Pick a better place and I'll count to ten."

But Josh doesn't move. She can't see him clearly. Just a shape, really, a small shape of red and yellow through the bright green leaves.

"Okay, if you don't want to play, fine," Linda tells him, snapping off a few more clusters. "Help me pick some lilacs."

But the shape on the other side of the bush still doesn't move. He's just standing there.

Why is he spying on me?

She strains to see him through the leaves.

That *is* Josh, isn't it?

Linda moves around the bush to see.

"Josh?"

She gasps, dropping the lilacs she carried in her arms.

No, it's definitely not Josh.

It's a demon in the shape of a boy—a *dead* boy, a boy *burned* to death—his skin black and charred, his hair scorched. Blank eye sockets glare out at her from his blackened skull. Only his clothing—the same that Josh had been wearing—remains unburned.

"Oh, dear God, no!"

"Were you calling me?"

She spins around. Josh is behind her. The real Josh, looking fine.

She whips her head back to where she saw the dead boy. He's gone.

I'm not going to react. They mustn't know I've had another one of these crazy visions. They mustn't know.

"I—I thought I saw you back here," Linda manages to utter, trying to steady her heartbeat racing in her ears.

"No," Josh says, eerily calm. "I was in the back-yard looking for my swing set."

Linda kneels, picking up the lilacs she'd dropped. "Your swing set?" she says, trying to keep her voice even, her thoughts collected.

"Yeah. When I was little I had a swing set back there. But Daddy told me he had it taken down be-cause it got all rusted and wasn't safe."

Linda stands, managing a smile. "And was it gone, then?"

The boy nods, and a little twinkle appears in his eyes. "If you get him to buy me a new one, maybe I'll be nice to you."

"Now, Josh," she says, "that's called bribery."

"Don't you *want* me to be nice to you?"

She tries to quiet her own fears, to force back her own anxiety, even as Megan's idea of Xanax is starting to sound better and better to her. She tries to see the boy's own pain in his eyes, his own fears.

But the face of that burned boy keeps getting in the way.

"I want you to be nice to me because you *want* to," Linda tells him, forcing away the image, "not because I did something you wanted me to do."

He shrugs. "Have it your way then."

"Josh, we can have fun this weekend. Really. If you give me a chance."

He has started to turn away, to push off into the lilac bushes his mother loved so much, but he stops. "Why should I give you a chance?"

"Because your father would like you to." No, that's not enough. "Because I'm a good person. A fun person. You'll like me. You'll see."

"I'm never going to like you."

Linda suddenly feels at a breaking point, as if the trauma of seeing that horrible vision has made this kind of sparring with Josh unbearable. All she wants to do is crawl into bed and pull the sheets up over her head and forget it all. Josh. Geoff's friends. These hideous visions.

"You may never like me, Josh," she tells me, "but you're going to have to get used to me."

"Why do I have to get used to you?"

She takes a long breath. "Because your father and I are going to be married."

The boy just stares up at her. This wasn't the way they'd planned on telling him, but it had just come out. Linda couldn't hold it back any longer.

"We might as well be friends," she says, trying to soften her voice. "You'll see I'm not so bad."

The child keeps glaring at her, saying nothing. His round blue eyes beam. His fair hair glows in the sun.

Linda tries to smile, offering her hand. "Come on, Josh. Let's go inside and you can help me put these lilacs in vases. We can talk. We can talk as long as you want. You, me, and your Dad."

"You can't marry my father," he finally says, his eyes still holding onto hers, in a voice that is low and deep, and that sounds nothing like a child's.

Linda can feel herself stiffening again. "Oh, no? Why can't I, Josh?"

"Because my mother won't let you."

It's as if he'd just reached over and slapped Linda across the face, or punched her straight in the gut. She staggers backward from the boy's words. Josh turns and runs off into the yard.

"Josh!"

Linda becomes aware of someone behind her. She turns around quickly.

It's Julia.

"What did you say to him?" the old woman demands. "How have you upset him?"

"I just—I was trying to talk with him."

The nanny pushes past her to go after the boy. "He is a sensitive child," she says. "He is upset very easily."

Linda becomes angry. "Oh, really now? He's a *rude* child, that's what he is."

The old woman gives her a furious look, then begins to run after Josh in her pink Nike sneakers

Linda begins to cry. "I told him his father and I were going to be married," she shouts after her. "And it's true! You'd *both* better get used to it! *Geoff and I are going to be married!*"

Josh is found sobbing beside the cement slab that once held his swing set. Linda watches as Julia leads him in to his father, cooing little reassurances over him.

"I'm sorry," Linda tells Geoff later, behind the closed door of the master bedroom. "I'm sorry it all came out that way. I know I should have waited for you but—"

"It sounds as if Josh was asking for it," Geoff says.

"No. He deserved to hear it from you. I just lost it."

Geoff sits down on the side of the bed and puts his face in his hands. "Maybe we shouldn't have come here. There are too many memories of his mother here." He slams his fist into his palm. "I've talked with him, Linda. I've asked him to give you a chance—"

"Oh, Geoff, it's easy to see why it troubles him.

Yes, he's angry and hostile. But he's a little boy abandoned by his mother. " She sighs, sitting down beside him. "We can still salvage this weekend. We'll make it work."

He looks at her with sheer adoration. "Thank you for not giving up."

She kisses him lightly on the lips. "I'm determined to win him over. Even if I did nearly blow it by losing my control."

Geoff holds her in his arms. "What was it that set you off? What put you on edge? Was it something Josh said?"

She remembers the strange, horrible voice that had come out of his mouth. The sinister phrase: *My mother won't let you.* But she can't pin her state of mind on the boy. Linda's nerves had already been rattled by that thing she saw in the lilac bushes.

The dead boy.

The dead, burned boy wearing Josh's clothes.

No. She *didn't* see that. She only *thought* she saw that.

She does her best to cover up. "I—I guess I was still—oh, I don't know—a little on edge from that dream. The same one that made me cry out at dinner last night."

Geoff looks at her with concern. "Did you call your doctor?"

"No."

"Sweetheart, I know the situation with Josh is causing you anxiety. That must be what's making you so jittery."

She smiles. "Megan suggests Xanax."

He smiles back at her. "Hey, if it helps . . ."

"I've never been a nervous person before," she tells him. That's not entirely true: anxiety is no stranger to her. Self-confidence has never been one of her strong traits, growing up in the shadow of a perfect sister like Karen. In school, Linda never excelled, never thought she could get marks better than Bs. In social situations, she's often felt anxious—look at that dinner with Jim and Lucy—but never has that anxiety given her hallucinations before, or torn through her dreams like a raging wildfire.

But she's never been in love before, either.

In love with a man far smarter, far more handsome, far more successful than she thought she'd ever find.

And with a son who seems determined to keep her from achieving the kind of happiness she never thought would be hers anyway.

"I understand why you're so anxious," Geoff says, as if reading her mind. "I see it on your face, darling, every time you're with Josh. I see the stress. I see the pressure you're putting on yourself." He sighs. "I'm sorry Josh is so obstinate."

"I meant what I said," she tells him. "I'm going to win him over. Let's go downstairs and order pizza and rent whatever video he wants. We'll make it his night and show him we can be a happy family."

"And if he brings up the marriage plans?"

She smiles wearily. "We'll acknowledge them, tell him we both love him, and that he's going to be a part of our life together. That's what he fears, Geoff. That he's going to be abandoned again."

Geoff nods. "You're right. I suppose if we can reassure him of that, he'll be okay." He slaps his legs. "All right. Let's go down and find him."

Linda wants to believe it will work. She *has* to believe. All of her dreams depend on Josh finally accepting her—even growing to love her, or at least to like her.

Still, walking down the stairs she can't seem to get the face of that dead little boy out of her mind, his scorched, blackened eye sockets staring straight into her soul.

But Josh refuses to talk. Pepperoni pizza, *Buffy the Vampire Slayer* videos, chocolate ice cream with peanut butter and hot fudge—none of it does the trick. Geoff asks him if he wants to talk about what Linda told him, but the boy pretends he's deaf, ignoring his father's pleas. Linda can see it breaks Geoff's heart. For a father and son this close, such hostility is almost physically painful. Geoff slumps down on the couch, miserable. Josh plops onto the floor in front of the TV set, stuffing his face with pizza, refusing to look around at either his father or Linda. The only one he responds to is Julia, who seems, Linda thinks, to enjoy the discomfort of the adults.

After Josh has gone to bed, Linda joins Geoff in the master bedroom. They've gone through a charade of pretending to have separate bedrooms for Josh's benefit. Julia had made quite the scene, insisting the boy not know if his father was "sharing his bed out of wedlock." The old woman had drawn herself up to her full height, puffing out her chest. "The boy is *pure*. He mustn't be corrupted at such a young age." How old-fashioned she was. How prim and prudish.

Linda tiptoes past Julia's room and slips into Geoff's arms.

"How come you always smell so good?" she purrs against his skin.

They make love. Linda revels in the feel of Geoff,

his weight on top of her offering such a sense of security and fulfillment. She runs her hands through his thick dark hair, kissing his neck and his ear. He is gentle with her but solid, too, self-assured and certain of his strength. He is the rock Linda has needed for so long, the surety she has craved.

Why has it been so difficult for her? Lying there in the sleepy afterglow, listening to Geoff breathe, Linda remembers how frightened she'd felt when she first moved to Boston, the sense of displacement, of inadequacy in the face of all these achievers around her. Her college classmates all had grand career plans. Her best girlfriends all came from well-placed Eastern families, assured of post-graduation jobs and, in many cases, marriages. So often Linda would think it should have been her sister Karen who had gone on to college, who left their farm in Michigan for a chance in the Big City. Karen had charisma and confidence to spare. But Karen also ended up married to a chicken-feed salesman.

"Don't worry, Linda," Karen had told her, as Linda adjusted her wedding veil. "You'll find Mr. Right someday."

"Yeah, whatever. Maybe your hubby-to-be has got some chicken-feed salesman buddy. . . ."

"Do you want me to ask him?"

Linda scowled. "No, thanks, Karen. I'm okay on my own."

"Why don't you become a career woman? You know, you're going to move away to a big city and become wealthy and powerful, while I sit home and make babies."

"Gee, thanks, sis, for the pep talk."

Karen laughed. "I just want you to be as happy

as I am, Linda. To have found a man who loves me—that's just so indescribably perfect."

Linda imagined it was. And now she had—hadn't she?

And she couldn't wait for Karen to meet Geoff.

Linda remembers watching her sister walk down the aisle. How everyone had turned to watch her. "What a beautiful bride," she heard more than one person whisper. "She's really the beauty in the family, isn't she?"

Then Karen exchanged her vows with her husband, and the whole church applauded them.

Just so indescribably perfect.

But I'll never know what that feels like, Linda thought.

Linda wanted her sister to be happy. Sure, she'd always been envious of her, but Karen wasn't a bad person. A little insensitive at times, a little bit self-absorbed—she really *did* want Linda to be happy, in her own way.

Linda can't deny a certain smug satisfaction that Geoff is far more handsome and successful than Karen's husband. He was handsome like—like Jake Gandolfini back in high school, the jock who had rubbed suntan lotion on Karen's back. The kind of handsome Linda thought she could never get.

And now she has.

Hasn't she?

Of course she has. By loving her, by wanting to marry her, Geoff has given her an unmistakable message: you are good. You are worthy.

She drifts off to a happy sleep, and no dreams disturb her.

When she wakes, the early morning sun is streaming through the windows, filling the room with a bright pink light.

But the first thing she realizes is that Geoff is no longer beside her.

She sits up.

He is sitting in the chair opposite the bed, staring at her with tired, dark-circled eyes. His face is white. He looks—dead.

"Geoff! What's wrong?"

He doesn't respond. He just keeps staring at her.

She hops out of bed and hurries to him. "Honey. Geoff. What's happened?"

"I had a dream," he rasps.

She kneels beside him. "A dream?"

"A dream," he echoes. "A dream of fire."

Linda's heart thuds into her throat. "Fire?"

He turns his bleary eyes to her. "The house was burning down. I saw the fire claim you. I saw you burn to death in front of my eyes."

CHAPTER 3

"Dear God," Linda gasps.

"Then I went to save Josh," Geoff continues, his eyes staring off into the distance at the memory of his nightmare. "But I couldn't. He just stood there in the flames. He didn't move. It was as if he just accepted he was going to die. That it was his fate. I watched as the flames consumed him."

"Oh, Geoff," Linda says, her whole body trembling. She wraps his head in her arms.

"It was horrible," he says, his face pressed against her breasts. "The worst dream I've ever had in my life. I've been up ever since. I was too scared to go back to sleep."

She places her hands on his cheeks and turns his face to look up at her. She stares deep into his dark eyes. "Listen to me, Geoff. It's the power of suggestion. You've been so empathic with me about my own anxieties, you took them on as your own. I've been going on about fire in my own dreams, and so you had one yourself."

He stands, breaking contact with her, staggering across the room.

"That's *got* to be what is, sweetheart," she says after him. "It's nothing to worry about."

But she doesn't believe it herself.

He says nothing. She watches as he scuffs into the bathroom and closes the door behind him.

It was a sympathy dream, that's all. The power of suggestion.

Except Josh had had a dream about fire, too.

Linda stands, looking out of the window into the glorious golden day.

What is happening? What do these dreams mean?

Below, in the yard, she sees Julia. The old woman is walking among the lilac bushes, breaking off a branch here and there. From this distance Linda can't be sure, but she could swear Julia's talking to herself. She catches snippets of words—"the boy"—"soon"—"the sun"—and she's certain she can see the woman's lips moving.

Linda turns and raps softly on the bathroom door. "You okay, Geoff?"

"Yeah," he grunts. She can hear the shower water turn on, splashing into the tub. "I just need to get my head clear."

"I'll see you downstairs then. I'll start breakfast."

She's not even at the bottom of the stairs when she sees what's happened to the white lilacs. They've all turned brown. Their purple sisters remain fresh and vibrant and fragrant in their vases, but the whites, despite plenty of water, have faded overnight.

Julia comes in through the back door, her apron filled with new purple flowers. "I told you we never have white," she says, pulling out the dead clusters and replacing them with new blossoms.

Linda says nothing, just heads into the kitchen.

She sees the nanny has already started breakfast. The room is filled with the aroma of fresh-baked blueberry muffins. A pan of scrambled eggs is being kept warm on the stove. A pitcher of just-squeezed orange juice awaits them on the table.

"I was going to cook," Linda says, her voice weak and ineffectual.

Julia doesn't respond.

"Where's Josh?" Linda asks.

"He's in the backyard," the nanny tells her. "He said his father promised to take him out on the lake. He's getting the boat ready."

Linda peers out the kitchen window. Sure enough, there's the boy, untangling the ropes that had tied the small wooden dinghy to the pier.

She walks outside and calls to him.

"Josh! Come in and have breakfast."

He ignores her.

"Tell me, Josh. Are there fish in that lake?"

She's walking toward him now. He doesn't look up as she approaches.

"Perch, maybe? Trout?"

"Yeah, there's fish," he says.

"Maybe you and your father can catch some when you go out. I can clean them and cook them for dinner tonight."

The boy looks up at her. "My father doesn't like to fish."

"Oh, no? Why not?"

"He can't stand putting the worms on the hook."

This surprises Linda. A little factoid she didn't know about Geoff. Mr. Dark and Handsome. Mr. Brilliant Professor. Afraid of a little worm guts. She laughs.

"Back home, my father would take my sister and me fishing all the time. There were a lot of lakes near where I grew up." Linda rubs her hands together. "Why, if we had some bait we could probably bring in quite the haul here."

For the first time something other than hostility registers in Josh's eyes when he looks up at Linda. There's curiosity. Interest.

"Would you want to go fishing, Josh? I mean, I know you don't like me much, but at least I have no problem with sticking nightcrawlers on a hook."

The little boy looks at her. He's clearly considering the idea, obviously intrigued. *This is it,* Linda thinks. *The breakthrough.*

"What do you say, Josh? We can go down to the general store, get some bait . . . I saw some fishing poles in the garage."

"I can't go," he says, turning away.

"Why not, Josh?"

"Because my mother will be here soon."

Linda lets out a long sigh.

She looks out over the lake. The day is clouding over. Before a minute has passed she sees the ripple of raindrops against the water's surface. Standing there beside Josh, she witnesses the day change from sunshine to rain in a matter of moments. Thunder rumbles overhead, and all at once the skies open and a torrential downpour drenches them on the spot. They both make a mad dash into the house.

"So odd," Geoff says, peering out the window, "this change in weather."

Rain pounds against the roof of the house. Linda sits reading a *People* magazine while her fiancé paces, still agitated by his dream.

"It was supposed to be sunny all weekend," he grouses.

"Maybe we can go to the movies," Linda suggests,

Geoff says nothing. He walks back and forth between windows, looking out of each of them as if one might suddenly offer him a better view.

Josh is at the dining room table, coloring with crayons in a large drawing pad. Julia has just popped him a bowl of popcorn, and he stuffs handfuls of it into his mouth as he remains intent on his work. The aroma of salty butter hangs over the room.

"It should clear up soon," Linda says. "It must be only a passing shower."

A great crash of lightning rattles the house, and the power shuts off.

"Oh, terrific," Geoff moans.

The electricity flickers back on, however, and Linda goes back to reading about Ben Affleck and J. Lo.

Despite Josh's ultimate refusal, she remains heartened by the look she had seen his eyes. *I can do it,* she thinks. *I can win him over. It's going to take a little time, but I can do it.*

She looks over at him now, so focused on his coloring, his angelic little face scrunched up and his tongue planted on his upper lip. He may be another woman's child, but he will become *her* son, too—her responsibility to raise and nurture and teach and love. Someday he'll go to college, and get married, and have babies of his own—and Linda will be right there, watching him, proud of him, at Geoff's side.

The day passes lazily, the rain showing no sign of letting up. Linda moves from Ben and J. Lo to

Jennifer and Brad, then on to Prince William and his sexy college roommate to poor old Bob Hope, a hundred years old and still hanging on. By the time she's finished, Geoff has gone elsewhere to pace and Julia has disappeared, but Josh is still at the table coloring, humming to himself.

Linda heads upstairs. She'll shower, fix her hair, try to keep the gloom of the day from oppressing her the way it's doing to Geoff. They'll go to the mall. Josh would love that idea.

She walks into the master bedroom to run smack into Julia.

"Excuse me!" Linda says in surprise.

The nanny arches an eyebrow at her. "May I help you, Miss Leigh?"

"I was just—I was going to take a shower."

"There's a bathroom in your room, Miss."

Linda can feel herself getting angry. "Let's make it clear, Julia. While we're staying here, this is my room. Geoff's room is my room."

"I don't think it's wise for Master Joshua to be exposed to such an arrangement."

"His father and I see no problem with it. Josh knows we're planning to be married. He needs to understand that I am going to be a permanent presence in his life."

The nanny says nothing, just hardens her jaw.

"And may I ask what *you* are doing in here?" Linda asks.

"Just freshening up the room." The nanny stares at her defiantly. "Making it the way Dr. Manwaring has always preferred it."

Linda glances around. There are purple lilacs in several vases on the table and the bureau. Candles are lit on the mantelpiece, flanking a small urn in which burns a tiny flame.

"I found it in the study," Julia says as Linda approaches the urn to study it. "I always remember it in this room. It was always lit."

Linda holds the urn in her hand. It's made of some kind of very old tarnished metal, with strange markings like hieroglyphics on its side. No more than six inches long by three inches high, it's filled with oil, a short wick flickering with a tiny bluish flame.

"I believe it was hers," Julia says.

"Hers?" Linda asks, her voice barely a whisper as she finds herself transfixed by the urn.

"Mrs. Manwaring's."

Linda sets the urn back down on the mantel. She shakes off the feeling that had come over her and turns with some indignation to the nanny.

"In the future, you should get Dr. Manwaring's approval before you bring anything into this room," she says.

Julia smiles. "Oh, but I did, Miss. Dr. Manwaring wanted the urn."

Suddenly Linda is aware of her fiancé standing in the doorway. He looks weary and sheepish. Dark circles remain prominent under his eyes.

"Thank you, Julia, that'll be all," he says as the nanny nods efficiently and slips out around him back into the hall.

Linda watches him as he closes the door and comes into the room. He sits on the bed and begins rubbing his temples with his fingers.

"You wanted this?" Linda asks. "You wanted this—whatever it is?"

"It's an urn. Gabrielle and I found it in Egypt on our honeymoon." He doesn't look up at her. "It's very old. It was a real find."

"But why do you want it in here?"

"I just thought—I don't know. Julia showed it to me and I said okay. Put it in the room."

"She's very loyal, Julia." Linda pauses. "To Gabrielle."

"They were very close."

"Well, I don't want it in here. I don't like it."

Geoff finally lifts his eyes to look at her. "The symbols—they translate into a prayer for eternal life. It's a piece used in veneration of the ancient Egyptian sun god, Ra. I've always viewed it as good luck."

"I think it's ugly," Linda says stubbornly. "I don't want it in here."

She turns back to the mantel, her hand outstretched to pick it up again.

"No!" Geoff is on her in a flash, grabbing her arm. "Don't put out its flame!"

"Dear God, Geoff! What's gotten into you?"

He snatches the urn into his own grip. "I—I just don't want you to damage it. The oil . . . I don't want the flame to go out. It could—damage the inside casing—"

"How could it do that?"

He holds the urn tightly to his chest. "If you don't like it, I'll put it in the study."

Linda makes a face. "You're behaving very strangely."

Geoff sighs. "Maybe. Maybe so. The dream . . . I'm still freaked out by the dream."

Linda gives him a small smile. "I guess I can understand that. My own dream kept me on edge for a couple of days."

He turns to leave, taking the urn with him.

"Geoff," Linda calls, "I didn't know you didn't like to fish. Josh really wants to try it. I'm going to bring it up with him again tomorrow if the weather clears up—"

But she finds she's talking to air. Geoff has hurried out of the room.

The rain finally starts letting up late in the afternoon. The mall idea fell on deaf ears. Geoff has become engrossed in grading his student papers, hunched over a pile in the study, that damn urn beside him, still burning. Julia has begun preparing dinner in the kitchen, and although Linda had wanted to make it herself, she makes no effort to confront the old woman again.

And Josh remains coloring in his pad at the dining room table.

"The rain's stopped," Linda tells the boy. "Maybe you might want to go outside and play."

He doesn't respond.

"What are you drawing, Josh? You've been so intent all afternoon."

For the first time Linda takes notice of the boy's work. There are dozens of sheets torn out from his pad scattered at the foot of his chair and under the table. What Linda notices first are the colors: only yellows, oranges, and reds. As she lifts one of the sheets to look at it, she glances at Josh's crayon box. All of the so-called cool colors—the blues, greens, and purples—remain untouched, their points still sharp. But tiny stubs of red and yellow crayons litter the floor.

"What are these, Josh?"

They're all the same: some kind of a figure—a bird, from the looks of it—surrounded by red, orange, and yellow scribbles. Linda picks up another sheet and then another. Some of the scribbles are rush jobs, but others are carefully rendered, colored in solidly. The look like—

Flames.

"What *are* these, Josh?" Linda repeats again, quieter now.

The boy doesn't answer. He's drawing on a new sheet now: the same birdlike figure, its head raised, two wings at its side, pointing upward on the page.

Linda's suddenly aware of Julia standing behind her.

"The boy has talent, don't you think?"

"Yes," Linda says. "I think Josh probably has many talents."

"Dinner will be ready soon. I'm making lamb chops. I hope that meets with your approval."

Linda turns to look at her. "Lamb chops will be fine."

Julia smiles.

"Tell me," she says to the nanny. "Do you know what these drawings are?"

"Not exactly. But the bird—it was a symbol his mother always used. She had a pendant in that shape, didn't she, Josh?"

"My mother's coming home," Josh says in response, not looking up from his drawing.

"And these lines," Linda says, indicating the yellow and red scribbles. "What are they supposed to be?"

"I'm not sure I know, Miss. Maybe you should ask Master Joshua."

Linda turns to the boy. "Well," she tries. "What are they, Josh?"

"My mother's almost here," he says.

Julia just smiles and returns to the kitchen.

* * *

The night is quiet. Earlier the crickets had been busy, but as the night went on they stilled their chatter, and now only the soft steady tick of the grandfather clock in the hall is all that Linda can hear.

Geoff sleeps soundlessly beside her. She's wide awake, feeling cold and uneasy.

Gabrielle Deschamps had been a fascinating woman. Geoff has only told her a little, but Linda's pieced in the rest through conversations with Jim and Lucy Oleson and others from the campus. In the beginning, Geoff and Gabrielle were madly, deeply, *dazzlingly* in love—or at least, Geoff was with her. Gabrielle, everyone agreed, kept her most private thoughts to herself. But there was no disguising the passion she had for certain things: academic debate, ancient history, travel, beautiful clothes, stunning jewelry, *men*. She was an impetuous flirt; no man was safe from her charms. Sit down at a table with her and she'd home right in, finding a man's eyes, touching his hand, taking hold of his spirit. She'd find his weakness, his vanity, and then she'd prick it, ever so skillfully, making the man hers in mind if not in body. It drove Geoff crazy with jealousy. It only made Gabrielle laugh.

"Borderline personality," Megan had diagnosed at hearing the description. Her husband, Randy, is a psychologist, so Megan thinks she has all the answers. "Gabrielle was a disaster waiting to happen. Geoff should be glad she's gone."

But is he? Linda looks over at him, sleeping peacefully. She's glad his nightmare seems to have passed. A good night's rest, some sunny weather, and they'd make up tomorrow for what they missed out on today.

Linda knows she's no great beauty like Gabrielle was. She's seen the photographs. How alive Gabrielle had seemed. Always laughing, always posing for the camera. She puckers up for a kiss in one; in another, she pushes up her breasts, accentuating her cleavage. There's a shot of her on some Mediterranean island—her honeymoon with Geoff, which took them from Rome to Greece to Egypt—where she looks like a sun goddess: iridescent blond-white hair, glowing golden skin, her face lifted to the skies.

"She walked out on him," Megan has reminded her, whenever Linda has gotten insecure, threatened by the memory of her predecessor. "Remember that. He found her in bed with a teenager! They say hell hath no fury like a woman scorned. Well, what's even worse is a man whose ego has been wounded. If Geoff ever felt anything for her, believe me, sweetie, it evaporated pretty quickly when he found her boning some pimply paperboy."

And how many others? Linda knows that's what Geoff wonders. How many others had she cheated on him with? Those men she'd dazzle at college parties. The students she'd tease when they came to the house seeking extra help from Geoff. How many did she seduce once Geoff was out of sight?

And Josh? Could they be sure he was Geoff's? He looked nothing like his father, so fair and blond and soft and pretty like his mother.

But no. Linda won't allow herself to think that way. She's seen the bond between them. She's seen the love, the connection between father and son. The way Geoff will hoist Josh on his shoulders and carry him across campus. The way they wrestle on the living room floor, Josh reduced to a giggly bowl of little-boy jelly. The way the boy will look at his father, his eyes filled with awe, with love, with a sense of who he will someday be.

Geoff has started to snore slightly.

Linda sits up in bed. She's wide awake. It was such a strange day. The weather. Geoff's mood. That urn. Those drawings of Josh's.

She stands, slipping into her robe. But the events of the day aren't the reason for his sleeplessness. There's something else. Something amiss. Something she can't quite put her finger on.

Josh. She needs to check on Josh.

She pads down the hallway silently. At the boy's door, she pauses. Downstairs she can hear the grandfather clock chime twelve. Midnight.

Linda pushes open Josh's door, careful not to wake him.

He's not in his bed.

That's what she felt was wrong. Josh—he's gone.

She hurries downstairs, hoping she'll find him back at the dining room table, coloring with the last tiny chunks of red and yellow crayons. But he's nowhere to be found. She looks around the room frantically.

The front door. It's ajar.

Linda hurries to the front steps. "Josh!' she whispers into the still-dark night. The only sound is the soft swaying of pine trees in the breeze. "Josh!"

In the moonlight she makes him out: a tiny figure in the driveway, staring out into the road.

Linda makes her ways through the dewy grass in her bare feet. "Josh!" she calls. "What are you doing outside at this time of night?"

The boy is in his pajamas. He just keeps staring out into the road.

Linda has reached him. She places her hands on his shoulders, expecting him to pull away from her. But he doesn't.

"My mother is coming," he says softly, almost hypnotically. "My mother is coming."

"Oh, Josh."

Linda drops to a stooping position beside him so that her eyes are level with his. She sees he's crying. Her heart breaks.

"Oh, Josh, your mother isn't coming. I know how much you must miss her. I know you must think I'm here to replace her, to make you forget her. But I'm not, Josh. I know I can never take your mother's place. She'll always live in your heart. I don't want you to forget her."

He turns his small face to look at her. The moonlight casts a soft white glow across his features. A tear drops down his cheek.

"But she's not coming, sweetheart. We don't know where she is. Your dad tried to find her. You know that. But she's gone. I know that's hard to understand. I wish I could give you a better explanation. But I can't."

Josh just looks deep into her eyes.

"Will you come in the house with me now?" Linda asks gently.

The boy begins to cry harder. He allows Linda to take him into her arms. He buries his face in the folds of her robe and sobs. She holds him tightly for several moments, then lifts him and carries him back into the house.

There's little chance of sleeping after that. She tosses and turns, dreaming of Josh, a little forlorn elf standing at the foot of the driveway. She sees his tearful face as she lay him back into bed, bringing the blanket up around him. She hears his muffled cries in her dreams, and she can sleep no more.

The sun is beginning to rise when she finally gives up on her rest. Geoff is snoring now, seemingly back to normal, rattling like a bear. Linda throws on a pair of sweatpants and a T-shirt. She peeks in on Josh. Sound asleep. She smiles and makes her way downstairs.

She's glad Julia isn't awake yet. She puts the coffee on herself. She mixes flour and eggs in a bowl for pancakes. Maybe things are changing. Maybe Josh will come around. He let her hold him. He let her pick him up and put him to bed.

The coffee helps to waken her, to throw off the lethargy of the night. Linda stands in the kitchen, sipping its warmth, leaning against the counter and watching the shadows of the room disappear. The pink light of dawn slices through the windows. It's going to be a beautiful day.

She walks outside into the yard. *This will be my house,* she thinks. *Our house. Mine and Geoff's. Mine and Geoff's and Josh's. Our family's house.*

The tulips in the side garden are beginning to open. Had Gabrielle planted them? It doesn't matter: they're Linda's now.

The sun is still low enough in the sky to cast long blue shadows across the yard. Linda loves the very early morning. She often gets up this early so she can jog or head to the gym before work. She'll do a run through Boston Common and marvel at the light, at the solitude, at the peacefulness. In a few hours the city would turn into a bustle of energy and frantic, angry noise, but at dawn it was quiet and respectful.

In the front yard there are daffodils, most past

their bloom, but a few still soldier on. She'll add more bulbs in through here, she thinks. Hyacinths and narcissi. Make it a vibrant spring garden.

Something catches her eye. Down in the road, there's a figure, still far off but walking this way. Someone else out enjoying the first light of day.

Linda watches. The person walks from the east, so is little more than a silhouette in the glow of the rising sun. Linda holds her coffee mug close to her chest as she keeps her eyes on the figure. She can't seem to move from the spot. The person gets closer, growing larger. Linda can make out a cloak, a long full flowing cloak. And a hood.

She suddenly feels cold terror. She wants to run, scream, hide in the house, but she's rooted in place, unable to look away. The figure approaches.

It is a woman.

Send her away, Linda prays. *Dear God, send her away.*

The woman has stopped now at the foot of the driveway, the same spot where Josh had stood last night, crying into the dark.

"Hello," she calls.

Linda doesn't move or respond.

The woman in the long black cloak advances up the driveway. In the trees, a large bird begins to caw manically. Linda can't see the woman's face, as it remains shadowed within her large, full hood. She braces herself. The woman keeps walking toward her.

"Hello," she says again.

"Hello," Linda whispers.

"I'm looking for Dr. Manwaring."

The woman has stopped just a few feet away. Linda still can't clearly see her face.

"Who are you?" Linda asks in a small, choked voice.

The woman reaches up and folds down her hood, revealing hair of startling gold. She smiles.

"I'm his wife," she says.

CHAPTER 4

"Gabrielle," Linda breathes.

The woman smiles again. "Yes. You know me?"

"I've—I've seen your picture."

"And might I inquire as to who you are? No, wait. I'm sure I know. Geoffrey must . . . Well, it's been a long time that I've been gone. I couldn't expect that he'd wait for me."

Linda finds her voice, feeling a surge of emotion—anger? fear?—rise inside her. "You can't just come back this way," she manages to say. "Not after so long."

Gabrielle smiles sadly. Her lovely face, as beautiful and unlined as in the photographs, appears pained. "I heard in town that Geoffrey was here, at the house. Word gets around. You see, I've been here in Sunderland a while. It was the closest thing to home I ever knew."

But Linda is adamant. "You—you just can't show up like this. It will upset them."

Gabrielle seems near to tears. "I hadn't planned on interrupting. I was just walking by the house, remembering. . . . Then I saw you standing here. It was an impulse to approach. I'll go. I'm sorry if I've upset you."

She raises her hood and turns to leave, but both of them are started by a voice.

"Madam! Oh, madam, you've come back!"

Linda turns. Julia has walked out onto the front porch. Her hands are outstretched, her face in a kind of rapture.

"Julia," Gabrielle says fondly.

"Oh, Mrs. Manwaring, I knew you'd come back. All this time I knew it." She rushes up to her, takes her hands in her own. "The boy—Joshua—he knew it, too!"

"Joshua," Gabrielle says with emotion.

"You must come inside. We will wake him. Go to his room—"

"No!" Linda shouts. They both turn to look at her. "You will not wake Josh up. It would only upset him terribly."

Julia throws her a disdainful look. "But he's been asking about her, insisting she'd return."

"No, she's right," Gabrielle says, patting Julia's hand and letting it go. "It would be too much too quickly." She looks up at the house sadly. "After all, I've been gone an awfully long time."

"I think you should go back to town," Linda says. "I'll tell Geoff that you came by." She's aware that Julia is glaring at her. "We'll let *him* decide when and if Josh sees you."

"Of course." Gabrielle tries to smile. "It should be Geoffrey's decision."

"All I know is Joshua has missed you terribly," Julia says.

"And I've missed him." Gabrielle sighs, and her

crystal blue eyes move off into the distance, seeming to fix on something Linda can't see. "I've missed him more than I can possibly say. More than I ever knew was possible. But he mustn't be forced into anything too quickly, Julia. I think our friend here is right."

Julia sniffs. Linda knows she considers her anything but a friend.

She watches as Gabrielle walks slowly down the driveway and back out into the street. Julia makes a little sound of grief and hurries back into the house. Linda keeps her eyes on Gabrielle, who returns the way she came, disappearing into the gathering light of day.

It was her. It was really her. Josh was right. Somehow he sensed it. His mother did come back.

Linda suddenly is overcome with fear. Her legs feel weak as if they can't support her weight. Her hands begin to tremble.

What will this mean? How will Geoff react when he knows his wife has returned?

Nothing is going to be the same. That much she knows. She starts to cry standing there, staring out into the bright light of morning. Nothing is going to be the same.

"Where is she staying in town?" Geoff wants to know.

"She didn't say." Linda's pancakes aren't being eaten. Geoff is just moving them around on his plate. Julia hovers in the background, listening as Linda tells him about Gabrielle's visit. "I told her you'd decide if she should see Josh."

"Where has she been all this time?" Geoff slams

down his fork and stands up. "I searched everywhere for her. Hired detectives, had the police scouring the whole goddamn country."

"We didn't speak very long, darling," Linda tells him. "I didn't want to engage her without you being there."

"Dr. Manwaring," Julia offers, "I'm sure Cal at the general store in town will know where she's staying. I'm sure you can contact her through him."

"Yes, yes," Geoff mutters.

"You're going to?" Linda asks, alarmed. "You're going to go into town to find her?"

"You're damn right I am," he says. "I want to know she wants. What she came back for. She's a crafty one. Always has been. The divorce is nearly final, and if she thinks she can fight me, get anything out of it, well, she's got another thing coming."

Linda breathes a sigh of relief. He's angry with her. That's good. He's not running off to Gabrielle so he can fall into her arms and welcome her back. Of course he's not. Geoff loves her. Linda. Why is she getting so insecure all of a sudden?

Still, she's cautious. "I'd like to go with you, Geoff, when you see her," she says.

"If you like." He's heading upstairs. "No mention of this to Josh when he wakes up. Understand?"

Linda notices the stern look he gives to Julia, who turns away, her lips pinched.

"Understand?" he repeats.

"Yes, sir," Julia says.

Linda smiles. She follows Geoff upstairs to get dressed. She's brushing her teeth at the sink when Josh staggers to the bathroom doorway in his flannel pajamas, covered in a pattern of airplanes and rocket ships. He's holding his crotch.

"Gotta go," he announces.

"Oh! Of course."

Linda spits toothpaste into the sink and hurries out of the bathroom. The little boy closes the door behind him. In moments she can hear the sound of his tinkle hitting the water of the toilet. Then the toilet flushes.

He opens the door looking at her.

"I dreamed about my mother," he tells her.

"Oh?" Linda asks, trying to be nonchalant. She resumes brushes her teeth at the sink. Josh stands at her side watching her.

"She looked very beautiful," the boy says.

"Well, I understand she was."

"Have you seen her picture?"

Linda's rinsing her mouth with water. She doesn't answer right away.

"Yes," she says at last. "I've seen her picture."

"So do you think she's beautiful?"

"Yes. She's very lovely."

"She's more beautiful than you."

Linda gazes down on the little imp. "Yes. I suppose she is, Josh."

"In my dream, she was the most beautiful ever. She was glowing in a bright light. It was all gold and yellow. And she was saying, 'I'm coming, Josh. I'm coming.' "

How is it possible? Linda keeps her gaze on the child standing beside her. Did he have some kind of telepathy? Was he somehow psychically linked to his mother?

But that's absurd, Linda tells herself. Josh has been obsessed with his mother for a long time. It's nothing new that he's thinking about her, dreaming about her. There's no way he could know that she really has come back.

But when he finds out . . .

"My father thought she was beautiful," Josh tells her.

Linda stoops down to face the boy. "Yes, he did, Josh. But you need to accept that your father loves me now, and we're going to married."

Josh remains silent.

"Nothing will change that, Josh. Nothing."

"My mother will," he says darkly, a sour little voice so unlike a child's.

"No, Josh. She won't."

He runs from her, scurrying back to his room and slamming the door. Linda stands, sighing. She tries to deny it, but the child has upset her, deeply. Gabrielle *was* beautiful. No, she *is* beautiful—and now she's back. She's back, just when her husband planned to marry someone else.

Me! He's going to marry me!

Linda looks down the hall at Josh's closed door.

And nothing will change that. Nothing!

My mother will.

Linda closes her eyes.

My father thought she was beautiful.

More beautiful than you.

Linda opens her eyes to see Julia standing in front of her, as if appearing out of nowhere. She gasps.

"Is everything all right, miss?"

The nanny's face is sweet and composed, but her eyes are blazing with hatred.

"Everything is fine," Linda tells her.

"Dr. Manwaring is downstairs waiting," Julia tells her. "He asked me to let you know he's ready to go."

"Thank you," Linda says, pushing past her.

"Is Master Joshua awake?" Julia asks.

"Yes," Linda says.

"Oh, good," the nanny says.

As Linda begins to descend the stairway, she

hears Julia open Josh's door. "Good morning, Joshua!"

"Good morning, Julia," she hears the boy reply.

"And did we have a pleasant sleep?"

"Oh, yes, Julia," Josh tells her. "I dreamed of my mother."

Linda and Geoff head out into town. Cal at the general store reports that Gabrielle is staying at a local inn. "Nearly blew my socks off when she walked through that door this mornin'," the storekeeper says. "I'd given her up for dead."

"No such luck," Geoff grumbles under his breath.

When they call her room, it takes nearly ten rings before Gabrielle picks up the phone. When she hears it's Geoff, she agrees that he can come upstairs to see her.

"Be calm," Linda cautions him. "Arguing with her will do no good if she starts making demands. We'll just call the lawyer."

Geoff grunts. They head up the stairs. He raps loudly on Gabrielle's door.

There's no answer.

"Gabrielle!" he demands.

"She just answered the phone," Linda says. "She's got to be here."

Geoff raps again. Still no response. He tries the knob. It turns. He opens the door.

They're immediately struck by the warmth of the room. The temperature outside is already in the high sixties and it's not even eleven A.M. But there's a fire blazing in Gabrielle's fireplace, and she's sitting in front of it on a hassock, staring into the flames.

"Gabrielle," Geoff says.

At last she turns, as if finally roused from a daydream. Was that why it took her so long to answer the phone, too? Had she been sitting there as she is now, lost in some sort of reverie in front of the fire?

"Oh, Geoffrey," she says softly, standing and facing them. "Oh, Geoffrey."

Linda watches her fiancé's face. She studies it for any sign of emotion, any lingering feelings of affection at seeing his wife again after so many years. But all that's there is anger and defense. His lips remain tight, his jaw firm.

"Geoffrey," Gabrielle says, approaching him, holding out her hand. Linda notices now what she hadn't earlier: the pendant around her neck, half-hidden inside her blouse. It's in the shape of a bird, almost exactly the shape of Josh's drawings. "How have you been, Geoffrey?"

He doesn't take her hand. "The time to ask that is over, Gabrielle."

"I suppose you're right." She withdraws her hand and her eyes flicker over to Linda. "I'm afraid I didn't get your name earlier."

"It's Linda," she tells her. "Linda Leigh."

"She's my fiancée," Geoff adds. "We're going to be married and I'm here to make sure you don't try to get in our way."

"Oh." Gabrielle's face is hard to read. Is she hurt? Sad? All Linda can read for sure is a certain wistfulness, her beautiful blue eyes looking away into the distance again. "Congratulations. When is the date?"

"We haven't set it yet," Linda tells her.

Geoff is quick to speak. "I've instituted divorce proceedings, and it should be final in a matter of weeks, if not sooner." He folds his arms across his chest. "I don't expect you'll contest it."

"Oh, no," Gabrielle assures them. "Honestly, Geoffrey, I have no intention of standing in the way of your happiness. Frankly, I'm surprised you didn't secure the divorce sooner. I assumed I'd come back and find myself a single woman."

"Maybe you could put that in writing," Geoff suggests.

Gabrielle smiles. "I'm sorry. I'm being a terrible hostess. Might I offer you a both a cup of tea?"

"No, thank you," Linda says.

"I'm sure it was difficult," Gabrielle says, returning to sit in front of the fire. She gestures for them to sit as well. Linda takes a seat on the edge of the couch, but Geoff remains standing. "Apologies are pointless. They would do no good, so I'm not going to ask you to forgive me. What I did was unforgivable. I do realize that, Geoffrey."

He says nothing, just stands over her, arms folded across his chest.

"I didn't return with any grand illusion that you might take me back," she says, making a point to look over at Linda before gazing at Geoff. "That's not why I returned to Sunderland."

"Then why did you return?"

"Because of Josh." She smiles. "Because I want my son."

Linda looks sharply over at Geoff. She sees his face redden, the veins in his neck jut out. She quickly gets to her feet, hurrying to his side.

"*You . . . want . . . Josh?*" Geoff asks. "Maybe you should've thought of that before you went waltzing off to God knows where with God knows who. Maybe you should've given some thought to him while you were out there fucking around! Do you know what your disappearance did to that poor kid? Do you know what he's had to go through?"

"My poor baby," Gabrielle says. "My poor, poor little baby."

"Don't start with that," Geoff snaps, "because I don't buy it. If you cared about him at all, you wouldn't have walked out on him."

"I can understand your anger," she says, nodding, turning from them now to look into the fire. "But regardless of what I've done, I'm still his mother, and a child has a right to see his mother."

"A *right!* He's been wanting to see you for the past four years!"

"Splendid," Gabrielle says, hardening a bit now. "So let him know I've come back and I'll be over to see him tonight."

"Absolutely not."

"But Julia said he'd sensed I'd returned! You can't deny that, Geoffrey. There's a bond between mother and child."

"A bond you forfeited," Geoff snaps.

"I regret that."

"You're not well! You're—unbalanced. I have the data to back me up. Any doctor would declare you unfit—"

"I've gotten better, Geoffrey. I'll take any mental test you want me to take to show I'm fit enough to be around my son."

"Look," Linda offers. "Let's all calm down. We'll go back home and talk about this. We'll give you a call after we get back to Boston tonight. If there's going to be any meeting at all, it's not going to be today and not here."

Geoff is still ready to pounce on his wife. "You have no idea, do you? No clue of what you put your son through."

"I want to make it up to him," Gabrielle says simply.

"It's too late for that!"

"You can't keep me away from him!" For the first time, anger creeps into Gabrielle's words. She stands defiantly in front of her husband.

Linda sees Geoff's face turn a deathly shade of white. She grips him by the arm. She can feel his body tensing, wanting to lunge at Gabrielle, to throttle her.

"Geoff," she says. "Stay calm. Let's go."

Reluctantly he allows Linda to turn him around and they head for the door.

"Please know I wish to cause no trouble," Gabrielle says behind them, her voice returning to a mild, cautious cadence. "Why don't you put the question to Joshua? Ask him if he'd like to see me. If he says no, I swear I'll go away and never come back. For only if Joshua *wants* to see me—only if he comes willingly—will there be any point in my staying around."

The wind seems to be particularly strong as they drive back home.

"Geoff," Linda says, breaking the stony silence that has settled over the car, broken only by the howling of the wind.

"What is it?"

"You know, it's weird, but I'm—I'm a little frightened."

He sighs, looking over at her. "Frightened?"

"Don't you think it odd that Josh has been predicting that his mother would come home, and then she does?"

Geoff shrugs. "He's being doing that, on and off, since she left."

Linda looks out the window at the trees, swaying

against the wind. It seems to be dying down now, the farther they get from the center of town.

And Gabrielle.

"I just feel uneasy," Linda says. "Like something's going on under the surface. Something we don't know about. Something we can't see. It's strange, I admit, but—"

"It's not strange. Not at all. I feel the same way."

"You do?"

"Sure as hell I do. Gabrielle's up to something. She put on quite the demure act back at the inn. All that sweet talk about not wanting to intrude. Wishing us happiness. But it's bullshit."

Linda looks over at him. His jaw is clenched tight, almost as tightly as his hands are gripping the steering wheel.

"You think so?" she asks.

"I know so."

"Then what is she after?"

"Who knows with her? It could be anything. But whatever it is, it will be extravagant. You can count on that."

"She seemed sincere," Linda offers. "She really did."

"Don't fall for her. Stick with your suspicions."

"The problem is, I don't know what I suspect. Just that—"

"Just that what?"

Linda shivers, and suddenly in her mind it's her dream again. The flames surging in at her. The voice tempting her to enter . . .

"Just that something is going on that we can't see," she continues, finishing her thought. As she does so she wraps her arms around herself. "I just know I'm frightened."

They turn onto their road. They can see the house up ahead.

"Now for Josh," Geoff mumbles.

"What will you tell him?"

"I don't know. I can't keep her away from him entirely. The courts would never go for that."

"He dreamed of her last night," Linda tells him.

"I'm not surprised."

"Geoff, we have to do this right. We have to handle telling him about his mother better than the way we handled telling him about the marriage."

Geoff nods.

"He's just a little boy, after all," Linda says. Her conflicted feelings for the child pass across her mind. On the one hand, she loathes him for the way he taunts her. On the other, she can't help but feel for him. How must any child feel who's abandoned by his mother?

And with that mother's return, what would happen now? How much more terrible might the boy's taunts get? She's right to be frightened, Linda tells herself. The whole situation may be on the verge of getting one hell of a lot worse.

They find him packed and sitting on his suitcase in the driveway.

"What's going on, champ?" Geoff asks, stepping out of the Range Rover. "Ready to go back to Boston so soon?"

The boy nods.

Linda walks around from the other side of the car. "It's still early, Josh. We could still go out fishing."

"I want to go home."

Geoff sighs. "Okay. We might as well at that. I've got a little packing to do myself. Linda, will you ask Julia to start shutting down the house?"

She nods. She looks down at Josh as Geoff strides into the house.

"Did you see my mother?" he asks her.

Linda's stunned. "How—how did you know? Did Julia—?"

"I know my mother's here. You told me she wasn't coming back, but you lied. You lied to me."

Linda kneels down beside him. "I didn't mean to lie, Josh. I didn't know."

"But I did."

She sighs. "Yes. You did. You were right, Josh."

"So you saw her."

Linda hesitates, but she can't lie to the boy. She wants to handle this correctly, and so she goes on instinct. If they start out lying to the boy, they might never regain his trust.

"Yes," she says. "Your father and I just saw her."

Josh's eyes grow wide as Linda admits the truth. "She came here, didn't she? She came to the house?"

Linda nods.

"And she didn't see me," he says, suddenly crestfallen. "She didn't want to see me!"

"That's not true, Josh."

Tears are falling down the seven-year-old's cheeks again. "Then where is she? How come I didn't see her?"

Linda grips his little hands in hers. "Do you want to see her, Josh?"

Little bloodshot blue eyes make contact with her own. Miniature versions of the eyes Linda has just seen at the inn.

"Yes," Josh says. "I want to see my mother!"

It's as if the boy is—on fire, Linda thinks, suddenly chilled to the bone. Every fiber of his body seems to quiver with excitement, pulse with possibility. He stands, gazing out down the road in the direction of town. The hair on his head seems to come alive, almost as if it were lifted by static electricity. His skin seems actually to glow.

"I want to see my mother!" he says again.

Linda looks up. Geoff is in the doorway, watching in utter astonishment the transformation of his son.

Inside, later, Julia denies ferociously that she said anything to the boy.

"I swear, sir, I never told him that his mother had come home. He just *knew.*"

Linda is inclined to believe her. She's seen the psychic connection between Josh and Gabrielle. Maybe she hadn't believed it before, but there's no discounting it now. *There is a bond between mother and child,* Gabrielle had said, and she's right.

"We've got to take him over to see her," Linda tells Geoff. "It's only right."

"Are you insane?" he shouts. "Get packed! We're going back to Boston."

"We can't keep them apart forever. She's back, Geoff. We have to deal with it. She's going to keep trying to see him. You said it yourself, that the courts will insist she see him eventually."

Seeing Josh so strangely energized at the thought of seeing his mother has made Geoff very reluctant to permit such a meeting. It unnerved him, Linda can tell. It's made him very defensive.

"I have custody," Geoff insists. "I'll have the courts declare her unfit. She abandoned him!"

"But he *wants* to see her! If we don't let him, he'll resent us!"

Geoff lets out a yell and punches the wall. It leaves a dent in the plaster. He turns away in a fury and stalks off down the hall.

How had everything changed so fast? Linda's worst fear has come true. Gabrielle—the mysterious entity of the past, the name that hovered constantly over her life—has returned. In the flesh. A real, living, breathing person. A part of Linda knew it would happen someday. Part of her fully expected that Gabrielle would not remain in the past, that she'd come back to push Linda out of the place in Geoff's life that she occupied so tentatively anyway. But the rest of her remains stunned, overwhelmed, by how quickly all her realities have changed. Yesterday their chief concern had been too much rain. Today it was Gabrielle wanting to see Josh.

What would she demand? Shared custody? Geoff would never agree to that. Regular visitation? The courts were always biased in favor of mothers, even ones who'd abandoned their children. And while Geoff might be able to show prior mental illness, Linda suspected Gabrielle would also offer evidence of being cured. She had seemed very grounded and self-assured during their meeting at the inn, only once raising her voice in even the slightest hint of anger.

The most Linda can imagine Geoff agreeing to would be supervised visitation. *We would always need to be present,* Linda thinks. *She might try to kidnap Josh. Take him away.*

The thought terrifies her and fills her with alarm. Yes, only supervised visitation. Otherwise, she'll try to take Josh away. Linda's sure of that.

Still, Gabrielle's words remain in her mind: *Only if Joshua wants to see me—only if he comes willingly— will there be any point in my staying around.*

Yet that's just it: Josh *does* want to see her. They need to take him to her, let them talk—and then get Josh out as quickly as possible.

She finds Geoff in the study, holding the urn in his hands. The little blue flame shivers inside.

"It won't be so bad," she tells him. "It may be even the best thing to do for Josh in the long run. It will put a human face on his mother. She's been just this magical image in his mind for so long."

Geoff just keeps staring down at the urn.

"We'll take him to see her, then go home to Boston. You can talk to your lawyer and make sure that all she gets are supervised visits. And on your terms, Geoff."

"Why did she come back?" he whispers.

"Geoff, I know it's hard. But at least now she's *here.* We can deal with her. She's a real, living, breathing person and not just some memory, some abstract idea. That was even more difficult."

She's speaking for herself. As much as Gabrielle's surprise entry into their lives has unsettled her, Linda realizes dealing with the person—that slightly distracted, somewhat penitent figure over at the inn—was far easier than living with the idealized image—the always laughing, always dazzling face in the photographs and in Geoff's memory.

"Maybe you're right," he says, replacing the urn on the desk. "For so long I've lived with the possibility that she might return. Now she has, and I can just go on from there." He looks at Linda. "I just don't trust her. She says she doesn't want to cause trouble, but she will. Mark my words."

Linda takes his hand. "Come on. Let's go tell Josh he can see his mother."

* * *

Julia is ecstatic with the news. "It's the right thing, Dr. Manwaring. You're doing the right thing."

He says nothing as he slides their suitcases into the back of the Range Rover. Josh stands beside him, looking up at him with wide blue eyes filled with wonder.

"I'm really going to see her?" he asks.

"Yup," Geoff replies, slamming shut the back door. "You're really going to see her."

"Does she still have blond hair like me?"

"Yes, she does."

"Does she still wear pretty dresses?"

"Well, when I saw her, she was wearing jeans. And a red shirt."

"A red shirt," Josh echoes, as if this were something rare and beautiful.

His father buckles him into the backseat. Julia slides in beside the boy and claps her hands. "We're going to see your mother!" she gushes.

Linda gets into the front seat with Geoff, who starts the ignition. She can't help a little wry smile from playing with her lips. What a queer way for their little weekend to end. Linda had entertained notions of winning Josh over this weekend. She had allowed herself to dream that this might be the moment they all became a family. And here they are, heading off to see Gabrielle.

Still, it's the right thing. If Gabrielle makes a stink in court, she can't say that Geoff was unreasonable, that he kept Josh from her. Geoff will be able to show himself as level headed and broad minded. And for Josh's own peace of mind, whisking him back to Boston without seeing his mother would do far more harm than good.

But in the short run, it will probably seriously derail any campaign Linda might have in winning the boy's affection.

As if to prove her point, Josh leans forward toward the front seat. "So does this mean you won't be marrying *her* anymore and you'll go back with my mother?" he asks Geoff.

"No, Josh, it doesn't mean that. Linda and I are still getting married. Your mother and I are getting divorced."

"I hate that word," Josh says, sitting back in his seat. In the rearview mirror, Linda sees Julia pat the boy's knee in sympathy.

They pull up in front of the inn. Linda wonders if perhaps Gabrielle will have gone out, if they'll miss her. They didn't call to say they were coming. Had that been Geoff's secret hope, that they'd get here and she'd be gone, so he could then say, "Hey, I tried"? But Linda thinks she's here. She imagines she's still upstairs in her room, just sitting there in front of the fireplace, even though it's warm enough outside for shorts.

Once again, it takes nine or ten rings for Gabrielle to answer the phone. Geoff tells her they've brought Josh to see her. "Yes," he says into the phone. "We asked him. And he said yes."

There's no waiting, however, when they head upstairs to her room. Gabrielle is in her doorway, her face alive with passion at seeing her son, who walks timidly between his father and Julia.

"Oh, Josh! My Joshua!"

She stoops down and throws open her arms. The little boy looks at her. To Linda's surprise, he doesn't rush into his mother's arms. He just stands there, looking at her.

It's been almost four years, Linda thinks. *He doesn't fully remember her. She's been just an image in his mind for so long.*

Gabrielle has to settle for a small handshake. She stands, a little ruffled by the less-than-enthusiastic greeting. "Well, shall we all go inside? I'll pour us some tea."

This time they accept her offer. Linda notices Gabrielle doesn't have a cup herself. Her attention remains riveted on Josh, who sits on the same hassock his mother had used and stares into the fire.

"How big you've gotten," she gushes, sitting beside him. "Mommy has missed you so much, Joshua."

Linda notices that Josh reacts slightly when Gabrielle takes his hand. He pulls back a little. As yet, he's said not a word to her.

Geoff has sat down uneasily in a chair across the room, watching his son with steely eyes. Julia is on the couch, beaming at this mother and child reunion. It strikes Linda as odd that the old woman would be so invested in seeing Gabrielle back in the picture. What connection was there between them? What's Julia's story anyway?

"What grade are you in school now, Josh?" Gabrielle asks.

The boy doesn't answer.

"He's in second grade," Julia replies for the boy.

Gabrielle smiles up at her then returns her gaze to Josh. "Summer vacation is almost here, isn't it? Maybe you'd like to come with me to the beach. Would you like that, Josh?"

"We're not making any plans here," Geoff warns her from across the room. "This is just an introduction. Nothing more yet."

Gabrielle frowns. Linda notices that she's possibly even more beautiful than her photographs. Her features are fine, like porcelain. Her fingers are delicate, and her lips full and red. But there's something else, too, something not at all beautiful: something—dare she say it?—hideous. It surprises Linda to think such a thing. She couldn't for the life of her say what it was. To all appearances, Gabrielle was a startlingly beautiful woman. In her jeans she reveals a figure far shapelier than Linda's, with a tiny waist and long legs. Her eyes are magnetic. And yet something—something is wrong. Something is off. Something is ugly.

No, Linda was right the first time. Not just ugly. Hideous.

"Do you remember," Gabrielle is asking Josh, leaning close to him, "when we used to take our walks into the woods out behind the house?"

The boy looks up at her uneasily.

"And I'd tell you stories! Do you remember, Josh? Stories about the trees and the flowers and the sun? Do you remember, Josh? The story about the magical sun up in the sky?"

"No," he finally says, a tiny little frog voice deep in his throat.

"You don't remember?"

All at once the boy stands. He looks down at Gabrielle. His face is twisted in terror.

"You're not my mother!" he screams. "You're not my mother!"

He bolts out of the room.

CHAPTER 5

Geoff follows his son out the door and into the hallway, calling after him.

Julia springs up from the couch to console a suddenly distraught Gabrielle, who covers her face with her hands. "Oh, how could he say such a thing?" she cries. "How could he say I wasn't his mother?"

"There, there, dear," Julia says, her arms around Gabrielle and patting her back.

Linda stands over them. "You've been gone for four years. You couldn't have expected him to just pick up where you left off. He's not even eight years old."

Gabrielle flashes her an angry look. "Do *you* have any children, Miss Leigh?"

Linda hesitates. "No. Not yet."

"There is a bond between mother and child. A *bond!*"

The phone rings. Julia picks it up. It's Geoff from downstairs. "Do you want to speak with Mrs. Manwaring?" the nanny asks eagerly into the phone.

Linda can see Geoff's answer disappoints her. She makes a face and hands the phone over to Linda.

"Josh is a wreck," Geoff tells her. "Get the hell out of there. Tell Gabrielle she has her answer. Josh does *not* want to see her."

Linda tells him they'll be down in a moment. She hangs up the phone and turns to Gabrielle. "I'm sorry," she says. "Josh is too upset to come back upstairs."

Gabrielle blinks back her own tears and stands. "Very well. Maybe I did try to rush things. This will take time. I need to accept that."

She's talking to herself as much as to them. Linda watches as she paces a bit, wringing her hands.

"I suppose you'll be returning to Boston," Gabrielle says. "Josh still has a couple more weeks of school before vacation."

"That's right."

"I'll come to Boston. We'll try again."

Linda moves toward the door. "You can work that out with Geoff."

"I'm going to see my son, Miss Leigh," Gabrielle insists.

"Of course you are, dear," Julia says. "He just needs a little time to adjust."

They say nothing more. Linda and Julia head down the stairs, the older woman ahead of her, her chin in the air. In the lobby Linda hangs back a bit, allowing the nanny to get outside. Then she doubles back to the front desk.

"Excuse me," she says to the clerk. "Could you tell me when Mrs. Manwaring checked in?"

She's not sure why she's asking. She's just curious all of a sudden.

"Only this morning, ma'am. Quite early, in fact."

Linda thinks of meeting her shortly after dawn.

Gabrielle had said then she had been in town for several days. Of course, she might have been staying elsewhere, but it just feels odd to Linda. Cal at the general store, too, had told them he'd seen her for the first time only this morning. It probably means nothing, but Linda files it away in her mind.

All the way back to Boston, Josh keeps insisting Gabrielle was not his mother. "That's not her!" he cries. "That wasn't her!"

"But it *was*, Joshua," Julia attempts to correct him.

"Let it go, Julia," Geoff commands. "If the boy says it wasn't his mother, who are we to argue?" He winks over at Linda. "After all, isn't there a bond between mother and child?"

Linda manages a small smile. She turns to watch the rolling green hills of western Massachusetts flatten out into the vast stretches of concrete of greater Boston. She knows this turned out to Geoff's advantage. He can tell the court he tried but that Josh ran from his mother in fear. *He doesn't recognize her. He insists she's not his mother.* Let the court psychologists make of that what they will. They'll conclude Gabrielle's abandonment had left a huge scar, and that Geoff was the only constant in the boy's life. Seeing his mother at all might be too traumatic. Gabrielle didn't stand a chance in winning any kind of custody rights. If she sees him at all, it will be just as Linda figured would be best: intensely supervised visitation.

And it cleared the way for her, too: with the angelic image of Gabrielle erased from his mind, Josh might finally start warming up to Linda. Really, the boy's reaction to his mother couldn't have been better for them.

Then why does she feel so sad? Linda spots the John Hancock building and the Prudential tower coming into view ahead of them. Home. They're home. And the little boy in the backseat is heartbroken. As rude and belligerent as he could be to her, Linda still aches for what Josh must be feeling. How excited he had been to see her! And then—such disappointment!

Just why he had responded the way he did remains a mystery. But who could explain all the nuances of a child's conflicted feelings toward a mother who abandoned him? Linda's own mother hadn't been perfect: she'd often been too demanding, too quick to show her preference for the perfect Karen. But she'd always been around, there when Linda got sick, there when she acted in the school plays, there when Linda had nightmares in the middle of the night. What would it be like to feel your mother didn't care enough to stick around?

She's consumed with these thoughts as Geoff drops her off at her apartment. Josh has nodded off to sleep in the backseat, so she just whispers a goodbye to him and Julia. The nanny just nods primly. Geoff walks her to the door and kisses her, thanking her for all she'd done this weekend. He'll call her in the morning, he promises.

Linda heads up the elevator. She leans against the back wall, watching the little red numbers tick upward. 8, 9, 10, 11, 12 . . .

And then the elevator jerks and stops.

"What the—" Linda says, pressing her floor number, 18, again. The elevator doesn't budge.

"Oh, great," she mutters. "What do I do now?"

Should she press the emergency buzzer? She's heard it before, when some kid in her building hit it accidentally. It's a horrible sound, shrill and piercing, bells and whistles worse than any car alarm. She punches her floor number again once, then twice, then a frantic machine-gun assault.

And the elevator door suddenly slides open.

Linda screams.

It's a raging inferno. Her building's on fire. She can see nothing but flames, and their heat singes her face. The fire makes a roaring sound and it appears ready to lunge at her, cooking her instantly within the oven of the elevator. In desperation she reaches out and hits the close-door button. The elevator doors mercifully slide shut.

She hears the gears shudder back into life. But instead of beginning to climb again, the elevator starts to drop. *Good,* she thinks instinctively. *Get me down to the ground so I can get out. Away from the fire!*

But the elevator isn't descending floor by floor. It's going far faster than it should be. "No," Linda gasps. "Oh, dear God, no!"

The elevator drops hard and begins to plunge.

"Noooooo!!!"

She's certain she will die. This is it, the end.

But all at once, as it nears the ground, the elevator suddenly slows and comes to a gentle stop at the ground floor.

The door opens with a peaceful "ping."

Linda stumbles out, leaving her suitcase and her purse inside. She runs screaming across the marble floor of the lobby to the concierge's desk. "There's a fire!" she shouts. "A fire upstairs!"

The concierge, sitting with his feet up on the desk reading Tolkein, springs to life. "Where? Where?" he barks, gripping the edges of the bank of security video screens, looking among them frantically.

"I don't know! The twelfth floor! The thirteenth! Somewhere below mine!"

"How do you know? How do you know?"

"The elevator got jammed! I saw it!"

The concierge, a genial Indian with oversized ears, can see no fire on his monitors. "A small fire. Was it a small fire?"

"No, it was raging," Linda insists. "The whole floor was ablaze."

The man looks desperately at his screens for some sign. "Here is the twelfth floor," he points to her, "and here is the thirteenth. No fire. You see, no fire."

Linda does see. But her face is still hot from its heat.

"I will have to call the fire department," the concierge says.

Suddenly Linda feels foolish. A vision? Another vision?

"Maybe," she suggests, "maybe we can just check before we—"

"No, the policy is to call. I'm going to have to set the alarm, too. If you say it was raging—"

"Well," Linda stammers, "I—I thought—"

The concierge has pressed the button for the alarm. A horrible wail echoes throughout the building.

"Yes, I've had a report of a fire," the concierge is saying into the phone. He gives the address, and within moments, Linda can hear the sound of sirens approaching. Terrible, hideous sounds, like the screams of banshees. Linda has to cover her ears with her hands.

Of course, no fire is found.

What's going on? Linda asks herself, staring into her mirror.

What are these visions I keep having?

Why so much fire?

She stands, exhausted, heading to bed. She thought about calling Geoff, but decided against it. He would just worry.

And besides, what would she say?

Oh, hi, Geoff, I just had another crazy vision about fire. Got the whole building in an uproar.

As if he doesn't have enough to worry about. No need to layer on top of that the fear that his fiancée might just be *losing her mind.*

She slips under the sheets, staring up at the ceiling.

That's what she fears. That she's going crazy. And that Geoff will decide she's not a fit mother for his son, after all, and since Gabrielle is back, and since she's much more beautiful and interesting anyway, why, he'll just decide to dump Linda and take Gabrielle back.

Stop it, Linda, she scolds herself. *Go to sleep.*

But she can't.

She's too scared.

She sits up in bed.

I'm afraid if I go to sleep, I'll dream that the fire has returned again, she admits to herself.

She turns over onto her side and pulls the blanket tightly up around her neck. *Count sheep,* she tells herself. *Count backwards from 100. Do anything. Just don't think about fire.*

But it proves futile.

"Why am I so frightened of fire?" she asks herself out loud, a tiny, shivering whisper in the dark.

Because all of your dreams are about to go up in flames, a voice tells her.

Whose voice?

The thing that torments her in her dreams?

Or . . . her own?

"Oh, God," she moans.

She swings her feet out of bed and scuffs across the floor into her bathroom. She flicks on the light and withdraws a sleeping pill from the medicine cabinet. She swallows one with a handful of water from the faucet.

No dreams, is what she prays for.

Her prayer is answered. She falls asleep in about fifteen minutes, and her rest is deep and untroubled.

But in the morning the fear is still there, and it never retreats very far for the rest of her day.

"It was *awful,*" she tells Megan over lunch.

"Sounds it."

"Everybody standing around, some in their pajamas, little kids crying." Linda shivers at the memory. "And no fire."

Megan laughs. "Linda, it's a crime to report a false alarm. Don't you remember those kids in high school who'd call the school with bomb threats? They always thought they'd get away with it, but nooo. Somebody always squealed, and the kids would get expelled."

"I didn't do it deliberately," Linda says, oblivious to her friend's attempt at humor. "I thought I saw it. And look." She thrusts her face across the table. "My nose and cheeks. They are singed."

It's true: she had to put aloe on them when she woke up this morning.

"Those flames were real," Linda says with mounting fear. "But real only for me."

"I don't understand, sweetie."

"Neither do I."

"You know, Randy has a theory, that if one has a strong enough belief in something, it can manifest. Like Padre Pio. You know who he was?"

"No."

"He was some priest in, I don't know, Rome or something. And he really, really believed that he needed to share Jesus' suffering on the cross and all that. And what happens? He gets those wounds on his hands and feet, just like where Jesus was crucified. It's called roseola or something—"

Linda can't help but laugh. "Stigmata, Megan. Roseola is a baby's rash."

"Whatever. Point is, he made it happen. With his mind. The mind is more powerful than we know. If you really believe you saw those flames, Linda, your cheeks might just turn up burned."

She sighs. The waitress brings them their salads. All morning long, Linda's had a hard time concentrating on work. What was happening to her? What did these visions mean?

"And this weekend, Geoff had the dream, too," Linda says, running her hands through her hair. "Josh has had it, too. Why are we all dreaming about and seeing visions of fire?"

"You think it has something to do with the creepy wife coming back, don't you?"

"I can't imagine how, but . . ." Linda's thoughts drift off. In her room at the inn, Gabrielle had seemed so focused on the fire. Was she affected by this craziness, too?

"I think it's some weird manifestation of all of your fears," Megan says. "Maybe you ought to talk with Randy about it. He does family counseling, you know."

"Well, it's true Gabrielle's return has sure thrown us into a state," Linda says, taking a bite of cucumber dipped in ranch dressing. "But these dreams and visions started before she returned. The first one I had was the night of my birthday."

"The night Geoff asked you to marry him."

Linda nods. "Yeah. That was the night."

"I don't know, sweetie. Do you want me to ask Randy to get you some Xanax?"

Linda smiles. "Yeah. Why not?"

"Good. Well, finish up that salad, sweetie. Remember that memo that came around saying we were to take no longer than fifty-five minutes at lunch. Hah! I don't know why they even still call it a 'lunch hour.' It's a contradiction in terms!"

Linda nibbles the last of her lettuce and tomatoes.

Some weird manifestation of all of your fears . . .

Yes, that's what this is. All of it.

But how? How and why?

And in her mind Linda has a very clear picture of Gabrielle arriving in Boston, planning her next move to see her son.

They don't hear from her right away, however. In some ways the next few days slide back into normality. There are no more dreams, no more visions. Geoff has a couple of frantic meetings with his lawyers, warning them that Gabrielle is back and they need to plan and adjust for that. That she doesn't plan on contesting the divorce is good news, the lawyers say, but legally now that she's back the process and paperwork is going to be a little different, and the divorce might not be obtained as quickly as they'd hoped before.

But with each passing day, with no word from Gabrielle and no more dreams to tear holes in their tensions, they settle into a kind of waiting period. Linda even feels some of the fear that's been gnawing constantly at the back of her mind begin to ease up. She takes a day to go shopping by herself, losing track of time as she pokes through the mall from shop to shop.

"Hello, Linda."

She turns. There's no one behind her.

She looks back the other way. No one there either.

It must have been her imagination. Or someone else in the store is named Linda. She's in a cute little sportswear boutique. She's considering a bathing suit. After all, the summer will soon be upon them, and they'll be spending more time at the house in Sunderland. There will be swims in the lake, lazy afternoons floating on inflatable rafts. She considers a bikini, but thinks it's too revealing, especially for being around Josh. A more sensible one-piece is a better choice—

"Especially since your body isn't half as curvy as Gabrielle's."

She spins around. Who said that?

Her heart is thudding in her ears. *My mind— playing tricks again—*

But she can't push away the idea that someone in the store is watching her. She glances around. Two salesgirls are leaning against the counter, talking to each other, oblivious to Linda. She could be a shoplifter and they'd never know. The only other person in the shop—that Linda can see—is an old woman trying on a pair of running shoes, grunting as she does so.

There's no one here, Linda tells herself. *No one but my crazy mind.*

She hurries out of the store. But she keeps turning around, suddenly paranoid that someone is following her. Someone unseen. Someone who means to do her harm.

I'm cracking up, she thinks. *I'm going crazy. I thought I was getting over it, but I was wrong.*

She pulls out her cell phone from her purse and pushes in Megan's number. She needs to hear her friend's voice.

"Megan, it's Linda."

"Hey, girl."

"I'm at the mall. Shopping. Come join me."

"Oh, I can't, sweetie. Randy's picking me up and we're going to some psychic fair. You know, talk to the spirits from the other side." She hums that weird *Twilight Zone* music.

"Stop. You're scaring me."

"Are you okay, Linda?"

She laughs. "I just have this feeling someone's following me." She glances over her shoulder again. No one that she can see. Just the usual mall shoppers, kids with baggy jeans and moms pushing strollers.

"Go someplace safe, honey. Stay in public. Ask someone to walk you to your car."

Her car. Linda freezes. No way is she going to walk through that dark parking garage alone.

"Is it just a feeling, sweetie, or do you see someone?"

Linda stops, leaning against a kiosk, and scans the crowd. A couple of teenage girls with pimply skin pass her, gushing about Justin Timberlake. A man with deep-set eyes is behind them, staring at the ground. Then along comes a woman with red hair, smiling crazily at no one.

"It could be anyone," Linda breathes into the phone.

"Sweetie, you need to talk to somebody. You know that, don't you?"

"Yeah," Linda admits.

"You go get a mall security guard to walk you to your car, and you go straight home. I'll call you tonight, okay?"

"Okay," Linda says, and she feels as if she might cry.

Even with the security guard, Linda still feels insecure and paranoid. She checks the backseat of her car before getting in. When she starts the ignition, however, she feels better, and by the time she gets home, she chalks the whole thing up to her imagination, overworked these days by her strange dreams and the events with Gabrielle.

But if Linda has been feeling uneasy, it's nothing compared to the strange mood Josh has fallen into. He makes no mention of his mother. All his previous ravings about her have ceased, and he sits for hours sometimes just staring into space. He keeps mostly to Julia. Geoff expresses concern.

"Maybe he ought to see Megan's husband, Randy," Linda says one night after dinner at Ambrosia, walking hand in hand with Geoff down Huntington Street. "Maybe he needs to talk to someone."

Megan's words haven't left her. Not only about Josh talking with someone, but herself, too. Though she hasn't had a repeat of the paranoia attack she'd had at the mall, it's still pretty vivid in her memory. They all need to talk to someone, Linda thinks. Though she knows Geoff won't be an easy sell.

As she predicted, he scoffs at the idea. "My fa-

ther always said seeing a shrink was a sign you'd already gone crazy."

Linda looks up at him imploringly. "There's nothing shameful about seeing a therapist, Geoff."

"I don't know. I was always taught you only sought
help for something you couldn't do on your own."
He smirks. "Like heart surgery."

Linda smiles. "You come from such classic New
England WASP stoicism."

Geoff shrugs. "My father wouldn't even let us go
to the dentist to get our teeth cleaned. 'You're supposed to know how to brush your own teeth,' he'd
say. 'Why pay to have someone do it for you?' "

Linda has stopped walking and is looking up at
him. "Your son needs help, Geoff. I know how much
you love him. I know you want to do the right
thing for him."

Geoff just sighs.

"Please, Geoff. The boy is terribly confused."

"Okay," he says quietly.

They resume walking. "We've all been under a
great deal of pressure and fear," she says. "I'm
looking forward to getting away for awhile."

That might do it for her, she hopes. Maybe she
can avoid therapy herself if she can just get away,
put all of the fears from the past few weeks behind
her. She's arranged to take two weeks off from
work once both Geoff and Josh go off for summer
vacation. They plan to head back out to Sunderland
and just relax. No worries, no deadlines, no fears . . .

But after this past weekend, she wonders if such
a scenario is possible in that place, so filled with
memories of Gabrielle.

That urn—that horrible urn. Geoff and Gabrielle
had found it in Egypt on their honeymoon. Why
had Geoff kept it? Linda plans to find it when they

go back. Find it and then conveniently lose it. She doesn't want it in the house.

She wonders where Gabrielle is now. She's somewhere in Boston. Linda's sure of it. Maybe she'll stay here when they all head out to Sunderland. Maybe she'll find a new life for herself . . . forget all about them . . .

Linda smiles to herself. Pipe dream.

Why had Gabrielle left her family? Geoff would only say that she was crazy. Psychotic. But there was more to it than that, Linda was sure. She knew there were women for whom home and family did not offer sanctuary but rather prison. She imagined Gabrielle was one of these, an antelope kept penned in by the cage of her family.

Since meeting her, Linda has become even more intrigued by her predecessor. She's asked Geoff for details on Gabrielle's life and was surprised by how little he knew. She was an orphan, he told her, and an only child. There had been no relatives from the bride's family at their wedding, held in the little chapel in Sunderland. Gabrielle had been born abroad, she explained, on an island in the Mediterranean or the Aegean—she was never sure which. Her parents had been archaeologists and explorers, and they never bothered to keep any records. Only through Geoff's connections at the college was Gabrielle able to secure a birth certificate that enabled them to be married.

The end came one day around this time of year. It was the end of the spring semester. Things had been bad between Geoff and his wife for some time; the affair with the teenager had only been over for a matter of months, and Gabrielle was surly and discontent around the house. One night they had a huge argument, with Gabrielle announcing she would go crazy if she remained in the house any longer. She said the walls were coming in at her, that she felt she would simply explode.

"There was never any great concern about Josh," Geoff says now, clearly mulling the same thoughts as Linda. "That's why this sudden interest in seeing him feels so odd."

"What do you mean?" Linda asks.

"When Josh was born, she showed very little excitement. I always thought mothers gushed over their newborns. Lucy Oleson threw her a baby shower and she got all these wonderful things, but they stayed in their boxes. If it weren't for me, we wouldn't have even put together a nursery for Josh. We wouldn't have even had a crib set up for when we brought him home."

Linda shudders. She can't imagine. Someday, when she hopes to find herself pregnant with Geoff's child, she's sure she will be decorating the baby's room with all sorts of stuffed animals and bassinets, toys, and diapers.

"Gabrielle seemed bored by her pregnancy. And after Josh was born, she'd play with him. They'd talk and she'd tell him stories. But she'd rather be out on her own, shopping, or laughing with friends, or—or flirting with strangers."

Linda can feel Geoff's hand tighten in her grip.

"Toward the end, when she was really chafing against being home in our house, she sometimes wouldn't even bother to get Josh dressed. I'd come home and he'd still be in his pajamas, sitting in front of the TV, eating a box of crackers for dinner. She'd be just sitting there, staring into the fireplace—"

"The fireplace?"

Geoff nods. "Yeah. Just like she was doing in the

inn. It was a habit of hers. She seemed to get lost in the flames."

Once again, fire.

"So this sudden conviction that she's his mother, that she has a right to see him, that there's such a bond between mother and child—" Geoff's words trail off. "It just seems like a lot of bullshit."

"Do you think there's some, I don't know, other reason she wants to see Josh?"

He laughs. "You mean, other than motherly love?"

"Yes."

Geoff nods. "Yes. Yes, I believe she has some ulterior motive."

"But what possibly could it be? She's said she doesn't want to contest the divorce. Do you think she's using Josh to get at you somehow?"

"I don't know. That's the thing, darling. I just don't know." He pauses. "And I never have where Gabrielle is concerned."

Back at Linda's apartment, there's a message waiting for them on the answering machine from Jim Oleson. "If you're there, Geoff, give me a call. I need to talk with you."

Geoff rings him up and is startled by what he hears. Linda can see his face go white. "What did she want?" he asks Jim, and Linda knows he means Gabrielle.

"Gabrielle went to see Jim?" Linda asks when he hangs up the phone.

"Yes," Geoff says. "It was very odd. She wanted to see him alone, without Lucy. So he told her to come by his office, which she did. He said she mentioned nothing about trying to see Josh. She was just interested in reconnecting. Jim thought it was very bizarre, and thought I should know."

"She just made small talk with him?"

"Yeah. Strange huh? They talked about old times and parties we'd been to on campus and friends who've moved away. Jim asked her a couple times if she came to see him for any reason, but she said no, that she just wanted to touch base."

"So why not have Lucy present?"

"Well, exactly, and Jim asked her that. Gabrielle said she thought Lucy didn't like her. Which is true, I suppose, but Lucy never showed it, Only after Gabrielle was gone did Lucy admit that she'd always had doubts about her."

Linda sighs. "Gabrielle's a very perceptive woman, I think."

"She's up to something. If she's out there courting my friends . . ."

"Put her out of your mind." Linda reaches up and kisses him. She hopes he'll stay, even for a little while, but he says that he promised to read Josh a story before bed tonight. Linda understands and walks him to the door. They kiss again and then he's gone.

She walks back into her living room. *That's odd,* she thinks. The candles on her table are lit.

I didn't light them. She examines them up close. *They've just been lit. They've barely burned down at all.*

She snuffs them out with her fingers as quickly as she can. Then she checks in every room, every closet, under every bed and table, to make sure she's alone.

She is.

Could Geoff have lit them when we came in? He must have. I was hanging up my coat. He must have lit them then.

But why?

And why did she persist in seeking logical explanations for things?

Her life was no longer logical.

Not since her birthday. Not since the night Geoff asked her to marry him.

Suddenly she's exhausted. She falls asleep almost as soon as her head hits the pillow. It's almost as if she's being pulled . . . summoned . . . from this waking state into the world of dreams . . .

Or nightmares.

But this time there is nothing terrible about her dream. No, not a nightmare at all. It is her wedding day. She is dressed in the most beautiful white lace gown, with a filmy white veil covering her face. Bouquets of roses and daisies are everywhere, and from inside the church she can hear the music starting. The wedding march. Her mother is embracing her now, her father standing over her with his eyes filled with tears. Her sister, Karen, is telling her how beautiful she looks.

Then, when she turns, looking down the aisle toward the altar, Linda can see Geoff.

Her groom.

How handsome he looks in his black tuxedo! And how his face beams with love for her.

She takes her father's arm and begins the walk down the aisle.

The church is filled with all of her friends. People from back home who had despaired of seeing her ever make a catch as good as this. Cousins who had called her plain. She holds her head up high, keeping her eyes on Geoff, waiting for her there at the altar.

There's Megan in the front row, crying with joy. Linda takes her hand as she passes.

"It's all going to be okay now," she whispers to her friend.

Her father hands her over to Geoff. Her husband-to-be takes her hand. They smile into each other's eyes.

But then, standing beside Geoff, Linda spies Josh, in a miniature tuxedo. His eyes are burning holes in the air.

"My mother will stop you," he tells her.

And suddenly there is a gasp from the crowd. Linda spins around. True enough, there is Gabrielle, in her own wedding dress, far more glittery and glowing than Linda's, walking herself down the aisle.

The entire church begins to shout out praise. "How beautiful she is," they exclaim.

"How stunning she looks," Megan says.

"How could you ever think you could compete with her?" Karen asks.

Linda looks over at Geoff. He is drawn by Gabrielle's glowing beauty, by the light that seems to shine from her eyes.

"No, Geoff, no," Linda cries.

But he bounds off the altar to meet her in the aisle, and they embrace.

The minister is pushing Linda aside. "Make way," he tells her. "Make way."

Gabrielle and Geoff step up to the altar, arm in arm, eyes locked together.

Linda staggers backward. Her eyes meet Josh's.

"I told you she would stop you," he says, grinning.

"No!" Linda screams.

And wakes, her hands in her hair.

"Ambrosia," she says, repeating the name of the restaurant she'd just left with Geoff.

Why is she thinking of that? The dreams recedes

quickly, almost to the point where she can no longer remember it. She knows it was bad, but just what it was, she can no longer recall. All she knows is that it concerned Gabrielle.

And that now she can't stop thinking about Ambrosia, the restaurant where she and Geoff had eaten only hours before.

She gets out of bed and dresses quickly. She retrieves her coat from the rack, not sure why she's doing so. But she puts it on and hurries out of her apartment. Out on the street, she traces backward the route she and Geoff had taken. Back down Huntington Street to Ambrosia. It's a cool night, and she pushes her hands down into the pocket of her coat. An ambulance siren wails from the street. Taxicabs bleat their horns. She dodges oncoming pedestrians with an urgency that surprises her.

Why am I going back to the restaurant? Did I leave something?

What am I supposed to see there?

Standing outside, peering through the windows at the diners inside, she finds out.

There, at the same table she and Geoff had so recently vacated, is Gabrielle. She's seated with Jim Oleson.

And they're kissing.

CHAPTER 6

Linda backs away quickly, not wanting to be seen.
He must have talked to Geoff and then hurried over here. To be with her.

Linda can't think. She can't even move.

"What was that phone call about?" she whispers to herself. "To throw Geoff off the track somehow? Why would Jim call and tell Geoff that Gabrielle had come to see him, then rush off to meet her for some romantic rendezvous?"

She suddenly realizes she must look like some crazy person standing here on the sidewalk muttering to herself, so she forces herself to walk. To stride as fast as she can away. To put as much distance between Gabrielle and herself as she could.

So she hasn't changed, Linda thinks.

But what had caused her to come here? What had motivated her to leave her apartment and head back to the restaurant?

And the candles . . .

"Dear God," she says out loud again, "I *am* a crazy person! These things can't be happening!"

She needs to see Randy as much as Josh does. Or someone. She needs to see someone.

She can't sleep at home tonight. She knows that much. She pulls out her cell phone from her purse and calls Megan. "Of course," her friend tells her. "Come over if you need to."

She takes the subway over to Cambridge where Megan lives. She meets Linda at the door, her husband hovering behind her.

"Come on in, Linda," Megan says, stepping aside. "You remember Randy?"

"Yes, hi."

He shakes her hand. "Would you like a drink? You look as if you could use one."

"Uh, yeah, thanks. That would be good."

"Scotch?"

Linda smiles weakly. "Sure. Why not?"

Megan gestures for her to sit on the couch. She fills her in, telling her about seeing Gabrielle with Jim. Randy hands her the Scotch and she takes a sip, hoping it will calm her nerves.

"I told Randy some of what you've shared with me about her," Megan says.

"I'd say she's at the very least personality disordered." Randy sits in the chair opposite her. "Not that you asked for a diagnosis, but thought I'd offer one."

He's a good-looking man in his forties, balding, with wireless glasses. Linda smiles at him.

"Please," she says. "Any insight at all will be helpful."

"Well, from what Megan told me while you were on your way over here, this Gabrielle seems very narcissistic and controlling. My guess is she *wanted* you to see her with this friend of Geoff's."

"But *how?*" Linda leans forward on the couch. "How did I know to go there?"

Randy scratches his bald head. "I don't know. Some call it intuition. A hunch."

"This seems like too much of a coincidence," Linda says.

Randy looks at her evenly. "I don't believe in coincidence, Linda. There is always a connection between events in life. We may not know why at first, but there is a greater force at play." He smiles. "You see, I'm what you call a transpersonal psychologist. That means I give credence to forces that aren't easily explained or written up in psych books."

Linda studies him. "You mean like ESP or something?"

He nods. "Sure. Extrasensory perception is one way of describing it, as good as any, I suppose. I like to call it *intuition*. I've done a lot of work with intuition. Everyone has it. And you'll find that a lot of folks trust their intuition to some degree—you know, people who don't get on planes that ultimately end up crashing, and the whole tradition of woman's intuition, which a lot of women swear by—but science, good ol' basic science, hasn't gotten around to officially embracing it yet."

"Do you think it ever will?"

"Maybe. I think that someday in the future we'll be able to explain such phenomena, to document scientifically how the neurons of the brain can predict what is going to happen or warn us about a danger or give us some insight that seemingly comes from nowhere. For now, I treat it as a matter of faith." He smiles at her. "You knew you had to go to the restaurant to see something, and see something you did."

Linda nods. She feels safe here. Their home is modest, a small apartment in an old Victorian not far from Harvard Square. The walls are covered with books and the couch is soft and frayed, embracing. She could sit here all night. Of course, the Scotch is probably helping too.

"There's also the possibility of some kind of hypnotic suggestion." Randy stands, walking around the room and gazing up toward his books as if he's mulling the idea over in his head. "Perhaps when you saw Gabrielle last weekend in western Massachusetts, she said something . . . something she wanted you to remember."

Linda makes a face. "I don't follow."

"If she wanted you to see them at the restaurant, maybe she implanted the idea with you earlier, so that on a certain day and time you'd act on the suggestion."

"She didn't say anything like that when I saw her."

"You wouldn't necessarily remember it consciously. She may be a very good hypnotist and suggested that you forget what she told you."

Linda laughs. "Well, I don't know about that. But maybe. Maybe there's something in what you say. Because clearly what's been happening defies any rational explanation."

"Sometimes psychotic people manifest the most effective psychic abilities." Randy folds his arms across his chest and looks down at Linda through his wireless frames. "She sounds like a fascinating case. I'd love to talk with her."

"If what Linda describes about her is true," Megan says, sitting down on the arm of the couch next to her friend, "you ain't going anywhere *near* her, hubby o'mine."

"But why? Even as we sit here struggling with the

how, I still can't imagine why she'd want me to see her with Jim."

"That I can't offer hypotheses on," Randy tells her.

"Should you call Geoff and tell him what you saw?"

"No," Linda says. "He's upset enough as it is. Jim is a good friend of his. I just can't tell him yet."

"Well, you ought to get some sleep, sweetie," Megan says. "The couch okay for you? We don't have a guest bedroom."

"Oh, yeah, this will be just fine," Linda tells her. "Thanks for letting me stay."

"Keep in touch with me about this Gabrielle," Randy says. "I'm intrigued."

Linda smiles. She considers telling him that she and Geoff would like him to see Josh, but that ought to be Geoff's place to say anything. She's not his wife yet. And, having heard Randy's rather unorthodox approach to psychology, she figures she may have a harder time than she thought holding Geoff to his agreement.

"Thanks for the Scotch," Linda says as Randy heads down the hall. He gives her a little salute.

Megan has come out with a blanket and a pillow. "I assume you'll want to get up a little earlier than usual."

Linda nods. "I'm going to have to head back home and change before I go to work."

Her friend fixes the pillow on the couch. "Sweetie, are you scared?"

Linda holds her gaze. "Yeah. I am."

"It's definitely strange, all of what you're describing. But it's not like she's evil, or anything like that, right? I mean, all she wants is to see her kid occasionally."

"Yeah," Linda says, kicking off her shoes. "I don't think she's evil. She may be a bit psychotic, but you're right. She's just a mother who wants to see her son." She yawns. "And maybe she's not even psychotic anymore. She seemed pretty sane to me." She stretches out on the couch. "She's just hot to trot, as we used to say in high school. She's one of those women who has to have every guy she lays eyes on."

"Randy is *so* not meeting her," Megan says, laughing.

"Good night," Linda says. "And thanks."

"Don't mention it, sweetie."

Megan switches off the light.

It's hard keeping a secret from Geoff. It's the first one she's ever held back, and she feels terrible about doing it. She just needs to find the right time.

And that time presents itself soon enough.

A couple of days later, with Geoff swamped with grading final exams, Linda offers to bring him dinner on campus. She gets take-out Thai food: chicken satay and spring rolls as appetizers, with a double-sized chicken- ginger-peanut as the entrée. She lugs the bag of food across the quad, nodding at students she recognizes, all wearing shorts and eager for summer. She finds Geoff's building, heads up the front stairs and down the main corridor to his office.

And as she's opening the door, she bumps right into Jim Oleson.

"Oh! Oh! I'm sorry!"

He's nearly knocked the food out of her hand, but she manages to keep it from falling, setting it down on Geoff's desk. Hopefully the sauce didn't leak out of the foil containers too badly.

Geoff's not here. She turns and looks at Jim, who's beet red.

"I'm so sorry, Linda."

"That's okay. No harm done."

She studies him. The fink. She can't resist a dig.

"Has Gabrielle called you any more? Stopped by to see you?"

"Oh, no," he insists. "Haven't heard from her."

You liar, Linda thinks. She's got to tell Geoff about this, and soon.

She notices Jim has some files under his arm. "Where's Geoff?" she asks.

"He's up at the dean's office, turning in some grades. He should be right back." Jim smiles awkwardly, patting the files under his arm. "Which is what I've got to do myself. Take care, Linda."

She gives him a small smile as he hurries out of Geoff's office.

What was he doing in here? She supposes it's not unusual for colleagues to be in and out of each other's offices, but ever since seeing Jim smooching with Gabrielle, Linda has known the man can't be trusted.

She tells Geoff about it when he returns but he brushes it off. "Jim's always in here borrowing books of mine. Hey! Chicken-ginger-peanut! Yum!"

She considers telling him then and there, but Geoff starts talking first, going on about how stressed he is, how many final papers are still sitting against his desk waiting for grades. "You don't know how much I am looking forward to just getting in my car and heading out to Sunderland," he says, biting into a spring roll.

It will have to wait, she decides. He's too caught

up in the end-of-the-semester madness. But he needs to know his trusted colleague is making out with his wife in public.

Josh has been upset the last two days because his favorite toy, the Captain Space Ranger doll with the light-up eyes, has gone missing.

"You've got to learn to put your toys back in the toybox, Josh," Geoff reprimands him gently.

"He was right here!" he insists. "He was right here on the couch with me because we were watching Justice League and then when I came back he was gone!"

"I've looked everywhere, sir," Julia says wearily. "But it's nowhere to be found."

"I want a new one! Please! Get me a new one!"

Linda had seen it as a golden opportunity. Buy the boy a new Captain Space Ranger and he'd love her. It wasn't easy locating one of the damn things: as it is with every new season's hot toys, supply doesn't meet demand—on purpose—so she was left hopping from store to store in search of one elusive doll. She finally found one and presented it to Josh earlier tonight, but he'd just rejected it straight out: it might be Captain Space Ranger, but it didn't have the light-up eyes. Which completely made it worthless.

"Linda bought you one, and you weren't satisfied," Geoff tells him.

Josh is near tears. "The only reason Captain Space Ranger is master of the universe is because he has the power in his eyes. That one's just a stuffed make-believe Captain Space Ranger!"

"Josh, I've had about enough of your whining,"

his father tells him. "I have too many papers to grade now."

The boy stomps off in childish pique, Julia following him uttering useless words of comfort.

"I suppose I can understand," Linda says after they're gone. "It would be like having a Beautiful Chrissy doll without the up-and-down hair."

"What?"

She laughs. "Never mind. Just a girl's version of Captain Space Ranger for my generation."

"So," Geoff tells her, not looking up from his papers, "I finally heard from Gabrielle today."

"Oh." She braces herself. They're both on the couch, Geoff with papers spread over his lap, Linda reading a John Grisham novel. She's got her feet tucked up underneath her and she's leaning on Geoff's shoulder. She puts the book down and looks over at her fiancé. "Tell me."

He sighs. "I don't know how she did it, but she seems to have gotten a look at all the paperwork my lawyer had prepared. She was ready for everything. All sorts of medical opinions on her fitness as a mother, signed by all these hotshot Ph.D.s and psychiatrists. She had my complete schedule for the fall semester. She saw how many additional classes I'm planning on teaching. She actually questioned *my* fitness as a parent, saying I'm going to be away from Josh so much!"

"Oh my God!"

"That's not all." He looks up at her, his face dark. "She questioned my relationship with you."

"Me?"

He nods. "She raised the issue of my 'cohabitating' with you when I wasn't legally divorced from her. She said it was a bad influence on Josh."

"Oh, Geoff." She feels as if she'll cry.

"Dr. Manwaring?"

They look up. Julia has come back into the room.

"I've gotten Josh ready for bed. If you and Miss want to come in and say goodnight—"

"Okay, Julia," he tells her. "In just a moment."

She smiles and heads back down the hall.

"Geoff," Linda says, "do you think she . . . ?"

"Well, she's made no secret of her disapproval, and she's clearly still loyal to Gabrielle." He sighs. "I'd get rid of her, but Josh is attached to her. It would just be further anguish for him."

"And Gabrielle would use it as ammunition," Linda considers.

"I just knew she'd start playing dirty," Geoff says. "I knew it. All that talk about not wanting to cause any trouble. Since when did Gabrielle not cause trouble?"

Linda stands, running a hand over her forehead. "Maybe I—well, it might be a good idea if I didn't hang out here so often for a while."

"Hey," Geoff says. "I'm not going to give in to her. We're engaged to be married."

"If Julia's told her about how often I'm here, or how often you're at my place, then I'm sure Gabrielle also knows that Josh doesn't like me." Linda folds her arms over her chest. "We can't give her anything to use against us."

Geoff sighs. "Damn her. She's always got something up her sleeve." He tosses a student paper back into the pile, having hastily scribbled a "B-" on top of it. "But how she knew so much . . ."

"Tell me, Geoff. Have any files gone missing from your office?"

He considers it. "I'm not sure. I've been so crammed with year-end grades, I haven't checked. Why? Do you think she had them stolen?"

She should just tell him, but she holds back, yet again. Maybe she's just trying to spare him one more indignity, and maybe it's something else. She figures she'll handle it on her own for now.

Linda leaves Geoff going over his grade reports and heads down the hall to his study. There it is. That accursed urn. Even from across the room she can see its blue flame flickering, like a little tongue wagging at her. She approaches it and stares down at it, remembering Geoff's fascination for it. She blows out the flame.

She feels such childish glee at doing so, as if she'd just done something naughty, something wicked, but was still so pleased at having done it.

But then the flame re-ignites, flickering faster than before, as if it were agitated, angry.

I should take it, throw it out, lose it, she thinks. But she doesn't. The thing frightens her. She just hurries out of the room and closes the door, so she doesn't have to see it.

She confronts Jim at his office the next day.

"Linda!" he says, immediately struck with a case of nerves. "How good to see you!"

"I hope you'll still think so after I say what I've got to say."

She looks at him. Jim Oleson—witty, erudite, quick with trivia about the Babylonian empire or ancient Greeks. How she'd once felt inferior around him and his equally articulate wife. But now he's just a man—a man with all the sorry weaknesses and frailties of most men.

"What is it, Linda?" Jim asks, jumping up from his desk and closing the door to his office behind her. "What's going on?"

"Maybe you ought to tell me."

He sinks back down into his chair behind his desk. His face is white. Dark circles ring his eyes, and Linda doesn't think they come only from late-night grading sessions.

Other kinds of late-night sessions produced those rings.

"I saw you," she says, cutting to the chase. "I saw you at Ambrosia with Gabrielle."

"Oh." It's a small sound, more like air escaping from between his lips than an actual word. "Oh."

"Do you deny it?"

"No." He begins fiddling with a rubber band. "We had dinner, yes. She was upset. I was just—"

"Kissing her," Linda finishes. "You were kissing her."

He drops his face into his hands. "Have you told Geoff?"

"Not yet. I wanted to hear it from you on my own first."

He pushes back his chair and stands, pacing back and forth in the small space behind his desk. "You don't know what she's like. She has this way over me. Always has."

A light goes on in Linda's head. "Always has? So this isn't new?"

Jim looks as if he'll cry. "We had a—oh, I'm not sure what you'd call it. A fling. It was—right before she left Geoff."

"You were cheating with the wife of your best friend."

His face is twisted in agony. "I couldn't help myself! You don't know what she's like! I tried to stop—

but I couldn't! I tried to stop it from happening again this time, too. I called Geoff, tried to be up front—you see, she came here, tried to get things going again, but I refused. Lucy and I have been to see a couples' counselor, for crying out loud! I have a problem—a problem with women—but I really was trying. I did not want to cheat on Lucy again!"

"So what happened?"

His face crumbles. "As soon as I called Geoff, it was like she knew. Somehow she knew. She rang me right back, as soon as I had hung up the phone. And she told me to look outside my window. There she was, on her cell phone. I agreed to have dinner with her. And then—"

"And then it started all over again."

He nods, sitting back down in his chair and covering his face in his hands.

"You got her Geoff's schedule for next semester. You got her copies of his lawyer's divorce plans. You got her everything she asked for."

"Please, don't tell Geoff. And please! Not Lucy!"

"I can't make that promise to you," Linda tells him.

"I'll stop seeing her! I promise!"

Linda just turns and heads out of his office, leaving him sobbing behind her.

She plans to finally tell Geoff what she knows. She takes a cab from the college to his apartment in Beacon Hill. It's started to rain. Light at first, then heavier. By the time she arrives it's a downpour, drenching her in the few seconds it takes to hop from the cab and into Geoff's building.

Linda glances at herself in the mirror in the elevator. She looks a wreck.

And of course, it's the worst possible moment for her to be looking a wreck.

"Who's in the living room?" she asks Julia when she enters, shaking her wet hair and hearing voices coming from inside the apartment.

Laughter. A woman's laughter.

"Mrs. Manwaring came by with a gift for Josh," Julia says, beaming.

"Mrs. Manwaring—?"

Linda hurries to the living room. She stares inside. In the corner, Geoff sits stiffly in a chair. Cross-legged on the floor sits Gabrielle, laughing and smiling as Josh, standing in front of her, presses a button on the back of a doll and light shines from its eyes.

Captain Space Ranger.

"Look what my Mommy brought me!" Josh says when he sees her, holding up the doll. "It's just like the one I lost!"

"It *is* the one you lost," Linda mutters under her breath.

"Excuse me," Julia says, tapping her shoulder. There's a very self-satisfied grin on her face. She passes by Linda into the living room with a tray of Rice Krispy treats.

"Oh, Joshua!" Gabrielle sings out. "Rice Krispys! These were our favorite!"

"Yes!" the boy replies, grabbing a handful. "You used to make them for me all the time."

Linda makes eye contact with Geoff. He looks beaten.

"Oh, hello, Miss Leigh," Gabrielle says cordially. "I guess it's started to rain, no?"

Linda catches a glimpse of herself in the mirror on the wall. Her hair is plastered to her face, her mascara has run, and her white blouse sticks to her skin.

Gabrielle, meanwhile, is radiant: her blond hair bouncy and nearly glowing, her trim little waist showcased in her tight jeans. She throws her head back and laughs as Josh demonstrates for her again how Captain Space Ranger can send light out from his eyes.

"Geoff, may I speak with you?"

He nods, standing up solemnly, walking past his wife and son cavorting on the floor. He and Linda move off into the kitchen.

"Her lawyer called mine. I had to agree to a visit to show I was being cooperative, that I wasn't putting up obstacles."

Linda glances over her shoulder and sees Josh throw his arms around his mother's neck. "He seems to no longer have any doubts about her."

Geoff snorts. "She bought his affection with that doll."

Linda gets angry. "Julia took it! That's where it went. She took it and gave it to Gabrielle so she could waltz in here and win his favor."

Geoff lets out a long sigh. "Prove it. The doll was wrapped in a box. To Josh it was brand new."

"We need to get rid of her," Linda says.

"Julia or Gabrielle?" Geoff laughs bitterly. "We've lost, sweetheart. Now that Josh has reconnected with his mother, the courts will bend over backward for her."

"No. Not after what I have to tell you."

"What's that?"

"Wait until she's gone."

Geoff moves back into the living room so he can keep an eye on things. Linda can't bear to watch or listen to all the laughter, so she excuses herself, explaining she's going down to the lobby to buy a newspaper. It will give her a moment to think, to plan how she should tell Geoff about Jim, and how it might help them in any court battle with Gabrielle.

Once in the lobby she finds the newsstand closed and the rain outside harder than ever. Thunder rumbles over the city's soundtrack. She stands staring out into the rain, catching her breath and listening to her heart beat, pulling back her wet hair into a ponytail with an elastic band she found in her coat pocket.

I can't stand to be up there with her there, she thinks. *She's a conniving, manipulating b—*

Her thoughts are interrupted by a man she spots standing on the sidewalk in the rain. He's staring at her through the glass. There's no question about it: he's staring right at her, getting drenched in the process.

She turns away. Strange street people do strange things.

When she turns back to again look outside, he's come closer—his nose nearly pressed up against the glass. Linda lets out a small yelp and steps backward.

There's no one in the lobby. Geoff has no concierge. Linda wants to hop on the elevator and hurry back upstairs but something compels her not to.

She looks back at the man.

Come with me, Linda.

His voice. She can hear his voice in her head.

You can trust me, Linda. Come with me.

She studies him through the glass. He has a small, thin, neatly manicured moustache on his upper lip. He wears a bowler hat—sopping by now, its brim filled with rainwater. He's dressed well, but in a style that seems old-fashioned to Linda, with a waistcoat under his overcoat and a high-collar shirt and tie.

Linda, come.

She can't help herself. It's like the night she wandered off to find Gabrielle with Jim at Ambrosia. She just knows she has to go.

She pushes out through the revolving doors onto the sidewalk.

The man has already begun walking down the block. She wishes for a moment that she had an umbrella, but she's so wet anyway it hardly matters. It's getting dark, and she worries she'll lose the man among the crowds hurrying past in the rain. She follows him down one street then turns onto another, and then another after that, always keeping at least three or four yards of distance between them. He never turns around, and in her head she hears no more commands. She follows the man in the bowler wherever he leads.

They turn into an alley behind one of Boston's old brownstone churches. The man makes a sharp right behind the church and disappears into a cemetery.

Linda feels utter terror. She stands at the cemetery's gate, the sky black by now, the thunder frequent. A bolt of lightning illuminates the old gravestones for a moment. But she sees no sign of any man.

Get out of here, she tells herself. *Turn around and run!*

But she can't. She is frozen to the spot, standing there at the gate, staring into the cemetery.

Gradually she moves one foot and takes a step inside. The rain shivers down her back, and her shoe immediately fills up with mud as she walks onto the grass. Another flash of lightning, and she sees a hideous carved skull face glaring out at her from an old gravestone. She shudders.

What is she here to see? Who was that man?

Suddenly she is assaulted by horrific images: A hand thrusting upward from the muddy soil, trying to grab her foot. A skeleton exposed behind a grave. A howling wolf with yellow eyes glaring at her in the dark.

She knows these things aren't real. She holds on to her sanity, determined to discover the reason she was drawn here.

At the next glow of lightning, Linda spots the man in the bowler hat. He is standing over a grave a few feet away, looking down, as if in grief. When the lightning disappears, so does the man, but Linda's eyes are still riveted to the spot where he had been.

She makes her way through the muddy expanse. Lightning crashes again above her, and the rain has turned cold now. She shudders but keeps moving, despite the terror, despite the increasingly gruesome images. A slaughtered corpse. A mutilated woman. Blood everywhere.

Something is trying to scare me away, Linda thinks. *Keep me from seeing what the man brought me here to see.*

And now: fire. She could have predicted it. A great ball of fire roars up in front of her, but Linda won't be daunted. She pushes on, and the fire disappears, as if extinguished by the rain.

She reaches the spot where the man had stood.

Here, she thinks. *This is where he was. This is what he brought me to see.*

Two white marble slabs are imbedded into the earth at her feet. She can't read the inscriptions. It's too dark.

But then once more a flash of lightning allows her a chance to see. In that brief moment of ungodly light, Linda reads the names, and she gasps.

GABRIELLE DESCHAMPS SINCLAIR
1895–1926

And beside it:

ARTHUR DAVID SINCLAIR
1918–1926
AGE 8

CHAPTER 7

"Gabrielle Deschamps," Linda breathes.

That's Geoff's wife's maiden name!

And her son—Arthur David Sinclair—died when he was Josh's age!

She decides not to go back to Geoff's. She hurries home, where she strips off her wet clothes and wraps herself in her robe. She considers turning on her gas fireplace and sitting in front of it, but opts against it. She's not sure why. She just doesn't want to.

Instead, she calls Megan.

"Well, it's an unusual name, but not *that* unusual," Megan says. "I suppose there could have been another Gabrielle Deschamps a hundred years ago in Boston."

"So why did whoever he was show me the stone? Ask Randy, Megan. Tell him what's happened."

Her friend laughs. "Here. Tell him yourself."

Her husband comes to the phone, and Linda blurts out the whole story.

"Wow," he says when she's finished. "I think you're

dealing with some kind of certified psychic phenomena here, Linda. This is beyond what I do. I
deal with hypnosis and meditation techniques. I'm
not a ghost hunter." He sighs. "I'm just not sure
what to tell you."

"I don't know whom else to ask. I want to tell
Geoff, but I can't make sense of it. What's going
on? Who was this man? Is the woman buried in the
cemetery an ancestor of Gabrielle's? What am I
supposed to learn from seeing the grave? And how
do the visions of fire fit in?"

Randy seems to be considering something over
the phone. "I tell you what. I have a colleague out
on Cape Cod. Let me call him. He's had experience in the paranormal, has written books on it, in
fact. Let me call him and maybe you can talk with
him."

Linda's near tears. "I'd appreciate it, Randy."

She dreams that night—not of fire, but of rain.
Pounding, driving rain, and a windswept cemetery,
the white marble of the stones glowing through
the darkness.

Linda . . .

Come, Linda . . .

Who is calling her? The same voice that tried to
summon her into the flames? The same beast of
the shadows who seemed intent on claiming her
very soul?

No, this voice is different.

This voice is good.

Linda, come. Come and look.

She pushes through the fierce, cold rain, the icy
liquid fingers slapping at her face. The cemetery is
quiet now except for the downpour. There are no
skeletons pushing through the earth, no wolves
with ominous eyes.

There is only the voice, entreating her.

Linda. Look down and see.

She is standing over the flat markers she had seen before.

Gabrielle Deschamps Sinclair . . . Arthur David Sinclair . . . Dead more than eighty years. What did it mean?

And who was the man who led her here?

You can trust me, Linda.

Is that who calls her now? Is it he who tells her to look?

Look, Linda. Look and learn.

Staring down at the gravestone, Linda feels the warmth of the flames before she sees them. But then, slowly at first, then with a terrible, insistent urge, flames begin to crackle around the cold, wet, solemn marble. It is as if they are pushing up from the soil. The very flames of hell itself bursting through the core of the earth.

Linda gasps, pulling back.

In the flames she sees a bird—a mighty creature of red and gold, its wings outstretched. It opens its hideous beak to let out a terrible cry, and in its blazing black eyes Linda sees herself reflected there.

She screams.

She sits up in bed, breathing hard.

"What is happening?" she asks the stillness of the night. "What is happening to me?"

In the morning, she tries to steady her nerves. She's got to ground herself, keep her mind sharp and refuse to give in to the fear. Dreams, visions, paranoia . . . she can't let them get the better of her.

So . . . first things first, she tells herself, making

mental notes for her day. It's the last day of school, and so Linda leaves work early to meet Geoff on campus. He embraces her warmly, and in his arms she does feel better, allows herself to feel safe. She sits down in a chair in Geoff's office and looks up into her fiancé's eyes. *He loves me,* she tells herself. *No matter what else might be happening, Geoff loves me, and so long as that's true, I can handle anything.*

"So how did it go with Gabrielle?" she asks.

He sighs. "She stayed only about an hour, but in that time seemed to have completely swayed Josh into accepting her."

"Oh, Geoff."

"They laughed, they carried on," he tells her, packing up his books for the summer. "It was as if no time had passed, and they were just a happy mother and child."

"I suppose," Linda says, trying to stay rational, "on one level that's a good thing. Good for Josh." But her heart isn't in what she says. She doesn't trust Gabrielle; she has far too many questions about her.

Geoff seems to hear the hesitancy in her voice. "Oh, sure," he says, "and a judge will make all sorts of happy noises about it, too. But if she's able to manipulate me, she'll do the same to Josh. Somehow I know this newfound commitment to motherhood isn't about what's best for him. It's for her own motives, whatever they are."

He explains that they've set a meeting with their respective lawyers for Monday to discuss custody issues. "She's got Garner Richards as her attorney. Garner Richards! Only the best, shrewdest, most aggressive divorce lawyer in the state. I saw him in action when Jim Oleson divorced his first wife so he could marry Lucy. How Gabrielle got him, I can't figure."

Linda hesitates, but can wait no longer.

"Geoff," she says, "I need to tell you something."

He looks up from his crate of books. "What's that?" He studies her. "I don't like the look on your face, Linda."

"The other night." The words stick in her throat like peanut butter. She has to force herself to take a deep breath and begin again. "The night we had dinner at Ambrosia. Do you remember?"

"Of course."

"Well, for some reason I went back there. It was just a feeling I had."

Telling him what she has to say about Gabrielle and Jim is difficult enough. She just can't bear to bring up all the dreams and visions and intuitions she's been having. Not yet, anyway.

"What is it, Linda?" Geoff has drawn in close to her and is looking her deeply in the eyes. "What are you trying to say?"

"I saw Gabrielle in the restaurant. With Jim."

"Jim?"

Linda nods. "They were kissing."

Geoff stares at her, dumbstruck.

"I didn't tell you right away because I couldn't bear it. There was so much happening."

"Kissing? Jim and Gabrielle?"

"I confronted him. He admitted it. He's promised to stop—"

Geoff heaves the book he's holding in his hand across the room. It slams against the wall, upsetting a shelf of other books, which also, one by one, drop to the floor.

"Promised to stop! *Bullshit!* So Jim is how she hooked up with Garner Richards!"

"Geoff, calm down."

"Calm down?" He slams his fist against his desk.

"The goddamn backstabbing asshole! I always sus-pected him of having an affair with her before! When we were married, before she left. I'd spot them together. I'd find Jim's business cards in her drawer. This cinches it!"

Linda is on her feet, pulling at Geoff's arm, try-ing to calm him down. "We just have to be very careful from here on in. Too many strange things are happening—"

Geoff is heading toward the door. "I'm going over to his office and beat the shit out of—"

"Geoff!" She grips him by his shirt and stares hard into his eyes. "That won't accomplish any-thing. That will just land you in jail and give am-munition to Gabrielle to use in court, that you have a temper and are prone to violence." She makes a small smile. "Besides. I checked on my way in. Jim's already vacated for the summer."

Geoff looks beaten. "Why did he call me, then? Why did he tell me she'd been by to see him? Was he trying to taunt me, rub it in my face?"

Linda sits down on the edge of Geoff's desk. "I don't think so. He was clearly very conflicted about it. He tried to keep her away."

"Oh, yeah! Tried real hard!"

"Look, Geoff. I think Gabrielle has some . . . some kind of hypnotic power. Don't laugh. It's possible. She could have made some kind of hypnotic sug-gestion that later made Jim act on it and follow her to the restaurant." She hesitates, remembering Randy's hypothesis. "She may have done the same to me."

Geoff narrows his eyes at her. "What do you mean?"

"I'm not sure. But something compelled me to go to the restaurant and see them." She considers adding the other salient fact: that something—or rather, someone, in the form of a man in a bowler hat—had also been compelled to go to the cemetery last night. But it feels like information overload. She needs to figure out more about what that means before bringing it up with Geoff. It would only make him more distraught.

"Even if that's possible, even if Gabrielle has picked up some hypnosis tricks while she's been away, why would she want you to see them? She's clearly been counting on Jim to be her mole. I'm sure he came in here and took my files. You were right, Linda. They *are* missing."

Linda admits to herself that Geoff has a point. Why would Gabrielle want her to find out about Jim? Vanity, perhaps, but she senses Gabrielle isn't interested in something as petty as that. She'd have no motivation for spilling any of her secrets, not if it interfered with her plans.

Then who wanted Linda to know?

The man in the bowler hat.

Yes . . . He led her to the cemetery. Maybe it had been he who compelled her to go to the restaurant, too. But why?

And, most importantly, who is he?

Megan picks her up early the next morning. Randy had gotten in touch with his friend from Cape Cod and had arranged for them all to meet at his office. Both Megan and Randy had sensed the creeping desperation in Linda's voice. "I really appreciate your doing this," Linda says. "I feel so foolish, in a way."

"Honey, if you're prowling around cemeteries in the rain, I want to do all I can." She laughs.

"Couldn't you have at least waited until it was sunny?"

"You don't know what it's like, Megan. This feeling that comes over me . . . It's irresistible. I just have to do what it wants me to do."

"No, I think I can understand," Megan says, pulling into her driveway. "It's how I feel when the box of Little Debbies starts calling me from the pantry. I have no control. I am powerless to resist."

Linda laughs. She's glad Megan is irreverent about the whole thing. She needs the release that a little levity can provide. For the last couple of days, her head has felt as if it would split open. She's been totally unprepared for the phenomena that's been happening. On the one hand, she wants to dismiss it all as coincidence or the result of too much stress. She wants to pull a Gladys Kravitz from the old *Bewitched* TV show. When anything unexplainable started to happen, Gladys's husband would tell her that it was just one of her headaches coming on, or too much Chinese food the night before. And the laugh track would roar. And the façade of normality would be preserved.

But that's all it is: a façade. Something unexplainable is indeed happening to her. The dreams and visions shared by Geoff and Josh. The candles that lit by themselves. The compulsion to head to the restaurant. The man in the bowler hat, and the gravestones he revealed to her. Gravestones that bore the same name as Geoff's wife, and a boy who was the same age as Josh when he died.

"Hello, Linda," Randy says warmly, shaking her hand.

"Randy. Thanks so much."

"No problem." He steps aside to introduce his

friend. "This is Dr. Kip Hobart. I've filled him in on what I could."

"Hello, Ms. Leigh," Kip Hobart says.

They shake hands. He's handsome, with startling green eyes, much younger than Linda expected. She guesses she thought a psychic investigator, or whatever Hobart was, would be some bearded, hunched-over old man with a monocle. But Kip Hobart can't be more than thirty-five. When he smiles, he has the most adorable dimples.

"It's good to meet you, Dr. Hobart," Linda tells him. "I hope my story didn't sound too weird."

He laughs. "Not at all. I've dealt with a *lot* weirder, believe me."

That reassures her somehow, knowing that her case isn't that odd. *He can help me,* she thinks as they all sit down, Linda once again settling into that comfy, frayed old couch. *This man can help me figure out what's going on.*

"Let me tell you a little bit about what I do," Dr. Hobart tells her. "Like Randy, I am a transpersonal psychologist. Part of my practice is very conventional, much like his."

"Conventional, huh!" Randy laughs. "Now, I resent that!"

Kip smiles, those dimples making Linda's heart leap. "Hardly a conventional therapist, Randy, but conventional cases. By that, I mean I work with people who are working on issues small and large, from quitting smoking to dealing with illness or death. We use various methodologies, from hypnosis and trance to traditional talk therapy and behavior modification."

"Okay," Linda says. "I follow so far."

"Transpersonal psychotherapy includes consideration of the spirit as well as the mind and body. What is our relationship with our higher powers? What are the truths of our core faith? By looking at such issues, we allow ourselves to deal with areas that other therapists might be a little afraid to touch." He smiles. "Randy works with intuition. I understand he explored some of that with you. I go even a little further afield than that."

"I'd say," Randy says, laughing. "If you call exorcisms further afield."

"Exorcisms!" Linda gasps.

"Now, Randy," Kip scolds gently, "I've only performed a couple—"

Linda is aghast. "Are you suggesting I need an exorcism?"

Kip's laughing. "Not at all. Randy is just trying to stir things up."

"If you don't behave," Megan says, shaking her finger at her husband, "you can be excused."

"All I was trying to do," Randy explains, "is to point out that Kip knows an awful lot. There's very little he hasn't encountered."

"I was very fortunate to work with a well-known parapsychologist, Dr. Stokes," Kip tells her. "We traveled a lot together. I got to investigate many different cultures and traditions. I've learned many rituals." He shoots a glance Randy's way. "Exorcism being but one of them."

"So what does all this have to do with what has been happening to me?"

"I'm not sure," Kip Hobart admits. "I'd say you've definitely had an encounter with some kind of spirit. The man who led you to the cemetery . . . You told Randy he was wearing what looked like old-style clothes?"

"Yes," she says.

"Similar to this?" He flips open a notebook that's been sitting on the coffee table. Inside is a photocopy of a photograph. The man wears a bowler hat similar to the one her guide had been wearing. And the high-collar shirt and tie and waistcoat are also very much like those she'd seen. Linda tells him it seems like a match.

"This photograph is from 1922," Kip says. "What was the death date on the gravestone?"

"1923," Linda replies.

"My guess, then, is that you're dealing with a ghost. The spirit of a man who lived in that time, who probably knew the people buried under those stones."

A ghost. A month ago, Linda didn't believe in ghosts. Oh, she liked to think of herself as open minded. She'd watch those shows on the Sci-Fi Channel like *Sightings* or sit riveted to psychic John Edward's tales of communication with the dead. She wasn't a skeptic the way Geoff was. He called the shows bunk and switched them off with the remote control. Geoff was a professor, a believer in facts and figures and dates. She wasn't nearly so cerebral, finding the stories entertaining. She even liked to think she believed some of them.

But underneath, she didn't. She didn't believe in ghosts.

"That's how most people protect themselves," Kip tells her, startling her.

"What?" she asks.

"You were just thinking about how you never believed in ghosts, not really. You could watch the TV shows and find them entertaining, even telling your boyfriend that you believed. But deep down, you never really did."

Linda feels the blood drain out of her face.

"How did you—how did you know what I was thinking?"

Kip shrugs. "Sometimes I get readings. You've seen it on John Edward's show. Sometimes things come through. Sometimes they don't."

Linda looks over at Megan, stunned. "That's *exactly* what I was thinking! He read my mind!"

"Doo doo doo doo doo doo," Megan sings the opening few bars from the theme from *The Twilight Zone*.

"What people do is convince themselves that the only reality is what they see. What they feel and touch and hear. Everything else is just the stuff of entertainment." He sighs. "Because when they start to actually and truly *believe*, well, then everything's up for grabs. All of their truths. All of their faith."

"What do I do?" Linda asks him in a small, frightened voice. "Where do I go from here?"

"I want you to write what was inscribed on those gravestones, as best as you can remember it. I'm going to go over and check them out, and then do a little research, find out who the people were."

"Why do you think it's the same name as Gabrielle? Both first *and* last names?"

"I can't even begin to conjecture at this point. But I'd like to schedule an appointment with you for Monday. Randy said we could use his office. I'd like to get the full story, everything you know about your fiancé's wife. In fact, maybe you ought to bring him—"

He stops. Linda smiles.

"If you've read my mind," she says, "you know that's not a good idea. Geoff would just call it hocus-pocus."

"Then just you for now." Kip shakes her hand. "Monday at nine?"

"Could we make it a little later? I told Geoff I'd go with him to meet with Gabrielle and her lawyer." She smiles wearily. "They want to see that I'm not the kind who'll be corrupting the boy's morals or anything like that."

"Eleven, then?"

"Eleven it is."

When she heads back out to Megan's car for the ride back home, Linda could swear she sees Jim Oleson sitting in a car across the street. But why would Jim Oleson be sitting in a parked car on a side street in Cambridge?

She only has to wait until Monday to find out.

"I'm sure Ms. Leigh is a fine woman," Garner Richards is saying, "though my client does have some concerns about the company she keeps."

Geoff looks over at her, suddenly alarmed.

Linda stares directly at the dapper attorney, done up in pinstripes and silk tie, gold and ruby cuff links glittering in the light. What is he implying about her?

They've met at his office, a plush retreat of spun glass and butter-soft leather. He was terribly gracious and accommodating when they first arrived with Geoff's lawyer, a somewhat awkward, soft-spoken man named Niles Witherspoon, who wore suits too large for him and had an annoying little eyelid twitch that sometimes fluttered for four or five minutes straight.

Gabrielle was already there, sitting in a swivel chair with her legs crossed, wearing a knockout black dress suit and sheer black stockings. She greeted both Geoff and Linda warmly, even clasping Linda's hand. Linda got a whiff of her perfume. Lilacs. Of course.

"Uh, uh," Niles stammers, "are you suggesting something about Ms.—Ms.—" He glances down at his notes.

Oh, great, Linda thinks. *He's forgotten my name.*

"Ms. *Leigh,*" Garner Richards reminds him.

"Yes." Niles stiffens, thrusting out his chin, trying to look indignant. "What are you suggesting about Ms. Leigh?"

"Only that the company she keeps is a bit, shall we say, controversial."

"That's crazy," Geoff says, interrupting. "Give us specifics."

Richards clears his throat. He's sitting behind his enormous mahogany desk, shined so much that Linda can see his reflection in it. He lifts a sheet of paper and reads. "On Saturday last, did you or did you not, Ms. Leigh, meet with a Dr. Kip Hobart?"

She's stunned. So it *was* Jim Oleson. He was *spying* on her. She spins her head over at Gabrielle, who just smiles at her benignly.

"Yes, but Dr. Hobart is not—"

"Oh, but I'm afraid he is, Miss Leigh," the attorney tells her. "*Very* controversial. Were you not aware of the, er, *exorcism* he performed on Cape Cod a few years ago?"

"No," she says in a little voice. She can feel Geoff's eyes burning into her.

"Well, he did, and a woman died. They were exorcising demons in an old church. *Exorcising demons.*" He turns, making sure the words are understood by Geoff's attorney. "The floor gave in, and the woman died."

Linda says nothing.

"Dr. Hobart has a history of dealings with voodoo and magic and ghost hunting. It says it all on his Web site, actually. He makes no attempt to hide it."

"I was there visiting a friend. Megan Riley. I work with her. Dr. Hobart is a friend of her husband's."

"Ah, yes. Randy Riley. I see here that he offers a plug for Dr. Hobart on *his* Web site, and there are plans for the two of them to start offering a series of psychic workshops together." He turns to Niles again. *"Psychic workshops."* He looks back at Linda. "Are you a member of one of these workshops, Ms. Leigh?"

"Hey," Geoff says, leaning forward in his chair toward the attorney's desk. "Who are you, Joe McCarthy? Linda can do what she wants on her own time."

Linda appreciates the defense but is sure she still has some explaining to do to Geoff after they leave.

"I'm just raising a concern of my client's," Richards says.

"It's nothing personal, Linda," Gabrielle says. "I'm just thinking about Josh."

Geoff explodes. "Thinking about Josh?" He stands up in his chair. "Were you thinking about him when you left him four years ago?"

Niles is on his feet, urging Geoff to sit back down. "Um, Geoff, let me, um . . ." He looks up at anxiously at Richards. "Well, as my client says, was she thinking about her son when she left him . . . uh . . . four years ago?"

Linda can see the flashy Richards clearly intimidates the nebbishy Niles. This is not going well. Not well at all.

"I don't dispute that I acted irrationally," Gabrielle

says, rising dramatically to her feet. "I wasn't well. I was . . . Well, you'll see the psychological reports. I was depressed. Clinically depressed. I left my son when he needed me most." A single tear runs down her cheek. "And I'm going to have to live with that the rest of my life."

Niles Witherspoon seems almost *moved*.

"But I'm well now. I'm cured of my depression, of all the human frailties that plagued me. You'll see that in the reports, too. I'm as fit as any mother could be." She smiles a little. *"More,* even, than most."

"Okay," Geoff says. "What is it that you want? Visitation once a week? I'm amenable to that. Providing there's some kind of supervision for a time."

"Yes," Niles echoes, "supervision for a time—"

Gabrielle has walked to the front of the room, turning around to face them as she stands against her attorney's desk, swinging her cascading blond hair so that it tumbles over one shoulder. Her black suit fits her perfectly, outlining her figure: her full breasts, small waist, round hips, and long legs. Linda can't deny Gabrielle's beauty, how classic she is, how absolutely stunning. *I can never measure up to her,* she thinks. *This is what Geoff had. How can he be satisfied with me?*

"I'm here to propose something, something radical, perhaps," Gabrielle says to them. Her voice is like honey. Even Garner Richards seems in awe of her. He just sits back in his chair and watches her, dazzled. Linda's sure they've rehearsed this scene many times, but that doesn't mean he can't enjoy the show.

"My radical idea," Gabrielle goes on, "is to let mother and son be together, to allow a mother back into her son's life." She smiles. "That's where a child *should* be. With his mother. What son hasn't benefited from a mother's devotion, from a mother's love? I want to give that to Joshua, to make up for the years I missed. I have so much to give him, so much that I want to share with him."

She looks directly at Geoff and widens her eyes.

"I want to take Joshua away with me."

It takes Geoff a few seconds to react. "Away with you?" he finally says, low and outraged.

"That's right. I don't want visitation. I want to take him away, to start over, in a new life. One you can't give him."

"I can give him everything he needs!"

"Not a mother! A boy needs a mother! A child *belongs* with its mother!" Gabrielle turns her ice blue eyes to Linda. "And he will never consider *her* his mother!"

"Is it not true," Garner Richards asks, poking his head around Gabrielle to be seen, "that Josh intensely dislikes Ms. Leigh?"

"I wouldn't say intensely—" Geoff begins.

Richards shrugs. "He told my client he was very unhappy living in a household that includes Ms. Leigh."

"Oh," Linda mutters, feeling the tears come on. It's all her fault. It's all because of her that Geoff might lose his son.

The son he loves more than anything.

More, probably, than even Linda herself.

"I am planning to sue for *full* custody," Gabrielle announces defiantly. "A court will decide." She looks utterly confident as she adds, "And *Josh* will decide. You'll see. A child's place is with his mother."

* * *

Geoff says little as they file out of the lawyer's office. "We'll talk," Linda promises, touching his hand, but his eyes are glazed over and he barely looks at her. Niles is escorting Geoff to his car and looks at Linda, assuming she's joining them. But she begs off from any post-meeting lawyerly talk so can keep her "doctor's appointment." Thank God she hadn't told Geoff what kind of doctor, or who.

"It's going to be okay, sweetheart," she tells Geoff.

But he just looks at her blankly, then follows Niles to his car.

On the cab ride to Randy's office, Linda feels her mind reeling from the meeting with Gabrielle. Is Geoff angry with her? He'll no doubt want answers about Kip Hobart. Linda had no idea that her quest for answers would endanger Geoff's custody of Josh. A woman killed during an exorcism? What kind of person had she gotten herself involved with?

She looks out the cab window. The day is bright and warm. The city is bustling with life. People rush through the streets on errands, chatter on their cell phones, hail cabs, and board buses. A busy hive of people, all with their own secrets, their own mysteries, their own fears. What might be going on in the life of that man over there, dropping letters into a mailbox? Or that woman, window shopping on Newbury Street? Or that teenage girl, walking alone and apparently lost, her eyes seeing not the world around her but someplace deep within her soul?

Linda settles back into the seat. What did she hope to find out from Kip? What kinds of answers would make sense? She doubts anything would seem rational after this. Her mind struggles to wrap itself around an explanation, a solution—but it's impossible. It feels like one of those calculus problems her teacher would set up in college. Try as she might, Linda just couldn't grasp what he was talking about. She couldn't visualize the problem, let alone propose a solution.

She wants to cry but doesn't. Has she lost Geoff? Is this the beginning of the end? She can just imagine calling her mother, telling her the wedding is off. Her mother would cluck sympathetically, but in her words Linda would be able to hear her real thoughts. *I didn't think it would work out. What was Linda thinking, playing so far out of her league? Who does she think she is? She's not Karen.*

"Shit," the cabdriver says.

Linda looks up ahead. They've crossed into Cambridge and run smack-dab into a traffic jam. She looks at her watch. It's nearly eleven. She'll be late.

"Could you find another way?" she asks the driver.

"I will try," he says. He slips out his map from behind the visor and studies it. He looks Filipino, and from his thick accent Linda figures he hasn't been in Boston long.

He turns the wheel sharply and heads down a side street. They make their way a few blocks, then run into more traffic.

"There must be something," the driver says. "Something stopping everybody."

"An accident," Linda muses, straining to see over the cars ahead of them. A plume of smoke rises to the air in the distance.

So she'll be late. There's nothing she can do. The cab inches ahead, bit by bit. The smoke up ahead grows darker and thicker.

"A fire," the driver says. "A building's on fire."

"Fire," Linda repeats.

Suddenly she knows.

"I'll get out here," she says. "I'll make my way faster on foot."

She pays the fare and hurries out of the cab. She walks quickly, then runs, in the direction of the fire.

She gasps when she sees it.

She was right.

It's Randy's office.

Where she was supposed to meet Kip.

Flames are shooting from the windows, licking their way up the outside walls, eating through the roof. Funnels of thick gray smoke pour into the sky.

"Linda!"

She looks in the direction of the voice. It's Randy. She runs to him.

"Thank God you're okay," she says, embracing him.

"Kip," he says.

"Is he—?"

Randy's face is torn with anguish. "He's inside. They can't save him. He'll burn to death."

CHAPTER 8

"Fire," she says weakly, staring into the inferno. "I brought this on him. It's my fault!"

Randy grips her by the shoulders. "Don't say that, Linda."

"He was helping me! He was going to give me answers!"

Randy looks from her back toward the burning building. The fire rages savagely. Angry flames roar as they burst up through the roof. It's like an animal, a living creature, intent on as much destruction as it can cause. Even from this distance, the heat is horrible.

"Kip," Randy mutters, near tears.

Linda puts her hands on his shoulders.

"I spoke with him this morning," he says, looking over at her. "He said he had information for you. I know he was researching what you'd told him."

An explosion from inside the building startles them all. New flames shoot toward the sky.

"Dear God!" Linda screams. "They've got to go in and try to get him out!"

Just then they witness a chunk of the building's roof collapse inward. Policemen are suddenly in front of them, pushing them and the rest of the crowd back. Linda stares with horrified eyes as fire-fighters aim their hoses and gush tons of water at the structure. But their efforts appear to do little good.

"Please," Linda begs, shouting to the firefighters over the shoulder of a policeman. The heavy smoke is making her eyes water, her nose burn. Her throat feels coated with soot. "There's still a man inside! You've got to rescue him!"

"They got everyone out," the policeman assures her.

"Everyone?" Randy asks, "Looking around, I can account for everyone but one."

The cop nods. "There was one man they took away, with severe smoke inhalation. I suggest you check the hospital."

"It's Kip," Linda says.

But they have to be sure. They manage to get out of the crowd and hop on the subway a few blocks away. And at the hospital, their hopes are confirmed. Kip Hobart has indeed been admitted, but he remains in critical condition, suffering from smoke inhalation and shock. No visitors are allowed at this time.

"It's all my fault," Linda tells Randy, shaking her head.

They head over to the cafeteria for coffee. "You've got to stop saying that," Randy tells her. "I'm the one who got him involved. And besides, you're drawing conclusions that might not be there. The fire department thinks there was an electrical problem. A simple, ordinary, everyday, very-much-of-this-world electrical problem. The fire could have nothing to do with what you're thinking."

"Randy, get real. My visions of fire. My dream. Geoff's dream . . . and now this." She gives him a wry smile. "And let's see if I can remember your words exactly. 'I don't believe in coincidence. There is always a connection between events in life.' Isn't that what you said?"

He sighs as the waitress brings over two cups of joe.

"Did you lose much in the fire?" Linda asks him, tearing open a packet of sugar and dropping about half of it into her coffee.

"Some records, but I got most of them. Thankfully one of the other therapists down the hall smelled smoke and we all had just enough time to gather some things and get out of there." He pauses. "But not Kip."

"Why? What was he doing?"

"I'm not sure. He was in my inner office. I banged for him to get out, but he didn't answer. I opened the door but saw the place was already filled with smoke. It was odd—"

"What was odd?"

"I couldn't see him, but I could hear him. He was talking. I couldn't tell what he was saying. I shouted to him, but he didn't respond. And then—"

"And then what?"

"There were flames everywhere. That's why I assumed he'd been trapped. There were flames, enormous flames, mostly blue. And I thought I saw—"

His words trail off. Linda reaches over and touches his hand. "You thought you saw what?"

"A bird."

Linda blinks. "A bird?"

"Yeah. Not a bird like we see every day. A huge bird. I guess it was just the flames, twisting into an odd shape. But for a fleeting second I thought I saw a giant bird, red and gold, rising up out of the fire."

Linda rubs her temples. The coffee is weak and bitter. "Kip was known to perform rituals. Might he have been doing something like that?"

"Maybe."

"Tell me about the woman who died in an exorcism on Cape Cod."

Randy looks at her strangely. "How do you know about that?"

"Gabrielle's lawyer has been doing a little snooping. He sprang it on us at his office this morning. They questioned if I was going to be a good influence on Josh if I was associating with people like Kip."

Randy sighs. "That woman was a close friend of Kip's. He was heartbroken. There were bad things going on in that town. Falls Church. Do you remember, a couple years ago, the mysterious deaths and the strife that went on out there?"

Linda thinks she vaguely remembers reading something about it.

"Well, Kip was one of those who helped beat back the forces. He's never given me all the details. To be honest, there are some things I don't want to know. But I know that I trust Kip. It wasn't his fault that the woman died."

They both push their coffees away from them. Randy tosses a few dollars down on the counter.

"Hey, I've got to call Megan. If she hears about the fire, she'll be anxious."

Linda nods. They promise to talk later with an update on Kip. They head their separate ways on the subway, and Linda trods home with a heavy heart.

They're supposed to leave tomorrow for Sunderland, she and Geoff and Josh. And Julia, too—Julia who's against her, who's in cahoots with Gabrielle. But just what is Gabrielle capable of doing? Could she somehow be behind the fire at Randy's office? Is that what Linda is thinking?

"I just don't know," she moans to herself, sitting on her couch, holding her head in her hands.

What was the information Kip was going to give to her? What had he discovered?

And was that the reason for the fire? Did someone—or something—not want that information passed on to Linda?

She sits there, listening to the muffled sounds of the city outside her window, the bleats and the sirens, the occasional boom of an airplane coming into Logan. She sits, not thinking, lost in the whirr of her automatic icemaker and the hum of the air conditioner. She begins to cry.

I've lost Geoff. I can't go on like this. If he connects me to this fire, he'll want to distance himself as far as he can from me. Whatever forces I'm stirring up, he will see them as a threat to Josh. I'm already a liability when it comes to keeping custody. My relationship with Geoff can't go on after all this.

I should've known it was too good to last.

Who did I think I was? Karen?

The phone rings, jolting her. It's Geoff. "Let's go today," he says in a tired voice. "Can you be ready in an hour, as soon as Josh is out of school? I can't stay in the city a minute longer. Let's go today."

So he still wants her. The idea gives her a little comfort.

But for how long?

* * *

The ride out to Sunderland is mostly silent. Linda doesn't mention the fire. Geoff still hasn't asked her about her involvement with Kip. Josh falls asleep in the backj174

seat of the car. Julia sits staring straight ahead, her hands folded primly in her lap.

Once they're there, however, Josh turns into a whirlwind of energy, running up and down the stairs and insisting they have hot chocolate. Julia heads into the kitchen to boil some water.

It's so peaceful in Sunderland at night. The sky is ablaze with stars and the tree frogs keep up quite the background chorus. Linda's always loved the "peepers," as Josh calls them. They only peep for a few weeks in the spring then disappear.

She stands on the front porch and stares up into the sky. What can she hope for during their time out here? Just a month ago she had hoped it would prove the start of her life with Geoff and his son. She had hoped it would make them a family. But now, what does she hope for? She can't seem to allow herself any room to hope for anything. Just peace. Just peaceful nights like this, with the stars and the peepers.

"What are you thinking?"

It's Geoff, coming up behind her.

"Nothing," she tells him. "My mind's a blank."

"I don't blame you, you know." His slips his arms around her, pulling her in close to him and pressing his lips against her ear. "Whatever that sleazeball lawyer tried to pull today was not your fault."

She feels as if she'll start to cry again. "Do you really feel that way?"

"I do."

She turns around in his arms and kisses him. As ever, he tastes so sweet. She looks up into his dark eyes and wants to believe him. But still she fears: if it comes down to choosing between her and Josh, he'll choose Josh.

"I only went to see Randy because I was hoping he might help Josh," she tells her fiancé. "He's a therapist. He's worked with kids."

Geoff nods. "I'm sure he's very good. Though with Garner Richards eagle-eyeing us, maybe we ought to wait on any child psychology sessions."

She agrees.

"What about this other guy he mentioned?" Geoff asks.

"Kip Hobart. He's—" Her words fail her. "Oh, Geoff, something terrible happened today."

She tells him about the fire. He listens but says nothing.

"Sometimes I'm frightened," Linda admits. She daren't tell him how frightened, but it feels good to reveal at least some of what she feels.

"I know what you mean," he tells her. "All this fire. But our dreams have stopped, Linda, haven't they? You've had no more visions of fire."

That's true, as far as it goes. The fire no longer exists in their minds: it's *real*. But she's had other visions, too. Visions she's on the verge of revealing to Geoff when Josh walks out onto the porch, holding his mug of hot chocolate in his hands.

"My mother's coming," he announces.

They release their embrace of each other. "What do you mean, Josh?" Geoff asks.

"I just know it. She's going to come out to Sunderland, too."

"Josh," Geoff says, "you know your mother and I are trying to figure out the best plan for you, so that you can see both of us."

The boy nods, sipping his chocolate. It leaves a brown mustache on his upper lip.

Geoff sits opposite the boy in an old weathered Adirondack chair. "What do you want, Josh? Tell me what *you* want."

Josh doesn't answer at first. He takes another sip of his hot chocolate, then looks up at the stars. The peepers seem louder in the trees, almost frantic.

"My mother wants me to go away with her," Josh says finally, in a low voice.

"Yes, I know," Geoff replies. "What do you think of that?"

"I want you to come, too."

"I can't, Josh. I have my work here." He pauses. "And Linda."

Josh doesn't answer.

"Josh," Geoff asks, "why did you change your mind about your mother? At first you thought she wasn't even really your mother."

"She brought me a Captain Space Ranger."

Linda sits down on the large flat arm of the Adirondack chair. She exchanges a look with Geoff.

"That can't be the only reason," Geoff suggests. "Is it, Josh?"

The boy turns and sits down on the step with his back to them. He keeps gazing up at the stars.

"No. It's not the only reason." Josh can't seem to

tear himself away from looking at the stars. "She tells me cool stories. I love her stories."

"What kind of stories, Josh?"

"About magical places. About the stars. About the sun."

"I'd miss you, Josh, if you went away," Geoff tells him, and Linda can hear the heartbreak in his voice.

His son says nothing in reply. He just sits there sipping his hot chocolate, looking up at the stars.

Josh is quickly proven right. The next day comes word through Niles Witherspoon that Gabrielle is indeed in Sunderland, staying back at the inn, and she wants to see Josh. He advises that Geoff grant her request. The visits should be supervised, he says, just to ensure she doesn't take off with the boy, but she should be allowed to see him. After all, she's his mother. That's what the courts will say.

"I wouldn't worry about her kidnapping him," Linda announces as they fix breakfast. Julia is out with Josh picking flowers for his mother.

"Why not?" Geoff asks. "I worry about it constantly."

"Something she said has stuck with me. She said she'd only try to see Josh if he *wanted* to see her. Only if he came willingly."

"We know that's bullshit, Linda. She tricked him with that Captain Space Ranger doll."

"Oh, I don't think she's above trickery," Linda says, sliding off some scrambled eggs from the pan onto the plate. "She'll win Josh over in whatever way it takes. But she won't take him away if he doesn't want to go."

"What if he wants to go?"

"He won't. He won't want to leave you."

She hands the plate of eggs to Geoff.

"And if I become a hindrance to that," she promises, "I'll go away."

"Don't talk like that."

She settles the pan back on the stove. "We have to be realistic. If Josh continues to resent me, then it might make him more likely to agree to Gabrielle's offer, even if it's just a way to spite you because of me. So if I have to discreetly fade into the background, I'm willing to do it."

She stares out the window into the backyard. Another gorgeous day. An unbroken blue sky—and that beautiful red-and-gold bird she's seen before, soaring gracefully from the treetops.

"I love you, Linda," Geoff tells her. "I want to marry you."

She looks at him. Why can't she allow herself to fully believe that when he tells her? She tries to smile but feels the tears coming again. She fights them back. Just in time, too, for there's a knock at the front door.

It's Gabrielle.

"Good morning, Linda," she calls cheerily through the screen door. "What a beautiful day, isn't it?"

"It is," Linda says, opening the door for her and letting her in.

The sunlight catches on the pendant hanging from Gabrielle's neck. Her bird pendant. A bird with its wings help upward.

In her mind, Linda sees the red-and-gold bird outside in the trees.

She can't take her eyes off Gabrielle's pendant.

It's a strange shape, really—as if the bird were flying straight up, away from the earth.

And Randy had said he thought he saw a bird—a strange bird of red and gold—in the flames at his office.

What does it mean? Linda thinks, shaking off the sensation and looking away. *What connection is there?*

As usual, Gabrielle looks like a knockout. In contrast to the all black she wore the other day, today she wears all white. A gauzy white blouse and white capri pants, and on her head she wears an oversized sunbonnet, white with a bright yellow sash.

"Is Josh up yet?"

"He's out in the back, picking flowers for you."

Gabrielle beams. "Isn't that sweet."

Linda heads into the kitchen, but Gabrielle stops her.

"I heard about that dreadful fire in Cambridge. Your friends. I hope they weren't hurt."

Linda turns around and faces her. "They'll be fine."

"I understand Dr. Hobart was hospitalized."

"Yes, he was."

"A terribly tragedy."

Geoff has come into the living room. "Good morning, Gabrielle."

"Geoffrey." She smiles at him, extending her hand. "I'm so glad we can all still be cordial to each other. None of this has to be personal. We all want what's best for Josh."

He shakes her hand. In her mind, Linda has a flash: Geoff and Gabrielle as young lovers, bound by passion, laughing and dancing and kissing. *What a beautiful couple they were,* Lucy Oleson has told her. *Everyone commented on how beautiful together they were.*

Yeah, Linda thinks, *and your husband and she were almost as beautiful.*

Linda watches Gabrielle sit down on the couch, removing her sunbonnet and placing it on her lap. How many others had Gabrielle cheated with? How many others had she caught in her web?

"I'll call Josh," Linda offers.

Outside, she finds Josh already knows his mother has arrived. "Where is she?" he asks excitedly, running past Linda and into the house. "Where is my mother?"

"He loves her so," Julia purrs, watching him.

"And he loves his father," Linda snaps. "Do you advocate him leaving his father to go away with his mother?"

"It's not my place, Miss. It should be whatever's best for the boy."

She's had just about enough of this nasty old woman. "And what is your opinion? What *is* the best for Josh?"

"Every boy needs a mother."

Linda knows Geoff's arguments against firing this creature. It would cause more instability for Josh. It would be ammunition for Gabrielle to use in court. But Linda's convinced Julia's working in league with Josh's mother. Julia's telling the boy he'd be better off leaving his father—Linda's sure of it.

She watches the nanny head inside. Linda sighs, heading off into the garden to clear her head. So much to grapple with. But topping it all is the unanswered question:

What had Kip Hobart found out, and what was he going to tell her?

* * *

She passes the morning reading out by the lake. At one point Gabrielle and Josh had walked up to the water. They were deep in discussion, about what Linda couldn't hear. But she did make out Josh asking Gabrielle if she wanted to go out in the boat with him. "Oh, no, Joshua," Linda heard her say. "You know Mother doesn't like the water."

Out of the corner of her eye, Linda can see that Gabrielle and Josh have settled on a bench in the middle of the garden. She sets down her John Grisham, careful to fold back the corner of the page she'd been reading. She knows she shouldn't eavesdrop—but if Gabrielle didn't play by the rules, why should she? The phrase "fighting fire with fire" pops into her mind.

Linda stands, walking out along the perimeter of the garden and then circling back through the tall blueberry bushes that grow wild toward the far end of the property. From here she can make mother and son out, and when the breeze dies down and the old weather vane on top of the house stops spinning and squeaking, she can just make out a bit of their conversation.

"—missed you so much during that time—you know that, Josh, don't you—"

"—but Daddy says—"

Linda decides to try to get a little closer. Hunching down, she makes her way through the bushes. At one point she steps on a twig, and it snaps underfoot. She freezes, holding her stillness for several minutes before resuming. She finally finds a spot only a few feet away from them, with the blueberry bushes offering a wall of protection.

"But if I went with you, Mother, what about Daddy? Could he come, too?"

"I'm afraid not, my love. He has to stay here." She pauses. "With her."

"But could I visit him?"

Gabrielle looks off into the distance. "Perhaps. But not for a long time."

"Why, Mother? Why couldn't I visit him?"

"Because, darling, where we would go is very far away."

Josh smiles. "A magical place, you said."

"Oh, yes. Very magical, Joshua. A place so beautiful, so unlike any you've ever seen before."

"Is that where you went when you went away, Mother?"

Gabrielle looks down at him sadly. "No, darling. I wasn't able to get there. But now we can go together."

Linda suddenly becomes aware of a presence, someone standing beside her. She turns.

The man in the bowler hat and high-collar shirt.

She gasps.

He beckons to her. Linda isn't afraid. Standing so close to him, he looks as real as he is. Kip had said he was a ghost. But Linda can see the pores on his skin. She can see the little red veins in his eyes. He seems kind. When he turns, she doesn't hesitate to follow.

He points behind some bushes. Linda looks in the direction of his finger.

It's the burned boy she'd seen before, his hideous, pulpy, black face staring up at her.

She screams.

"What is it?" she hears Gabrielle call. "What is wrong?"

Linda spins around. The man is gone. And now Gabrielle and Josh are running toward her, having discovered her in the bushes.

She looks back where she saw the burned boy. He is, of course, not there.

But something else is.

"Linda!" Gabrielle says. "Are you all right?"

"I—I was startled, that's all," she replies.

On the ground, where the burned boy had stood, lies a large dead bird.

It looks *charred*.

"What is it?" Josh asks, stooping down to examine it.

"Oh, Joshua, come away," his mother says in horror.

The boy keeps staring at the dead and blackened bird. Linda can't take her eyes off it, either. She knows what it is. It's the red-and-gold bird she's seen flying in the trees. So beautiful, and yet so ominous too.

She looks over at Gabrielle. There's terror on her face. Revulsion.

"Come away, Joshua," she says again, leading her son away by the hand.

Linda stares at the dead bird for a few moments longer, then hurries into the house.

"Are you all right, darling?"

Geoff spots her, steadying herself against the kitchen sink.

"I—I'm not sure."

"You look as if you've seen a ghost."

She looks up at him and laughs. Crazy laughs. She can't stop laughing, in fact.

Geoff smiles. "What did I say that was so funny?"

"Geoff, the visions haven't stopped." She grabs him by the shirt. "I just had another. It was—"

They're distracted by a loud rapping on the front door. They peer through the archway into the living room to see who it is. Beyond the screen door, they see a policeman.

Geoff goes to the door. "May I help you?"

"I'm here to see Geoffrey Manwaring."

"That's me."

"May I come in?"

"Surely." Geoff opens the door for him and the policeman steps inside.

"I'm Sergeant Wilcox of the Massachusetts state police. May we sit down?"

"Of course." Geoff gestures into the living room. Linda watches the two men as they sit opposite each other, Geoff on the couch and Sergeant Wilcox in a straight-back chair. The policeman holds a clipboard in his hands, with some papers secured to the front. He's old, gruff, and solid looking; Linda trusts him immediately. She tries to quiet her heart that's still racing from what she saw outside. But now she's anxious all over again. She listens to what the policeman has to say.

"We had a bit of a time tracking you down," Wilcox says. "Finally, the college told us they thought you were out here."

"What's wrong?" Geoff asks eagerly.

"Well, I'm afraid I have some bad news for you, Dr. Manwaring."

Linda can see Geoff steel himself. She walks over to the couch and sits down beside him in support.

"We got a call from the New York state police. It's your wife, sir."

"My wife?"

"She's dead, Dr. Manwaring. I'm sorry to tell you, but your wife is dead."

CHAPTER 9

Geoff lets out a laugh. "But that's impossible, Sergeant!"

The old policeman furrows his brow at him. "Why is it impossible, sir?"

"Because she's outside in the backyard right now with my son."

Sergeant Wilcox sits back in his chair.

"It's true," Linda offers. "I was just out there with them."

"Well, I—" The policeman scans the papers on his clipboard. "It says here that Gabrielle Deschamps Manwaring, age 28—"

"Did I hear someone mention my name?"

They look up. Gabrielle and Josh are in the doorway from the kitchen, having come in through the back door.

When she lays eyes on the policeman, Gabrielle leans down to Josh. "Run upstairs, Joshua," she tells him, "and get ready for lunch."

The boy glances over at Sergeant Wilcox, then

makes a beeline up the stairs, running as fast as his legs will carry him.

"Are you Mrs. Manwaring?" the policeman asks, standing.

"Yes, I'm Gabrielle Manwaring."

He removes his hat and scratches his head. "I'm not sure what to make of this report, then."

"What report are you talking about?" Gabrielle asks.

"We had a report in from New York. Upstate town, just over the border of Massachusetts. A woman was killed, identified as Gabrielle Manwaring."

Geoff has stood now, too. "How could that be possible?"

Gabrielle laughs. "Well, it's clearly *not*. I'm standing here right now."

"It was the town of Hudson, ma'am. Did you have an apartment there?"

She looks deliberately into the policeman's eyes. "Yes. I stayed there for a bit before coming back here."

"On the night of May fifth, ma'am, your apartment building was destroyed by fire."

Linda grips Geoff's arm.

"There was only one fatality," the policeman continues. "The body of a woman was recovered from your apartment."

"And so it was assumed to be me."

"Yes, ma'am."

She holds his gaze. "But clearly it wasn't."

"The body was burned beyond recognition. But the height and general build seemed consistent with what your landlady described as you. Tell me, Mrs. Manwaring. Did anyone else have a key to your apartment?"

"I—I'm not sure. No, wait. Yes, of course. I had a

cleaning lady. She had a key." Gabrielle moves closer to the policeman, looking into his eyes. "And she was my height and coloring, too. Oh, I do hope it wasn't her."

"Do you have a name for this cleaning lady?"

Gabrielle puts a finger to her lips. "Her name was . . . Mildred, yes, that's it. Mildred."

"A last name?"

"You know, I never found out. I always paid her in cash."

Sergeant Wilcox is writing this down on his clipboard. "An address? Any family you might know?"

"None. She came recommended to me by someone else in the building."

"And that person's name?"

"I've forgotten."

Linda notices the look the sergeant gives Gabrielle, and the hard-eyed stare she gives him back.

"When did you leave Hudson, Mrs. Manwaring?"

"Why, that very day. May fifth. It was an impulsive move, I suppose. I was eager to get back here to reacquaint myself with my son."

"So you just took off?"

"Yes, I did. It was a furnished place, so there was very little for me to take. I planned to send my landlady the last month's rent and let her know I wouldn't be returning. I must admit, with all that's been going on with my son, I've neglected to do it."

The policeman has been writing all this down. "Any reason why this cleaning lady would be in your apartment late at night?" he asks, looking up at her. "Because that's when the fire apparently began."

"I haven't a clue."

Wilcox sighs. "Well, I'd better get this information back to the New York police so they can try to identify this Mildred and let her family know."

"If there's anything I can do for them," Gabrielle says, "please let me know."

Sergeant Wilcox nods. "Thank you for your time. And Dr. Manwaring, I'm sorry if I alarmed you."

Geoff walks with him toward the door. "Just a moment," Linda says suddenly, coming up behind him. "How did the fire start?"

She can feel Gabrielle's eyes on her.

"Investigators aren't sure," Wilcox says, glancing down at his clipboard. "Seems to have been no cause they can pinpoint. They do believe it started in Mrs. Manwaring's apartment, however. That's where the devastation was the greatest." He pauses, looking up at Linda then back over at Gabrielle. "Strange thing. They think the door to the apartment was locked. From the *inside.*"

He wishes them good day and departs. Geoff and Linda turn to look at Gabrielle. "A terrible thing for that woman's family," she says, "don't you think?"

Josh has reappeared at the top of the stairs. "Can we have lunch now?"

"Yes, Josh!" Gabrielle sings out. "Come on down. Julia's making us sandwiches. She'll bring them to us in the garden!"

Geoff and Linda watch the two of them run off into the backyard.

"May fifth," Linda says after they're gone.

Geoff turns to look at her.

"My birthday. The night of the fire was the night of my first dream."

* * *

Geoff determines there are too many unanswered questions, too many strange mysteries going on, and that they all seem to center around Gabrielle. He decides to talk with her, to confront her about these queer experiences they've all been having. Especially after this latest episode—not to mention what Linda tells him she saw and heard in the garden—Geoff is determined to find some answers. Gabrielle agrees to a "face-to-face" that afternoon. "Whatever you want to know, Geoffrey," she says, "I'm glad to tell you. You'll see my only interest is in Joshua's well-being."

Geoff suggests they head into the village to talk; he doesn't want Josh overhearing. Gabrielle agrees, showering kisses on the top of Josh's head and promising to be back real soon. "Now you think about what we talked about, okay?" she coos in his ear just before she and Geoff head out the door.

Linda watches the little boy nod his head slowly. He watches his parents depart with a terrible sadness on his face, then heads back outside to sit at the side of the lake, throwing stones into the water.

"That was quite magnanimous of you, Miss," Julia observes, appearing in the doorway to the kitchen drying a plate.

"What?"

The nanny smiles. Her faces creases in a dozen directions. Linda notices the white roots of her jet-black hair are starting to show.

"That you would allow your fiancé to head out alone with his wife." Julia shrugs. "I suppose one cannot stop the natural flow of events."

"They've gone to talk about Josh, how best to resolve this."

"And I wonder what they'll come up with."

Linda approaches her. "Let me tell you something. When Dr. Manwaring and I are married, we'll no longer have need for a nanny. Or a housekeeper.

Or a cook. Or whatever role you've carved out for yourself in this family."

The old woman's lips tighten into a small white line. "When my services are no longer needed," she says evenly, "I will be glad to go."

Linda moves past her out into the yard. If she had stayed there any longer, she's afraid she would have slapped the old bitch. That wouldn't do.

She walks out through the garden. The dead bird, as she might have expected, is gone. What strange force did it represent? She prays Geoff will find out something from his confrontation of Gabrielle. But what is he going to say? Linda can't even frame the questions for the answers they're seeking.

"You like the water, don't you?"

Linda looks up. It's Josh, calling to her from the lake.

She approaches. "Sure. I like the water."

"And you used to go fishing," he says, remembering.

Linda smiles. The boy was actually engaging with her. "Sure, I went fishing all the time with my father."

Josh looks up at her and then out onto the lake. "You think there are fish out there?"

Linda stoops down so that she's eye level with the boy. "You want to find out? You want to go fishing with me?"

He looks directly at her. "Yeah," he says simply.

"Well, then, let's go." She straightens up. "Time's a-wastin'. Best time is early morning, but we'll just have to surprise 'em on their lunch hour. First we've got to go into town to get some bait, though."

Josh says nothing, just stands and follows her.

Geoff took the car, so they take a pair of bikes

from the shed, pedaling the few blocks into town. Josh is determinedly quiet, but when they start checking out the bait, squiggly worms and some large centipedes, he comes alive, giggling and holding out his hand so that the owner of the bait shop can let him feel the creatures. As they take the bait to the register to pay, Linda gets a look outside the store at the café across the street. She spies Geoff coming outside with Gabrielle. They're chatting amicably. He walks her to his Range Rover, opens the door for her, then hurries around to the driver's side. They pull out down the road.

They'll be there when we get back, Linda thinks as she and Josh mount their bicycles. I hope Gabrielle won't distract the boy's attention just when I'm making progress with him.

But there's no sign of Geoff's Range Rover when they return. He probably took her back to the inn. Good. This way Linda and Josh can stick with their plans to go fishing.

The boy's chattering like a parrot now. "How do you start the motor? How fast can the boat go? My dad hates worms. I've never been fishing before. I didn't think girls liked to fish. How many fish do you think are in this lake? Five million? Do you think there are any eels? How come I have to wear this life preserver? Is the lake really deep? If we put our house in here, do you think the water would cover all the way to the roof?"

She does her best to answer what she can. The sun is high in a perfect blue sky, sharp and clear. Sunlight reflects off the water in a pattern of white lights. The boy cries, "Wheeeee!" when Linda pulls the ripcord and starts the motor, the boat bursting into sudden energy like a bronco at a rodeo, cutting through the water toward the center of the lake.

Once there, she cuts the motor and they set about hooking their bait. "This is the part Daddy says he hates," Josh tells her conspiratorially. "This is why he's never taken me fishing."

"He doesn't know what he's missing," Linda says, showing him the best way to spear a worm.

"Worm guts are weird," Josh says, observing the goop on his fingers "Not bloody. Just yellowy."

"Here, wash your hands in this," she says, offering him a pail of water.

"My mother doesn't like the water," Josh says, dunking his hands into the pail.

Linda doesn't miss a beat. "We've all got our likes and dislikes."

Now comes the quiet part, she explains, the waiting game. "The fish have to first find the bait, then decide to take a bite." They cast their lines and sit back. "Now, remember, if we talk, it needs to be in whispers. Otherwise we'll scare away the fish."

Josh nods. "Do fish have ears?"

"Hmm. That's a good question, Josh. I've never seen any. But I know they can hear. Or at least sense vibrations from sound."

"Maybe they hear through their gills."

"Maybe."

The boy seems pleased with himself for having thought of the possibility. "You'll show me how to cut their heads off and clean them so we can eat them later on?"

"I sure will."

"Can we eat them tonight? Do you think Julia will know how to cook them?"

"We don't need Julia to cook them. I know how

to make the best fish and chips this side of London, England."

Josh smiles. They settle into place, holding their fishing poles, waiting.

And waiting.

Josh begins to fidget. "How long does it usually take?"

"Hard to say," Linda says. She sure hopes the fish are biting. After all this, to go back empty-handed might upset Josh's mood and promptly spoil all the progress she's made. *Come on, trout, don't let me down.*

She notices Josh studying her. She smiles.

"My mother wants me to go away with her," he says softly.

"Yes, I know," Linda replies. "What do you want to do?"

He shrugs, saying nothing. He lifts his eyes to peer over the side of the boat to see if there's any movement at the end of his line. There isn't. He settles back. Linda sees the sunlight reflecting off his little face. Josh is clearly troubled.

"I don't want to leave Daddy," he says at last. "But Mother promised to take me to all sorts of magical places."

Linda knows she has to be careful here. To bad-mouth his mother would backfire. To overly plead Geoff's case wouldn't work either.

"I just know how much your father loves you. And you know what, Josh?" She finds his eyes. "I love you, too."

He doesn't know what to say. *Maybe it wasn't a good idea to say that,* Linda thinks. *Maybe it's just pushing it too far. He'll start thinking I want to take his mother's place.*

But to her surprise a small smile starts to move the boy's lips. "I don't hate you anymore," he tells her.

She feels as if she'll start to bawl, right here in the middle of the lake.

That's when she feels the nibble at the end of her line.

"Hey, Josh," she says, "would you mind switching poles with me a minute? My shoulder is . . . uh, it's kind of getting tired."

"But what if a fish starts biting on my line when you have it?"

She grins. "We'll switch back."

He grunts, agreeing to the trade-off. She maneuvers around him, taking his pole and giving him hers. Josh moves over to where Linda had been sitting. She prays the fish is still on the line.

She waits a minute or two so as not to be completely obvious. "Um, Josh," she says finally.

"What?" He laughs. "You want to switch back *again?"*

"No. But I think you ought to look out at your line."

He suddenly seems to notice the pressure, the pull. "A fish!" he shouts. "I've got a fish!"

"Way to go, Josh!" She moves over to help him reel it in. The fish puts up quite a fight, but Josh uses all his strength to win this tug-of-war. The shiny trout breaks the surface in a spray of water. "Hooey!" Linda shouts. "He's a big one!"

They swing it around and unhook it, dropping it into the pail. Josh is beaming, ecstatic, so pleased with himself.

"But it was your line," he says all at once.

"Hey, that baby didn't bite until you had it, Josh. It must have been the way you were holding the line. I just have to accept it. That's *your* fish, buddy boy."

He grins, showing every one of his baby teeth. He looks over the rim of the pail at the trout, still jumping and flapping, its fins flicking back and forth, its gills opening and closing, gasping for air.

And his grin, so big, so wide, begins to shrink.

Linda watches him.

Josh begins to cry.

"Josh, what's wrong?" she asks. "Baby, what's wrong?"

"We killed him," he says, tears running down his face and dripping off his chin. "We killed him!"

"I—I thought you wanted to—to eat fish tonight."

"He's trying to breathe," Josh just says. "Look. He's trying to breathe."

Linda's heart melts. "Do you want to throw him back?"

Josh looks up at her with swollen eyes. "Yes," he says. "Please."

So they do.

Josh sits back in the boat and wipes his eyes.

"Are you mad at me?" he asks her.

"Let me tell you something, Josh," she says, sitting next to him. "What you did just now was a wonderful thing. You saw a living creature and you felt connected to it. You wanted it to live." She taps his little chest. "That means you have a good heart, and that's better than knowing how to go fishing."

"We killed the worms, too," he says.

She sighs. "Yes. I suppose we did. But you gave that fish another chance to live. Too many people don't even think about what they do. But you have a good heart, Josh. You love life. You love living creatures. And that's the most important thing, over everything else."

They head back to shore. The sun is lower now, and shadows are beginning to stretch across the yard. Julia walks out to them as they're tying up the boat.

"The boy's mother doesn't like him on the water," she says.

"My mother isn't the boss," Josh says defiantly.

The nanny seems surprised. Linda smiles. "Is Dr. Manwaring back?"

"No," Julia answers. "He hasn't returned."

How odd, Linda thinks. She decides not to dwell on it. She turns to Josh. "How about pizza for supper to-night?"

"Yeah!" he shouts.

"Will you order us a pizza, Julia?" Linda asks as she takes Josh's hand and heads toward the house. "We'll be in the living room playing video games."

Geoff returns as they're cutting the last piece to divide it between them.

"Darling," Linda calls, "we're in here."

He pokes in his head. "I—I've got a headache."

Linda's on her feet. "Are you okay?"

"I said I had a headache."

She turns to Josh. "I'll be right back." He nods, his eyes intent on the video screen, the remote control in his hands.

Geoff is already halfway up the stairs when Linda catches up with him. "Darling, did everything go okay?"

He keeps walking. "It went fine."

"But you were gone hours."

He spins on her. "I said I have a headache. *Would you leave me alone?*"

Linda staggers back from his words. "Geoff, what is wrong?"

"Nothing." He stops on the stairs, his hands in his

hair. "I'm sorry I shouted. I just have a killer head-ache. I want to take some aspirin and go to bed."

"Darling, I wanted to tell you about my day with Josh. It went so well. We've really connected. For the first time, I—"

"Tell me in the morning," he says, stopping her with his hand. He resumes walking. "I just want to be alone for a while. Please give that to me, Linda. Okay?"

She says nothing more. She just watches him head up the stairs.

She hates sleeping alone in this house. She feels like such a stranger, such an outsider. Lying in Geoff's arms made her feel part of the place, gave her sense of security. *I am his fiancée. He is going to marry me. I will be his wife.*

But sleeping alone makes her feel as if she is simply intruding into all of their lives, an inter-loper getting in the way of a happy family reunion. She knows it's absurd to feel that way, but she does. Even with all her suspicions about Gabrielle, when she lies here in the cold bed of the guest room, she really does feel that way.

Outside, a broken shutter begins rapping against the side of the house. Linda tries not to pay it any mind. She tries to shut out everything—all sounds, all thoughts—and just go to sleep. It had been a good day, after all. Such wonderful progress with Josh.

But then, Geoff.
Would you leave me alone?
I just want to be alone.
"What's happening?" Linda whispers into the dark.

What's happening is that you're going to lose him.

"No," she whispers.

You were foolish to think you could ever keep him. You. Little Linda Leigh. The little mousy schoolgirl.

"Geoff loves me," she says.

She knows all too well the identity of the voice that taunts her.

It is not Gabrielle, nor some shadowy beast from the flames. It is no ghost, no spectral spirit from beyond.

It is herself.

Her own voice.

"Geoff loves me," she says again.

And the thing is, she really does believe that. For all of her old self-doubts, for all of the fears that have plagued her, somewhere she has come to believe that. She has gotten stronger. She's no longer just "little Linda Leigh."

Except—except when she sleeps alone.

The wind outside starts to howl through the eaves. Linda closes her eyes and tries to force herself to sleep.

Geoff loves me.

I just want to be alone.

The voices compete in her head until, out of sheer exhaustion, Linda finally drops off to sleep.

In the morning, it's more of the same. Geoff skips breakfast, not appearing at the table. When Linda knocks on the door to his study, he tells her he has work to do. He's presenting a paper on Egyptian mythology in Kansas City in a month and hasn't done any planning for it. "Leave me alone," he insists. "Don't disturb me."

She puts her hand in the way of his closing the

door. "Did something bad happen with Gabrielle yesterday? Is that why you're acting so strange?"

He glowers at her. "Nothing bad happened with Gabrielle."

"Josh won't want to go away with her," Linda says. "I know he won't."

"She's his *mother*," Geoff snarls, and slams the door in Linda's face.

She's stunned.

She stands there, staring at the closed door, terror gripping her throat.

What does this mean? Has Gabrielle managed somehow to—to get control of Geoff?

And if so, how? How did she do it?

The way she gained control of Jim Oleson?

"Miss Leigh?"

It takes a few seconds to realize Julia is calling to her from the foot of the stairs.

"Miss Leigh?"

"What is it?" she snaps.

"You have a phone call. From Boston. A Mr. Randy Riley."

"Randy," Linda whispers.

She hurries downstairs and takes the phone. "Oh, Randy, it's so good to hear from you."

"He's coming out of the shock. Kip. Kip Hobart."

"He is? He's going to be okay?"

"I don't know. He comes and goes. The docs can't figure it out. They say they've never seen shock like this. It's more like he's—"

"Like he's what?"

Randy sighs at the other end of the phone. "Like he's in trance. But he's talking. He makes contact. And he's asking for you. He wants to see you."

Linda looks up at the clock. "I can be there in an hour and a half."

"Okay. I'll meet you at the hospital."

Geoff makes no reply when she says through the door that she needs the car, that she wants to go shopping. She finally hears him grunt his assent, convincing her at least that he's still alive in there. She's terribly worried about him, but she knows she can do nothing for him without more information. She has to understand what they're dealing with. She prays that Kip Hobart will be able to tell her something that might help, that might shed light on all of this.

She tells Josh she'll be back in a few hours, that he shouldn't bother his father, but that he also shouldn't leave the house without his father's permission.

And if Gabrielle came right now to take the boy away, would Geoff allow it?

She's his mother, he had snarled at her.

What did she do to him? Linda thinks the whole way to Boston. *What has she done to Geoff?*

She feels as if it's all starting to come to a head. All their fears, all their visions and premonitions . . . This is it. It's happening. But just what "it" is she still can't figure out. She knows now that Gabrielle has some sort of connection to something supernatural, something larger than all of them. Just what is it remains a mystery. But whatever it is, she appears more than willing to use it to help her gain custody of Josh.

And with Geoff out of commission, it may fall to Linda to stop her.

Driving into the city revives her spirits a bit. Seeing the John Hancock Building and the Prudential Tower and the crush of motorists backed up at the tollbooth on the Mass Pike has the effect of jarring her back to reality. The city is alive with people—real people with real lives, free from the kinds of weird suspicions and supernatural fears that have been tormenting Linda. The simple wave of a truck driver gives her hope; the vibration of rap music from a car behind her makes her feel connected and strong.

But then, approaching the hospital, a woman walks into the street without looking, right in front of Linda's car.

Linda slams on her brakes as the woman turns.

It is Gabrielle.

Linda cries out loud as Gabrielle's face changes from blond loveliness to a decaying skull.

"Dear God!" Linda screams, swerving the car instinctively, going up onto the curb at the sidewalk, nearly missing two pedestrians.

One of them, a teenaged Asian boy, runs up to her window.

"Lady, you okay?"

"Did you see? Did you—?"

But even as she speaks Linda can see there was no woman in front of her car. No Gabrielle.

"You okay?" the boy asks again.

"Yes," Linda says. "I'm—I'm sorry."

The teen backs away as Linda puts the car in reverse and backs up off the sidewalk, hoping no cop has witnessed her little stunt. She manages to glide back into traffic, trying to steady her nerves.

She doesn't want me to meet with Kip, Linda tells herself.

Kip holds answers. She's frightened of Kip.

"Well, I'm not frightened of you," Linda says out loud, trying to sound convincing.

Because it's a lie.

She's terrified.

* ~~*~~ *

The hospital is starkly white and intimidating. Linda always feels so *small* in hospitals, as if the very proximity to life and death has made her puny by comparison. She's never liked them, not since she was a girl and had to have her tonsils out. A simple enough operation, but she vomited blood into a bedpan while her sister Karen stood there watching her, calling her gross. Linda had thought she was going to die.

"He was talking earlier," Randy says as she enters the hospital room. "But now . . ."

Kip Hobart lies peacefully in his hospital bed. His eyes are open but he doesn't move, doesn't speak. His handsome face is thankfully not scarred; he appears not to have suffered any injuries from the flames. What had he seen that had so shocked him into this state? Or was his condition not the result of shock, but induced by some power no medical doctor could possibly understand?

"Kip," Randy is saying, holding his friend's hand. "Kip. I've brought Linda Leigh. You were asking for her. You wanted to talk to her, tell her something."

"Hello, Kip," Linda says. "I'm so sorry for what happened."

There's nothing. No sign of recognition.

"Kip?" Randy calls. "What do you have to tell Linda?"

She begins to fear her drive back to Boston had been in vain. She's suddenly terrified it had been some sort of ruse, some terrible trick, designed to get her away from Geoff and Josh. She ought to go back. They may need her—

"Lin . . ."

"He's speaking!" Randy says.

"Kip? It's Linda. I'm here."

"Lin . . . da . . ."

"Yes, yes, Kip, it's Linda."

His eyes don't move. They continue staring straight ahead. But Linda can still see the effort he's making. His jaw, his neck, his arms . . . They're all straining, all fighting, all trying desperately to push off whatever force that holds him back.

"Gabrielle," he manages to say.

"What about her? What about Gabrielle?"

"Ssss . . . ssss . . . ," he says, a tremendous will of effort.

Linda and Randy draw in close.

"Sinclair." The word pops out of his throat like a belch.

Gabrielle Sinclair. The woman with the same name as Geoff's wife buried in the cemetery.

"Her death," Kip rasps. "Her death."

He begins repeating the same two words over and over.

"Her death. Her death. Her death."

After about ten minutes, it's clear that's all he's going to be able to say.

"Gabrielle Sinclair's death," Linda says. "He wants me to find out about her death."

"You have the year," Randy tells her. "You could go over to the Registry of Vital Statistics and get her death certificate."

She agrees it's a plan. Randy stays with Kip in case he says anything else. Linda fights the traffic into downtown and then braves her way through the halls of the Registry. At first she's at a loss: too many rooms, too many card files, too many microfiche indexes. But then she finally finds a list of deaths in 1923.

And the two Sinclairs on that list.

Gabrielle Deschamps Sinclair and Arthur David Sinclair.

She orders certificates for both.

As she waits at the counter, she feels very strange. All these people around her, coming and going, bustling through their lives. Welfare mothers towing a line of small children applying for birth certificates for some governmental program or another. Lawyers and title searchers, lugging around banged-up briefcases, researching some legal case. Blue-haired old ladies digging up their roots.

And Linda.

Linda, trying to save a little boy and the man she loves.

From what?

"Here are your certificates," the solemn-faced young woman behind the counter intones. "That's twenty dollars."

Linda hands over the money and takes the two pieces of paper, stamped with the official seal of the Commonwealth of Massachusetts.

She looks down at them.

Gabrielle Deschamps Sinclair.

Arthur David Sinclair.

Died on the same day in 1923. June 1.

Five days from now.

And the cause?

Linda gasps.

"Burned to death," she reads.

CHAPTER 10

It's not that she's surprised. Of course she could've predicted it. She *should've* predicted it. Maybe she just had not wanted to. Maybe some part of her didn't *want* all this to come together.

Because it was becoming far too terrifying to contemplate.

From the Registry she heads over to the Boston Public Library, to the Microforms Department. Into the reading machine she threads a microfilm of the *Boston Globe* from 1923. She cranks the handle until she's reached the date she seeks.

She stares down at the headline in the newspaper, glowing up at her in a pale amber light, reliving a horror of eighty years ago.

MOTHER AND SON PERISH IN BLAZE

"Dear God," she whispers.

She reads on:

> *Firefighters struggled in vain last night to contain a blaze at 444 Chauncey Street, where Mrs.*

*Edwin Sinclair and her eight-year-old son were trag-
ically burned to death. Despite the best efforts of the
hosemen from Companies No. 4 and 5, the fire
quickly spread from a basement room through the
rest of the house.*

*Mr. Sinclair was on the scene and had to be re-
strained by firefighters from entering the inferno.
He was in shock late last night. He claimed that his
wife, Mrs. Gabrielle Sinclair, had been trapped in
the burning basement room and had called to her
young son for help, whereupon the lad himself became ensnared by the flames. An unidentified
woman on the scene attempted to lure back the boy,
witnesses said, but to no avail.*

*Mr. Sinclair has been distraught for several weeks,
neighbors said, claiming all sorts of delusions, and
it was thought that this latest tragedy would only
add to the disturbances of his mind.*

Linda sits back in her chair. In that florid, old-
style reporting, there was a dark echo of today. A
distraught father. A mother named Gabrielle. An
eight-year-old boy.

And fire.

So much fire.

She prints out a copy of the newspaper report.
She considers heading back to the hospital, to see
if any of this might jog a reaction from Kip. But
she realizes she's been gone too long. She has to
get back to Sunderland. She's worried about Josh
and Geoff's states of mind.

And what about her own?

When will another hallucination occur? Will
she be forced off the road again by some hideous
incarnation of Gabrielle?

Or another assault of fire?

She holds the wheel steady as she drives back down the turnpike.

What has she learned? Can she make sense of any of it?

The urban landscape of concrete gives way to passing fields of green and silvery lakes reflecting the low rays of the afternoon sun.

What do these people from almost a century earlier have to do with them today?

What connection between the two Gabrielles is there?

And what might Linda find when she returns to Sunderland? Will Josh be gone, taken by a devious mother for reasons none of them can yet comprehend?

And what of Geoff? Would he be gone as well—physically still present, but gone in spirit? Ensnared by the terrible power of his wife—a power they understand only its potency, if not in its detail?

At first glance, when she arrives at the house, it seems as if Linda needn't have worried at all. Josh still sits in the living room, playing video games. He greets her with a cheery, "Hi, Linda!" She smiles, relieved that their budding friendship seems to still be on track.

Even Geoff offers her a tentative smile when she finds him in the kitchen, sitting over a cup of coffee.

"Good shopping day?" he asks her.

She hesitates. "I didn't see anything I liked."

"I'm sorry if I was so brusque before. I just—I just had a lot on my mind."

She sits down opposite him at the table. She with-
holds the information she's discovered. Something
tells her to say nothing. *Intuition,* Randy would call
it.

"I've been thinking," Geoff says.

"About what?"

"About Josh. And Gabrielle."

She steadies herself.

"You know, a child *should* be with his mother."

"Geoff, you can't be serious."

He looks pained. He closes his eyes suddenly, as
if the headache that had plagued him has suddenly returned. He puts his hands to his temples,
takes a breath, then opens his eyes again.

"All I know is," he tells her, "Gabrielle loves him
very much."

"What did she do to you?" Linda asks in a low
voice.

"We just had a talk. A good, honest talk."

"Geoff, she has some kind of power. I don't
know what it is. But she's making you think this
way."

"She's beautiful, isn't she?"

Linda says nothing. She just stares at Geoff in
terror.

His eyes are looking at something far-off in the
distance. He speaks as if in a dream. "I remember
when she first walked into my graduate class in ancient philosophy. How radiant she was. How the
eyes of everyone in the room were upon her. She
has that way about her, don't you think?"

He looks at Linda as if he has no idea how his
words might affect her.

Maybe he doesn't.

"Oh, everyone on campus thought she was magnificent," he continues. "And her *laugh*. You've heard her laugh, haven't you? How beautiful her laugh is. How magical. Musical."

His words stab into Linda's heart. She can't speak.

Geoff is in rapture. "She's the most beautiful woman I've ever known. I thought so then, and I think so now. She was every man's dream, and I wanted her. I wanted her so bad I made an exception to my rule of never socializing with students. We met for coffee. She wanted to discuss Aristotle and Alexander the Great. She was both beautiful and brilliant. She captivated me. I was completely enthralled. Never before or since had I met such a woman—"

"I don't want to hear any more of this," Linda says, backing up in her chair.

"We would go dancing, and everyone watched us. We were good together, Gabrielle and I. We laughed. We danced. We talked about everything under the stars. She could keep up with me. She challenged me. She taught me things—"

Linda stands, the tears falling now.

"And in bed—oh, in bed! She was the most exquisite lover I've ever known. What passion we had! The things she did to my body, my mind, my soul—she was spectacular!"

"Stop it, Geoff!" Linda screams. "Stop it!"

Josh hurries to the doorframe of the kitchen, attracted by her cries. Geoff notices him.

"There he is," Geoff says, beaming at the little boy. "The product of our love. And doesn't he look like her? So fair. So radiant."

Linda can't stand it anymore. She turns, running past Josh in the doorway. She heads up the stairs and throws herself down on the bed in the guest room and cries into the pillow.

It's Gabrielle speaking, she tells herself. *She's making him say these things.*

But they're true nonetheless.

They're true!

Geoff loved her with a passion he can never love me with.

"Linda?"

She looks up. Through her tears she can see Josh, his face blurry and distorted in her watery vision.

"Are you okay?" the boy asks.

"Oh, Josh," she cries, wrapping her arms around the boy's neck.

"My Dad still likes you. I know he does."

She sobs in the little boy's arms.

She lies awake that night staring at the ceiling. Once again she's not sharing a bed with Geoff. *It's over,* she says to herself. *Gabrielle's won. She's gotten Geoff and now she can have Josh. There's nothing I can do to stop her from taking him if Geoff actually* wants *his son to go away with her.*

What is she even still doing in this house? She considers calling a cab in the morning, getting the hell out of here. She'll pack, say goodbye to all this craziness, put it all behind her. *What was I thinking?* She scolds herself in her mother's voice. *Did I actually think I could make a go of it with a guy as spectacular as Geoff?*

Who do I think I am? Karen?

She would leave here in the morning. She would go back to a simple life, free of all this stress, all these mysteries, these terrors, these visions. . . .

She sits up in bed, listening to herself breathe in the dark.

Mrs. Gabrielle Sinclair, trapped in the burning basement room, called to her young son for help, whereupon the lad himself became ensnared by the flames.

What did it mean?

Kip had told her to find out about Gabrielle Sinclair's death. And she had.

But what could it possibly *mean*?

But she knows one thing, sitting there in the dark.

She can't leave Josh.

She may be all he has left now.

The phone cuts through the morning like the scream of a child. Linda jumps. Julia's gone to the market. Geoff's once again barricaded in his room, surrounded by piles of books, refusing any contact, seemingly oblivious to the effect his words yesterday might have had on Linda.

She hurries into the kitchen to answer the phone.

"Yes? Hello?"

"May I speak with Dr. Manwaring, please?"

The voice. She recognizes it but can't place it.

"He's busy. . . . He's asked not to be disturbed."

"I see. Well, if you could have him call Sergeant Wilcox."

"Sergeant Wilcox," she says. "This is his fiancée. I was here the other day when you stopped by."

"Fiancée, huh? A fiancée *and* a wife."

Linda pauses. "He and Mrs. Manwaring are getting divorced."

"I see. Well, have him call me—"

"Might I tell him what this is about?"

The policeman is quiet for a moment on the other end of the line. "Well, I suppose so. We just had a call from the police over in Hudson, New York. A rather strange development has occurred that I thought I should let him and Mrs. Manwaring know about."

"If you can tell me, I'll make sure they know."

"The body in the morgue. The woman burned to death in Mrs. Manwaring's apartment. Her *cleaning lady.*" He says the words as if he doesn't believe them.

"Yes? What about it?"

"It's disappeared."

"Disappeared?"

"Yes. No one knows how it's possible. But they pulled open the drawer this morning and it was gone. Just gone!"

Linda doesn't know how to respond.

"Actually, I'd be very interested in talking with *Mrs.* Manwaring, but I don't know how to contact her. Will you give her the message?"

"Yes," Linda manages to say. "I definitely will, next time I see her."

Wilcox thanks her. She hangs up the phone.

"Linda?"

She looks up. It's Josh.

"Yes, Josh?"

"My mother's coming."

She eyes him. "Did she call?"

He shakes his head. "I just know."

Linda feels white terror throughout her entire body.

She buckles the seat belt around Josh in the front seat of Geoff's Range Rover. On the kitchen table she left a note. *Josh and I out for the day. Linda.*

She knows she has to get him out of Sunderland.

"Let's go to the museum," she announces, sliding behind the steering wheel.

"In Boston?" the boy asks.

"Yeah. The Science Museum. It's really cool."

"My mother will be angry."

"Oh, she won't mind, Josh, I'm sure—"

"Oh, but I will."

Linda freezes, her hand on the key in the ignition.

"Mother!" Josh says, seeing Gabrielle standing outside his door.

"I told Josh we would have a picnic today," Gabrielle says.

Julia's behind her, holding up a picnic basket with a smug little grin on her face.

"A picnic!" Josh exclaims.

"With lobsters," Gabrielle tells him.

Josh looks over at Linda. "Do you want to come with us?"

"Uh, I—"

Gabrielle is opening the car door now, hand outstretched to help Josh step down. "Now, you mustn't bother Linda any longer. She clearly has errands to do in Boston."

Josh smiles, unhooking his seat belt. "We'll go to the museum another time, Linda," he tells her.

She sits there behind the wheel, mute.

Gabrielle walks around the car to come face-to-face with Linda through the driver's side window. "Thank you for looking out for my son while Geoffrey's been so preoccupied. I do appreciate it."

"You won't win," Linda tells her.

Gabrielle smiles. "I already have."

"Mommy! Mommy!" Josh is beside her, tugging at her sleeve. "Can we have marshmallows at our picnic? You said we could toast marshmallows!"

"Yes, of course, darling. We'll build a fire."

"No," Linda says weakly. "No fire."

Gabrielle gives her a smile as if to say she's being foolish. "But without a fire, Linda, dear, how can we toast our marshmallows?"

Linda can do nothing. She can't overpower both Gabrielle and Julia and steal the boy away. She has no legal standing to get in the way. She can't go to the police. She can do nothing.

She watches the three of them walk away, Josh holding on to his mother's hand, happy as happy can be.

Her cell phone rings, jarring her back to reality.

"Linda, it's Randy. Can you get back to Boston? It's Kip—he's snapped out of it. He's insisting on being discharged right away! We can't hold him down!"

"I am *fine*, Doctor." Kip is dressed and packed when Linda arrives at the hospital. "You can plainly see that."

"Truthfully, there doesn't seem to be anything wrong with him," the physician in the white coat admits, shrugging to his nurse.

Kip's face lights up when he sees Linda enter. "Linda! I'm so glad you're here. We have so much to do."

"Hey, buddy," Randy says, stepping in. "Yesterday you were barely coherent. Take it slow."

"I'd advise the same," the doctor says. "You don't want a relapse."

"There will be no relapse," Kip tells him. From

inside his shirt he withdraws a chain. On the end of the chain hangs a small gold amulet, imbedded with a blue stone. "I wouldn't have had to fight so hard to come to my senses if you hadn't taken this off me in the first place."

The doctor gives him an indulgent smile. Turning to his nurse, he says, "Kip believes that amulet is what snapped him out of his shock."

"Out of my trance, you mean." Kip sits down to tie his shoes. "If you'd left it on me, I'd been able to fight her off. Now, with it back on, you can see I'm fine."

"Fight who off?" Linda asks. She's noted his use of the pronoun *her.*

"Whatever creature it is we're dealing with here," Kip answers, standing back up.

After he's signed all the papers releasing himself from the hospital, Kip asks Randy to bring his car around and meet them out front. "That will give me a chance to catch up with Linda," he says. "I assume you did what I asked? Looked into the death of Gabrielle Sinclair?"

They're going down to the first floor in the elevator. "Yes. She died in a fire. She and her son."

"Exactly. And I have a hunch we're going to find out even more about her."

She's thinking of Josh, walking off with his mother to their picnic. "Will that amulet protect others, as well as you?"

"I'm afraid not. It was given me by my mentor, Dr. Stokes. It's been divined to attune only to my aura. And it doesn't even completely protect me, either. Surely not enough to keep me from getting overpowered by that thing in the fire." The elevator drops from floor to floor, 12 to 11 to 10 to 9. "But it sure would have sped up my recovery had those fool doctors not removed it from my neck. Thank God Randy saw it on the side table and recognized it as something I was never without. He placed it back on me, and well, here I am."

"I was hoping it might . . . transfer to someone else."

He smiles at her kindly. "You're not thinking of yourself, are you? You're thinking of the boy."

Linda nods.

"If we hurry, he may not need any magical amulets. We can maybe find all the protection he needs through our own research."

The elevator slows to a stop. They're only at floor 3. Kip had pushed floor 1.

The door begins to slide open.

"I suggest you close your eyes, Linda," Kip warns.

She does, but not before she sees what's beyond the elevator doors. A roaring inferno of flames, rushing in at them. The heat makes her wince.

"Begone, you ridiculous creature!" Kip shouts, and indeed the doors to the elevator slide shut again and they continue their descent.

"She knows we're on to her," Kip says, almost nonchalantly.

Linda opens her eyes. "Gabrielle?"

"Yes."

The elevator comes to its final stop. The doors open. Linda follows Kip as he hurries through the lobby.

"What was the thing in the fire that you shouted at?" Linda asks, breathless behind him.

"A bird. Some kind of bird made out of fire. Quite the sight, really. Never seen anything like it."

"What does it mean?"

"I have my suspicions."

Randy's pulled up with his car. Kips hop in the front, Linda slides in back. "Where are we going?" she asks as Randy pulls out of the hospital parking lot.

"You brought my laptop?" Kip asks.

Randy nods. "At your feet."

"Ah, yes." Kip leans down, lifts it out of its case, and hits the power button. Linda hears it *dong* into life.

"I wish you'd tell me what we're doing," Linda says.

"You did say that the name of your husband's wife was the same as that on the gravestone. Both names. First and last."

"Gabrielle Deschamps. The same."

Randy's nodding, typing furiously on his laptop. "You know, some of the most brilliant magic has nothing to do with hocus-pocus. I mean, look at this. I'm wirelessly connected to the Internet here, going through thousands of death records from the Commonwealth of Massachusetts in instants. Amazing."

"What are you doing?" Linda asks, leaning over the front seat.

He adjusts his computer so she can get a look at the screen. "Today's genealogists have so much on their predecessors, who were stuck with card files and flaking parchment. Now these databases have been entered online. I can search for every Gabrielle who died in the Commonwealth for the past two hundred years and . . ."

He waits. Linda watches the little hourglass on the screen.

Suddenly a list of names appears. All with the first name of Gabrielle.

"Voilà!" Kip exclaims. "Now of course, some of these won't be Deschampses. These are probably married names in most cases, and maiden names weren't always provided on the old death records. But I have a hunch."

"What's that?"

"We're going to find a number of these Gabrielles died by fire. And each and every one of them is going to be named Deschamps."

Linda's befuddled. "How can that be?"

"How can it *not* be, when we've been presented with the evidence so far?"

She looks up. She sees they're headed back to the Registry of Vital Statistics.

"Okay. Copy these names down with their death dates." Kip hands the laptop over the seat to Linda. "It will make searching faster."

"I don't see how this is going to help Josh," she protests.

Randy's pulling into the parking garage. Kip's already gripping the door handle, practically out of the car already.

"She's won in the past because no one could figure out what was going on. No one could believe it." He winks over at Linda. "That's not going to be the case this time."

Sure enough, they find three other Gabrielles who died by fire. Gabrielle Starr, 1793. No maiden name given there, but given what they find on the other two, it's pretty easy to assume. Gabrielle Deschamps Harris, 1841. Gabrielle Deschamps O'Brien, 1888.

"And look," Kip points out, holding open the volume of death records for her. She gazes down at the flowery writing of another century. "In two instances, her child burned to death in the flames along with her. Jeremiah Starr, age 8. Caroline Harris, age 8."

"So she's the same person, is that what you're saying?" Linda asks, desperate to understand. "Like reincarnation or something?"

"Maybe like that," Kip says, tilting his head. "And maybe not."

"Oh," Linda says, deflated, hoping she was starting to figure it out.

"What about the O'Brien child?" Randy asks, looking over their shoulders at the volume of deaths. "You said in two instances a child burned to death with her. What about the third?"

Kip smiles. "There's no death of an O'Brien child in 1888." He looks between the both of them. "Do you know what that means?"

Linda's more confused than she ever imagined possible. "No. I have no *idea* what means. Tell me. *Please.*"

"It means there's hope. That she doesn't always win. Somebody must have saved the O'Brien child in 1888. And we can save Josh today."

"I want so much to believe that," Linda says.

Her mind is swirling around as if she'd been drinking way too many margaritas. She can barely keep up with Kip's energy, let alone his thought process. But all this talk about fires and children dying in the flames has left her very, very uneasy.

Because back in Sunderland there's a little boy too sensitive to kill even a trout, and he needs her.

Kip's scribbling into his note pad. "Perfect," he's mumbling. "Perfect."

"What's perfect?" Randy asks.

"Gabrielle Deschamps Harris is buried in the

North Hill crypt. I know where it is. I've been there. It's completely deserted and remote."

"So what does that mean?" Linda asks, becoming suddenly more terrified than she's been since she watched Josh walk away, hand in hand with his mother.

"Deserted and remote," Kip repeats, a little grin creeping across his handsome face. "A perfect situation for us to go and pay her a little visit."

This is the stuff of nightmares. When she was a girl, this is what Linda would dream about. This is what would cause her to wake up screaming in the middle of the night, calling for her mother in an icy cold sweat.

A dark, forgotten cemetery in the far reaches of town, huddled under shadows as dusk overtakes the day. Tall grass and weeds grow unchecked through the broken slabs of brownstone and granite. White marble angels have lost their wings. A headstone has fallen flat against the earth, its death's-head facing up at the sky.

"Over here," Kip says. "In back."

Ahead of them looms a brownstone crypt. Into its face are etched the words *North Hill*. A rusted iron gate leading inside sways slightly in the cool breeze of early evening, a low, creaking sound that makes Linda even more afraid.

"I don't understand what we're doing here," she says, a sudden chill upon her. She wraps her arms around herself.

"Linda," Kip says, looking over at her. "Do you trust me?"

She returns his gaze. "I'm not sure."

He laughs. "Any other answer would have been

dishonest. Good for you. Well, I hope I will have earned your trust when all this is done."

He opens the iron gate, which seems to creak in pain along its hinge, and he steps inside the crypt. Randy comes up behind Linda. He's carrying a crowbar.

"What is that for?" Linda asks, aghast.

"He asked me to get it out of the trunk of the car." Randy's face is white. "I think he means to open a grave."

"Open a—!"

"In here," Kip calls. "Linda, you come inside, too."

She grips Randy's arm. "What should we do?"

"This could land us in jail," Randy admits, then smiles. "Well, I'm already late for dinner. Boy, won't I have a story for Megan when I get home."

He heads into the crypt. Linda hesitates only a second, then she follows.

It's dark inside, with just a sliver of light falling through a cracked, stained-glass window. She can make out cobwebs and bird droppings, and a determined vine of ivy has crept through the cracks in the stone to grow along the far wall. The rest is in shadows. What lurks within? Rats, bats, and more, she fears.

Kip takes the crowbar from Randy. He's looking along the face of the marble stone wall. A dozen or so individual slabs bear the names of those interred behind. He runs his hand along each, trying to read the inscriptions in the fading light of day. Francis Chillingsworth 1779–1854. Marguerite Desmarais 1802–1860. George Adams III 1799–1845. Calvin Comfort Starr 1811–1859. And then, nearly eye level:

Gabrielle Deschamps Harris 1813–1841

"Here she is," Kip exults.

"What is this going to prove?" Linda asks, her stomach roiling, the skin on her arms breaking out in cold, tiny bumps.

Kip ignores her question. "Randy, you'd best stay outside on guard. If you see anyone, call in to us and we'll stop."

Randy nods and heads back out of the crypt. Linda imagines he's grateful.

"Stand back, Linda," Kip warns.

He lifts the crowbar and begins prying at the slab bearing Gabrielle Harris's name. All he manages to do for the first few minutes is chip away considerable stone dust.

"These things usually come off much more easily," he grunts. "Usually they just pop—"

All at once the slab breaks away from the wall, revealing the dark chasm behind.

"—right off!" Kip proclaims, dropping the crowbar, which clatters horribly against the marble floor of the crypt. He rushes up to the slab so it won't slide off the wall and smash. He grips it with both hands, breaks the rest of it free, then lifts it off and sets it down against the wall.

The setting sun reveals a pine box inside. The coffin of Gabrielle Deschamps Harris.

"Help me here, Linda."

She no longer protests. Does she trust him? She supposes she has no choice. Not here, in the gathering night, in a forgotten crypt, surrounded by the dead.

They each take a corner and slide the coffin off its shelf and lower it to the floor. It's ungainly and heavy, and Linda thinks she pulls a muscle in her back as she settles the filthy thing down. There's no odor, as she feared there might be. And although one side of the box has collapsed inward, it has not decayed as much as she would have expected after more than a hundred and fifty years.

"Are you ready?" Kip asks her.

She looks up at him and nods. What can she say?

"Open it," she tells him.

What will it reveal? Kip seems to think it will tell them something, the remains of this long-dead woman.

But what could possibly be left of her?

With the crowbar, he breaks the seal. Then he grips the edges of the coffin's lid and lifts, a terrible squeak causing the bats in the shadows to rustle.

They peer inside.

CHAPTER 11

The coffin is empty.

Even in the dim light they can see that. Empty. Completely, utterly empty.

"Well," Linda offers, "it *has* been over a century."

"Even so there should be *something* left behind," Kip tells her. "Bone fragments. Cloth. *Dust,* even." He runs his hand along the inside of the box, making Linda cringe. "But nothing. As if nothing were ever here."

"Did they inter an empty coffin?"

"No." Kip stands, looks around the crypt. "I imagine they came here, conducted the standard Christian burial service. Gabrielle Harris's body, as charred as it was, was inside that box."

"And then it disappeared?"

He nods.

"Just like the body of the woman in the morgue in New York," Linda says, suddenly understanding. "Gabrielle's *cleaning lady.*" She says the words in the same way Sergeant Wilcox had, as if she doesn't believe them.

"Precisely," Kip says. "And I suspect that if we went back to that cemetery your ghost led you to and we dug up the coffin of Gabrielle Sinclair, we'd find it similarly empty. As would be the coffins of all those other Gabrielles we discovered in the records today."

"It's all too bizarre," Linda says, a hand to her head.

"Randy!" Kip calls outside the crypt. "Help us get this back into the wall."

Linda places her hand on his shoulder. "But what does this really tell us? How can it help Josh?"

Kip smirks. "I'm working on that. Believe me, I'm working on it." He lifts the back end of the coffin. "Randy!"

But it strikes them, at the same time, that Randy hasn't come back inside.

"Randy?" Kip calls cautiously, peering outside the gate. Still no one. He steps onto the first step leading back into the cemetery. Linda follows closely behind.

"Randy!" he calls again.

"Oh my God!" Linda calls. "There!"

Ahead of them, about three feet away, Randy lies face down in the grass.

Linda runs to him. And as she does, she senses someone behind her. She spins around. A glint of steel flashes through the moonlight. She feels the sharp slice of metal against her arm as she lifts it to her face to defend herself. No pain at first. That comes later. First, it's just the cold sting of the knife's blade. She screams.

Kip has lunged onto her assailant. They struggle, and the sky darkens. The sun is gone, but now heat lightning burns the edges of the horizon. It lights up the cemetery as Linda, gripping her arm and feeling the blood ooze between her fingers, tries to see who it was that attacked her.

Kip has the man pinned to the ground now. Her assailant screams. As he does, Linda sees his face.

Jim Oleson.

"He's under her control!" Linda shouts to Kip.

"Break free, man!" Kip commands. "Break free of her!"

Jim merely struggles under Kip's hold, screaming again.

A tree behind them spontaneously combusts into a roaring torch of fire.

"Break free!"

"I can't! I can't!" Jim's voice is horrible, ragged and beastly. "She won't let me! I'm hers!"

"Here," Kip says, yanking the amulet from under his shirt and letting it drop into Jim's face. "Take hold of this. Try to hold it. Try to break free."

But Jim merely thrashes his head back and forth. "I've failed her! I've failed her!"

"Break free," Kip urges once more.

"Nooooo!"

Linda screams.

Jim has burst into flames.

Kip leaps off him. He stares down at the man who, moments before, had been alive and struggling beneath him—the man who, now, is nothing but a burning piece of meat, crisping and curling up in a horrible paroxysm of death. Linda can't bear to watch. She turns away, the stench of burning flesh in her nostrils, the taste of charred blood on her tongue.

"Are you all right?" Kip asks her, looking at her forearm.

"I think so," Linda says. "The wound wasn't that deep." Still, she feels light headed and faint.

Kip removes his jacket and tears off a sleeve. He wraps it tightly around Linda's arm as a bandage.

"We've got to get out of here," Kip says. "Someone is sure to have called the fire department. These flames are getting higher."

"Randy," Linda says.

Thank God. Her friend is coming to, rubbing his head. They each grab him under an arm and hurry him out of the cemetery. Linda eases him into the backseat while Kip starts the ignition. They speed out of the cemetery, praying no one has seen their car.

Poor Lucy, Linda thinks, behind the wheel of her own car now, heading back to Sunderland. *Poor Lucy. To lose the man she loves . . .*

But has the same happened to Linda?

What will she find when she gets back to the house? Will Geoff even still be there? Or will he be gone? Will he and Josh and Gabrielle be off to whatever horrible fate she has in mind for them?

Her cell phone rings.

"It's not Geoff she's interested in," Kip tells her.

She smiles. "You were reading my mind again."

"Sorry. It just came through."

She looks up into the rearview mirror. The headlights of Kip's Mini Cooper are behind her. He's following her back to Sunderland. Thank God for that.

"It's only Josh she wants. She'll use Geoff to get Josh, but in the end it's just the boy."

"In all these instances, all these other Gabrielles, they've somehow managed to lure their children into the flames. Why?"

"That's still a missing piece to the puzzle. But

the *why* isn't as important right now as the *when*. We've got to get Josh away from her."

Linda feels panic grip her gut. "What if we're too late? He was walking away with her when I left."

"I don't think we're too late. I have a hunch."

She laughs again. "You always have hunches, Kip. Wouldn't Randy call them *intuition?*"

"Whatever Randy wants to call them is fine with me. After what he's been through today . . ."

Megan had been nearly hysterical when they brought him home. Thankfully he wasn't hurt badly. He hadn't been Jim's ultimate prey: that had been Linda. Randy had been worth only a bang on the head. Linda was intended to get a knife through the heart. Randy will have quite the bump and bruise, but plenty of ice and Percocet should have him on the mend. As for Linda's arm, she probably should've gotten a stitch, but she settles for some gauze and first-aid tape from Megan. The bleeding has stopped, and the pain has settled down to a dull throb. They chose not to stop by any emergency department because the police were surely on the lookout for anything suspicious. After all, they had the death of a man by fire and a cemetery desecration to investigate.

"So what's your hunch about Josh?" Linda asks into her cell phone, not wanting to think about being a fugitive. She moves her eyes back up to the mirror. Kip's headlights give her some comfort.

"Well, it's something you said, how Gabrielle told you unless he went with her willingly, there would be no point in her taking him. Isn't that true?"

"Yeah. She said something like that."

"And he's not yet completely willing, is he? He's

torn about leaving his father . . . and, I think, about leaving you."

Linda sees the exit up ahead. She switches on her turn signal.

Could he be right? Could Josh have developed enough feeling for her to resist his mother?

"Do you really think Gabrielle is the same person as all those other Gabrielles?"

"What has Geoff told you about her? Any family?"

"None."

"Have you seen any childhood photos of her?"

"None."

"Any evidence of any life whatsoever before she met Geoff?"

"No." Linda sighs. "So what did she do? Just appear one day?"

Kip seems to consider the question. "Yes. I suppose that's exactly what she did."

"But she clearly had a life *after* she left Geoff. She had that apartment in upstate New York. The body they found in the fire—"

"Hers. It was her body."

"I don't understand."

She hears Kip let out a long sigh. "I don't either, Linda. This is like nothing I've encountered before. But some things *are* starting to come together."

"Well, what are we going to do when we get to the house? We're only just down the street here."

"I'm not sure," Kip admits. "But whatever we do, we're going to do it very, very carefully."

Kip parks in the road, his Mini hidden by trees. Linda pulls up alongside him. He's rolled down the window and is handing her something. It's his amulet.

"But you said it would only work for you."

He smiles sadly. "I was hoping its power might rub off a little. Poor Jim didn't give it a chance. Just take it, Linda." He sighs. "It's all I have to give you right now."

She accepts it, then turns up the driveway to the house.

All the lights are on, seemingly in every room of the house, burning into the dark night. Linda heads up the front steps, passes across the front porch, pulls open the screen door. It squeaks in her hand. From inside she can smell baked bread. As she walks through the living room she hears laughter from the kitchen.

And then she sees them.

The happy family.

Geoff and Gabrielle at the table with Josh, Julia serving them a platter of roast pork.

"Well," Geoff says, looking up at her. "I was wondering when you'd return the car."

"Hello, Linda," Gabrielle says pleasantly, nothing revealed on her face.

"Hey, Linda!" Josh calls out. "I saved you a place. They said you weren't coming home, but I said you would."

"Oh, really?" she asks, aware how shaky her voice comes out. She tries to steady her nerves as she slides into a seat next to the boy. "I guess you're the only one with faith in me, Josh."

She looks across the table at Geoff and Gabrielle, sitting nearly shoulder to shoulder. *Why am I here? She's his wife. I'm no one.*

"Hey, Linda, see what I made today?"

Josh holds up a crayon drawing. A bird, surrounded by flames. It's like the ones he made before his mother returned, only more carefully rendered now, with more attention to detail. The bird is in profile, its black, solitary eye the only dark spot in the picture. The rest is orange and gold and red, with flames surrounding the bird as it the rises from a fire.

Linda looks from the drawing to Josh.

He's why I'm here.

And why I'm not going away.

"Put the drawing down, darling," Gabrielle tells her son with a cool, even voice. "I'm sure Linda is hungry."

Linda makes eye contact with her rival. Gabrielle is a Grace Kelly ice queen tonight, in a light pink suit and pearls. Her hair is tied back in an elaborate knot. Her lips are full and painted scarlet.

Julia resentfully places a plate of food in front of Linda.

"Smells delicious," Linda tells her. Should she be worried it's poisoned? No. They hadn't expected her back. This was supposed to be their little family reunion celebration. By the end of the night, with Linda gone, Josh would have agreed to go anywhere with his mother. Oh, maybe it would have taken until tomorrow sometime, but he would've gone.

"Aren't you warm, Linda dear?" Gabrielle asks.

Linda looks down at herself. She had pulled on a bulky, heavy sweater she had in the car to cover the wound on her arm. "No," she says, taking her first bite. "In fact, I'm a bit chilly." She glares up at Gabrielle. "We ought to make a fire tonight."

She sees the surprise in Gabrielle's eyes. She wasn't used to being taunted. Linda can see that.

There's a sudden rapping at the door. "Who the hell—?" Geoff grouses, pushing back his chair and standing to go see who it is.

He hasn't looked at her since she sat down. Linda feels his cold distance, his hostility. But also his struggle. He may be in Gabrielle's control, but he's not happy about it. Deep down, he wants to break free. Linda has to believe that. Deep down, he still loves her.

She hears the voices in the living room. Kip's voice. She freezes.

"You don't have a cell phone?" Geoff is asking.

"No. I'm afraid I'm behind the times."

She hears Kip laugh. What's he planning?

"All right," she hears Geoff say. "The phone's in the kitchen."

Kip appears now, Geoff following behind.

"Sorry to disturb your dinner, folks, but my car broke down outside. I appreciate your letting me use the phone. A lot of people these days wouldn't let a stranger into their homes. Not that I blame them." He laughs. "Just glad you're not them."

"The phone's on the wall," Geoff grumbles, pointing.

Kip doesn't look at her, but Linda notices he got a glance in at Gabrielle. There's a sudden rise in the temperature in the room, like the blast of a furnace. Linda looks up at Gabrielle. Her face is tight, her lips are trembling, and she stares down at her plate.

Kip's punching buttons on the phone. "Hello, Triple A? Yes, my name's Tom Andrews, and my car's just konked out. . . ."

He rattles on with his information. Geoff stands with his arms folded across his chest, watching him. Gabrielle continues staring down at her plate.

"Mommy," Josh says, reaching over to her. "Are you okay?"

"Yes," she says, in a small voice. "Yes, I'm fine, Joshua."

"Okay," Kip's saying into the phone. "Yes, I'll wait out by my car. Thank you so much."

He hangs up the phone.

"Thank you again," he tells them all. To Geoff he says: "You're right. I need to get a cell phone. That way, I could've called and had the whole thing resolved, say, in fifteen minutes!"

Geoff grunts.

Linda's heard the code words. Cell phone. Fifteen minutes.

Once Kip's gone back out into the night, she stands and carries her plate over to the sink. "What a wonderful meal, Julia," she tells the old woman. "So glad I made it back in time. Next time, don't count me out so soon, okay?"

Julia just glares at her.

Linda excuses herself and heads upstairs. In the guest room, behind closed doors, she sets her cell phone to mute. In precisely fifteen minutes, she feels the vibration.

"What was that all about?" she whispers. "Your car breaking down?"

"I had to get a glimpse of her, feel her vibration," Kip tells her. "I think we're still safe. She doesn't have the boy yet."

"So what are you going to do?"

"I'm heading back to Boston. There's a little more research I need to do. I think I'm starting to understand. I saw the boy's drawing."

"Wait, Kip. You can't leave me out here in the middle of the woods all alone."

"If you think you're in danger, you should leave. But I think you're all right."

"All right? Why can't she just spontaneously combust me like she did to Jim?"

"You're not under her power. She recognizes how strong you are."

How strong I am. What a strange concept. Little Linda Leigh. So timid, so mousy. *And here I am fighting off supernatural creatures, getting wounded in battles with men wielding knives.* Even with all her fear and worry, Linda can't help a little smile when she hears Kip's words. *She recognizes how strong you are.*

"Keep the amulet around your neck," Kip warns. "She's not going to do anything like set the house on fire. That would just frighten Josh. She's got to be very careful so she doesn't upset his psyche. She wants him to come willingly and full of love for her."

"But why, Kip? Why does she want him to—to burn alive?"

"That's what I'm heading back to find out. Meet me at Randy's house tomorrow at four. I should have found out enough by then."

"What are you going to do?"

"Do you trust me, Linda?"

She hesitates.

"Yes," she says. "I trust you."

"Okay, then. I'll see you at Randy's at four."

She can't sleep. There was no question of her sharing Geoff's bed again. She just said goodnight as they all sat in the living room, Geoff reading some history book, Josh playing with video games,

Gabrielle sitting at the hearth and staring into the fire. The happy family. Linda crawled into bed, trying to will sleep to come. She had a feeling she was going to need it.

But even with all that had happened today, she feels her body fighting the lure of sleep. She tosses and turns, sitting up occasionally to peer through the darkness at the clock. Eleven-thirty. Midnight. One A.M. She clutches Kip's amulet around her neck. *Work with my aura,* she pleads. *Rub off on me.*

How the Linda of two months ago would laugh at her. Using words like *aura.* Believing in things like magical trinkets.

She finally, thankfully, nods off to sleep. How many hours? Three, maybe four. It's not yet dawn when she sits up, awake. A stillness hangs over the house in the dark. The stillness of a country night, when even the crickets are silent. How she longs for a siren, a honk from an automobile, the rumble of a subway. But nothing.

Nothing except—

"Oh, my darling . . ."

Gabrielle's voice.

Linda slips out of bed and pads into the hall. There's a flicker of candlelight coming from the master bedroom. It had been her bedroom, hers and Geoff's, when she first came here.

"Oh, Geoffrey . . ."

She sees them through the crack in the door. They're making love. The candlelight is enough to illuminate Gabrielle's porcelain skin as she moves sensuously up and down on top of Geoff.

"No," Linda cries, immediately covering her mouth with her hand.

It's the one sight that she cannot bear. Rotting

coffins, burning men, the roar of fire—but this is far worse. Geoff—the man she loves . . .

"Oh, darling . . ."

She turns away, wanting to scream. But that's what she wants her to do. That's what Gabrielle wants. She wants a scene. She wants a chance to destroy Linda's will.

She recognizes how strong you are.

Linda manages to stumble back into the guest room. *Yes, strong. I'm strong. But I won't be if I stay here any longer.*

The tiniest flecks of pink sunlight now filter their way through the darkness. Dawn will be here soon. She'll make her way to the village, then call a cab on her cell to take her to Boston.

But she'll be back.

She dresses hurriedly, throwing a few things into a bag. She tiptoes back out into the hallway. The door to the master bedroom is now closed.

She slips into Josh's room. The boy sleeps peacefully in his bed.

"Josh," she whispers, nudging his shoulder.

"Huh?"

"Josh, wake up a minute."

He stirs, opening his eyes and looking at her.

"I'm leaving for a bit," she says. "But I'll be back."

He sits up, rubbing his eyes. "Where are you going?"

"I have some things I have to do. But I want you to know I'll be back. If anyone tells you I won't be, like last night, tell them they're wrong."

"Linda, are you still going to marry Daddy?"

She feels as if she might cry. "I hope so, Josh."

"I think he likes my Mommy again."

Linda doesn't know how to respond.

"But he still likes you, too," Josh tells her. "I think he doesn't know who he likes better."

"I hope he figures it out soon," Linda says, kissing the boy on top of his head. She looks him in the eyes. "I'm very glad we finally became friends."

"Me, too."

"Josh, if your mother asks you again to go away with her, what will you say?"

He makes a face. "I don't know."

"Do you want to go away with her?"

"If she stays with my Daddy, we won't have to go away."

"Josh, she's not going to stay with your Daddy. She's going to want to go away and take you with her. Will you go?"

"Maybe." He looks up at her with honest blue eyes. "Maybe I will, because my Mommy says it's a magical place, and I'll have so many presents there."

"Josh, I need you to promise me one thing." She looks him straight in the eyes again. "I'm not going to try and persuade you one way or another. I don't think that would do any good. But promise me, if you do decide to go with her, you won't leave without saying goodbye to me."

He nods.

"You promise?"

"Yes, I promise."

"So you can't leave until I come back. Tell her that. You won't go willingly with her until you've had a chance to say goodbye to me. Okay?"

"Okay, Linda."

"Promise again."

"I promise!"

"And one other thing." She slips the amulet from around her neck and places it over Josh's head.

"Wear this until you see me again. Don't let anyone take it off you."

"Hey," Josh says, holding the amulet in his palm
and looking down at its bright blue stone. "Cool."

She kisses him again, then hurries out of his
room, crying all the way. Behind her, in the master
bedroom, she knows Gabrielle is awake, lying in
Geoff's arms, her head resting on his chest. Maybe
they'll make love again this morning, Geoff once
more knowing the passion he'd never know with
Linda. Brilliant sunlight fills the house as she
pushes open the screen door and runs down the
front steps. She runs all the way into town, not car-
ing who sees her cry.

"Randy's gotten involved in some wavy-gravy
things before," Megan is saying, "but this beats
them all."

They've gathered at her house in Cambridge,
Kip jumping back and forth between poring over
papers he's brought and looking things up on the
Internet. He's barely said a word to Linda since he
got there, just made sure everything was okay, and
then announced they'd be holding a séance.

"A séance!" Megan exclaims. "I mean, that tops
it all!"

"What kind of séance?" Randy wants to know,
but Kip waves him off, intent on reading something from his stack of papers.

"You know," Megan says, taking Linda aside. "He's
cute, but I think he's a little crazy."

"I trust him," Linda assures her friend.

Megan frowns. Linda knows she's not happy with
what happened to them yesterday. Earlier this afternoon she took Linda to the doctor for some

stitches. She made her eat a good meal of baked tofu and asparagus, and even insisted Linda take a nap, though Linda only rested. "I'm worried this is all getting out of hand," Megan confided to her. "Randy will do whatever Kip tells him. He respects him that much."

Linda couldn't exactly promise Megan everything would turn out okay. But she told her she felt they were on to something.

"And just what *is* this something?"

Linda could only shrug.

"All righty, boys and girls," Kip says, rubbing his hands together. He switches off his computer and clears the papers from the table. "Let's start!"

"I feel like Velma in *Scooby-Doo,*" Megan cracks.

"Can't you at least tell us what we're doing with this séance?" Linda asks.

Kip is lighting three candles he's placed in the center of the table. Randy is pulling the drapes closed. Megan has been instructed to dim the lights and turn the ringer off on the phone.

"We are hopefully going to get the kind of information I can't glean from old death records and obituaries," Kip says. "We are going to talk directly to Edwin Sinclair."

"The husband of Gabrielle Sinclair," Linda says.

Kip nods. "And the father of Arthur David Sinclair, the little boy she lured into the flames."

"Darn," Megan whispers, leaning into Linda's ear. "Here I was, hoping we were calling Elvis."

"Everyone hold hands and concentrate," Kip says. "That's right. Just like you've seen it in the movies. It's all pretty straightforward."

Linda sits between Megan and Randy, clasping each of their hands. She stares across the table at Kip.

"All right. Look into the candles. Push away any extraneous thoughts and remember we're here for a serious purpose. To help a little boy. Our goal is pure. Our thoughts are focused on that one idea alone."

Linda keeps her eyes on the flickering flames of the three candles.

"A little boy is in danger today, much as a little boy was in danger eighty years ago, in this same city of Boston, and from much the same forces."

The candlelight has an almost hypnotic effect on Linda.

"We're calling a spirit who carried the name of Edwin Sinclair in this life. Edwin Sinclair. Born eighteen hundred and ninety-two and died nineteen hundred and thirty-nine. I know you can hear me. You've been expecting us."

Nothing.

"Shouldn't we have hung a chandelier so it can start tinkling about now?" Megan asks.

"Don't make jokes," her husband scolds her.

"Edwin Sinclair!" Randy calls, louder this time.

And in the candlelight, Linda can see him.

The man in the bowler hat with the high-collar shirt and tie.

Suddenly she feels strange. Cold. Suddenly she realizes she's no longer inside the house, but outdoors. In an automobile. A strange, high, rattling automobile.

"You!" comes a voice.

She turns.

"How did you get in here?"

Linda looks into the face of Gabrielle.

CHAPTER 12

"This was *my* cab," Gabrielle is insisting. "I never would have taken it if I thought it was already occupied."

Linda can't speak. Where is Kip? And Randy and Megan? She tries blinking herself out of this strange vision, but can't change her surroundings.

She's in a cab.

An old-fashioned kind of cab, with large seats and a high roof, like she's seen in old movies.

But even more startling: she's with Gabrielle, who's just stepped into the cab dressed in a gown made of yellow feathers and wearing a cloche hat and a veil.

Linda gasps.

Outside the cab's windows is Boston—but not the Boston she knows. It's the Boston of the Roaring Twenties. She recognizes it from books Geoff has shown her. Early twentieth-century Ford automobiles. Some roads still unpaved. A few horses and buggies still lingering around corners.

"Where am I?" she blurts out.

"Beacon Hill," Gabrielle says resentfully. "Is this your stop?"

"Yes," she says, not sure what else to say.

She just knows she wants to get away from Gabrielle.

"Driver!" Gabrielle calls, snapping her fingers officiously. "Pull over and let the lady out." She sniffs, looking Linda over. "If lady's what you call it."

The driver obeys. Linda knows she has no money to pay him, so once out of the cab she makes a beeline into the crowd of people milling around the square. She suddenly becomes aware of her clothing, and the reason for Gabrielle's disdain. She's wearing jeans, a University of Massachusetts sweatshirt, and sneakers. Hardly the typical garb of 1923.

For that's where she is. She's certain of it. Somehow the séance has sent her back into time. She's arrived the year Gabrielle Sinclair died in the flames.

"Excuse me."

She turns around, startled.

"I saw you just get out of that cab."

"I'm sorry. I had no money. I—"

Linda realizes to whom she's speaking.

It's Edwin Sinclair. He tips his bowler hat in greeting to her.

"Oh, I don't mind about that," he says. "Let my wife pay for you. She's taken everything from me, she can afford it. My money. My son."

"Mr. Sinclair," Linda breathes.

"So you know me."

"Yes. I know who you are."

But it's clear he doesn't know Linda. Of course not. They won't encounter each other for another eighty years, when he'll be a ghost.

"I was hoping you might know my *wife*, actually," says Edwin Sinclair. "I was hoping you might tell me where she's been and where she's going." The man looks as if he might cry. "She's always flitting about from one party to another, speakeasy after speakeasy—"

"Mr. Sinclair, I want to try to help you."

His small, round eyes—like a teddy bear's, Linda thinks—implore her. "Help me? But how?"

She gestures for him to move away with her to a more private space beside a front staircase to a brownstone row house. "My name is Linda Leigh, Mr. Sinclair, and I need for you to tell me about Gabrielle."

"Tell you what?"

Linda looks deep into the man's eyes. "Edwin," she says, "you can trust me."

They are the same words his spirit will use with her eight decades from now. Somehow they resonate for him. "I can trust you," he repeats.

A light flickers in his eyes, and it's almost as if Linda can see right into his mind. *The séance— somehow it's given me some kind of telepathy. Edwin's spirit, eighty years from now, must be aiding me.*

Linda can see Gabrielle in Edwin's mind. A laughing, high-spirited, vivacious young woman. She dazzled the young insurance broker, right out of university. He met her at a café. She flirted with him across the room. He walked up to her and introduced himself, politely removing his bowler hat.

"I am Edwin Sinclair," he said. "Might I inquire as to your name?'

"Gabrielle Deschamps," she replied, batting her eyelashes and extending her hand. Linda can feel the surge of power that took over Edwin's mind and soul then, the rush of desire that claimed all his reason. Was that the way it had been with Geoff too?

"And where are you from, Miss Deschamps?" Edwin asked his future wife.

She smiled. "Do you know I'm not quite sure, Mr. Sinclair? Someplace far away, that's all I can remember."

"A woman of mystery," Edwin said, completely ensnared.

Linda watches almost as if a movie is unreeling before her on a screen. There is a slow fade and then she glimpses a new scene, this time of the couple's wedding. Gabrielle is all in white with flowers in her hair, and carrying a bouquet of lilacs. Purple ones, Linda notices.

And then she sees Gabrielle in bed, holding a baby wrapped in a blanket. Edwin is passing out cigars to his chauffeur, butler, and valet, but Gabrielle is staring down into her child's face with a look of horror.

"What is it?" her husband asks. "My darling, what is it?"

"I see fire in his eyes!" she screams. "Fire!"

"Darling, that is impossible—"

The new mother is so upset her maid takes the baby from her arms. Gabrielle dissolves into tears and falls backward into her pillows. "My baby will die! My baby will die!"

"He is fine and healthy, my darling," Edwin says, trying to reason with her.

A doctor is called. He tells Edwin that new mothers often go through depression and disorientation. It is nothing to worry about.

But Linda knows otherwise.

She sees Edwin pacing the empty rooms of his

house, his footsteps echoing down the long corridors. He asks a maid if she has heard from "madame."

"No, sir, she still has not come home."

Alone in his room, Edwin collapses in a chair. He covers his face with his hands and cries out loud.

"Why has she changed so? What has come over her?"

Linda's heart breaks watching him. She knows how Geoff will go through the same anguish eight decades later.

"Please!" Edwin cries out in agony. "Is there nothing I can do? Is there no one who can help me?"

Linda grips his hands as the images in her mind fade away. "Edwin," she says. "I've come to help you. I've come here from the future. I've come back to 1923 to find out what I can about Gabrielle."

He blinks as he looks back at her. "You are confused."

She smiles. "You can trust what I say, Edwin. I know it's difficult to believe, but I *am* from the future. Why do you think I'm dressed like this?"

"No. I mean you are confused about the year. This isn't 1923. It's 1921."

Linda pauses. But Gabrielle Sinclair died in the flames in 1923. *Dear God! Don't let it be that I'm trapped here for two years waiting for that event to happen!*

"I *do* trust you," Edwin says. "For some reason, I just do. Maybe my reasoning is faulty. They say that about me, you know. That I'm dotty and befuddled. They say because I cannot control my wife I must be soft in the head. An idiot."

"You're no idiot, Edwin," Linda tells him. "But

tell me what you mean when you say you can't control your wife."

He looks away. "She has become no wife to me. She has others. Other men." He looks back at Linda and once again it seems as if he'll burst into tears standing there. "She spends her days with strange people, gambling and drinking. Look at how she was dressed in that cab—and in the middle of the day! All she cares about is living the high life—and not a whit about our poor son, Arthur, who cries for his mother to come home."

"And yet she cared about him once," Linda says. "Enough to cry over him at his birth, terrified that she saw fire in his eyes."

Edwin nods. "Yes, I believe you *can* help me, if you know that. How much else do you know?"

"Not much, I'm afraid," Linda says. "That's why I need to talk with Gabrielle. I need to find out as much as I can about her."

He beams. "Whether you're from the future or the moon or the Salvation Army, I don't care. If you can do anything to help change Gabrielle, I would be so grateful."

"But I need clothes, Edwin. I'm already attracting enough stares as it is. I need to find an outfit that fits 1921."

He nods. "Of course. Come with me to the house. We've recently had a maid quit who just could not take Gabrielle's imperious behavior anymore. She left behind some clothes. She was about your size. You can wear something of hers."

So she follows Edwin down the block to his townhouse, a red brick and oak building, 444 Chauncey Street, which Linda knows will burn to the ground in two years' time. She suppresses a shudder as they make their way inside. Is this it, then? Is that what the séance sent me back here to see? Is it something inside this house?

"Oh, Patra," Edwin Sinclair calls. "Will you please fetch this young woman one of the dresses Molly left behind? And a pair of her shoes?"

A young, small, Arabic-looking woman in a maid's uniform appears in the entrance to the parlor. She takes one look at Linda and frowns, but obeys her employer's order. She returns with a plain green dress and some lace-up shoes. Mr. Sinclair gallantly steps out of the parlor for Linda to change, but Patra remains, watching her uneasily.

"What a lovely and unusual name," Linda observes.

"Egyptian," the maid tells her.

Linda smiles. "Ah. Like Cleopatra."

"Yes. Like Cleopatra."

"Are you from Egypt, then?"

"My parents were."

"A fascinating culture, I think."

A small spark glimmers in Patra's eyes. "Then you think correctly."

Linda has finished buttoning up the front of the green dress. "Have you been there? To Egypt?"

"No," Patra says, and her face takes on a great sadness. "But I hope to one day. To see the pyramids, the great temples—"

"These things mean a great deal to you."

"Oh, yes," Patra says. "My family comes from a long line of Egyptian priests and teachers."

"I see," Linda says, arranging her hair in a mirror. "Have you worked here for the Sinclairs long?"

"I work for *Mrs.* Sinclair."

Linda lifts an eyebrow at her with interest. "Oh, I see. Her personal maid?"

"That is correct."

"And I assume she shares your interest in your Egyptian heritage?"

Patra lifts her chin. "She does. Madame is very knowledgeable, and becomes more so, every day."

"I want to meet her," Linda says, lacing up her new shoes. "Actually, we've already met. I need to repay her for a taxicab ride."

"She said she would return in an hour."

"I'll be back."

After Patra has left the room and Edwin Sinclair returns, Linda asks him for cab fare. "It's good that I trust you, Linda, " he says with a laugh, "or else I might think you were just trying to get a new dress and a few dollars from me."

She smiles as he hands her the money. Not dollar bills, but silver coins.

"What's the best way to win her trust?" Linda asks him. "How can I get Gabrielle to talk with me?"

"Flatter her," Edwin says simply. "Her vanity has always been her weak point."

Linda nods. She hurries outside to wait in the park across the street. Eighty years from now, she knows there will be a parking garage here, tons of concrete poured over the grass and rosebushes that now grow wildly, where children play with balls and chase butterflies with nets. And across the street, where Edwin's town house is, will stand a convenience store. Christy's. Part of a chain.

If she weren't so terrified, if she weren't so focused on her cause, she might find all of this terribly fascinating. She's actually seeing the world as it was. How much she could learn! How Geoff would be enthralled. As a historian, he'd love the chance to actually see the past. The old-style autos, honking as they pass. The movie theater at the end of the block, with Charlie Chaplin and Gloria Swanson films on the marquee.

Linda sits on a bench and waits for Gabrielle to return. Her mind wanders. *Why am I here? Am I really here or is this some sort of delusion? How long will I remain here? I need to get back—Josh may be in danger. Is this a nefarious trick of Gabrielle's to get me out of the way? Is she capable of such a thing? Is her power that great?*

And if not—if I am here to discover some truth that will help me save Josh—then what is it?

She spots Gabrielle's bright yellow dress moving among the passersby across the street. Linda watches as she enters the house. She gives her a few minutes. Then she stands, crosses the street, and knocks on the door.

Patra opens it. She doesn't greet Linda, simply turns to her mistress behind her. "It's her, madam. The woman I was telling you about."

Gabrielle pushes her aside to appear in the doorframe. "The little lady from the cab," she says, apprising her. "Why did my husband give you our maid's clothes?"

"I am a poor woman, madam. He took pity on me. That is all."

Gabrielle sniffs. "Edwin has a soft heart."

"But with these good clothes I was able to find employment just now." Linda removes the silver coins from her pocket and holds them out to Gabrielle. "I received an advance on my pay. And I wanted to pay you back, first thing, for the cab fare."

Gabrielle looks surprised. She says nothing but accepts the money.

This close to her, Linda realizes that Gabrielle is

different. Haughty and imperious, yes, just as Linda knows her in the twenty-first century. But here she seems not nearly so—so—ethereal. She seems more *real* somehow, more of this earth. She does little things that Linda can't imagine the Gabrielle of the future doing, like fiddling with a piece of hair that's fallen in front of her face, or scratching her head, or sniffing as if she might be coming down with a cold.

"Mrs. Sinclair," Linda interjects before Gabrielle has a chance to close the door, "I come to you for one other reason. A favor."

Gabrielle eyes her suspiciously.

"I am new to the city. I am but a poor woman from the country and find it difficult to understand all the manners and ways of city life."

"So what do you ask of me?"

Linda smiles. "I have asked many people who it is that is the most enchanting, most fashionable lady in Boston, and was told 'Gabrielle Sinclair,' time and time again."

She notices the little flicker of pleasure in Gabrielle's eyes.

"I wish to be as stylish as you. I want so much to be successful in my new position, but to accomplish that, I must be sharp. I must know the latest fashions. I am hopelessly out of style, coming from the country. But you—you are perhaps the most beautiful, most elegant woman I have seen since I have come to Boston. You put Gloria Swanson to shame!"

Linda can see it's working. A smile creeps around Gabrielle's lips.

"Might you tell me which shops, which dresses—?"

Gabrielle laughs. "And here I was, thinking I was in for the afternoon! Patra! I am going out again! A tour of Boston's best boutiques with this poor lost soul here!"

"Yes, madam."

Linda hadn't quite expected this. She had thought maybe a conversation in the parlor, but this is even better. Gabrielle wraps a cloak around her shoulders and sweeps out the door, already two paces ahead of Linda.

"This way!" Gabrielle exults. "Watch and learn, little country girl. I will show you what you need to know."

Linda can scarcely believe it. Here she is, traipsing off down the street with her nemesis, the feathers of Gabrielle's yellow dress fluttering in the breeze. Passersby eye her as if she were a lady of the evening daring to show her face during the day.

And maybe she is.

"Follow me," she tells Linda. "You must know where to buy clothes and where to find the most perfect hats."

"Oh, yes, thank you, Mrs. Sinclair."

"Call me Gabrielle. I hate being called 'Mrs.' "

"All right," Linda says. "Gabrielle."

"And your name, little farmer's daughter? I assume you have one."

"It is Linda."

"Linda," Gabrielle echoes. "Linda."

Gabrielle knows all the shopkeepers and she introduces Linda to each one of them. Maurice. Benoit. Gregory. Enrique. She seems delighted to be able to show off her style, her sense of extravagant culture. Linda says little, just following her, observing her.

"Italian silk scarves are the best," she says. "Irish linen blouses. French gowns."

"I doubt I can afford it all."

Gabrielle laughs. "When you find a husband, he will pay for it. That's what husbands are for."

"Not for love?"

Gabrielle's face darkens. "Love? What is love? Love is nothing. It can only lead to death."

"Do you really believe that, Gabrielle?"

"You poor little country bird. But you will see. You will see."

Finally, after the sixth shop, Gabrielle professes to be tired, and they sit at a sidewalk café. "Tonio," she says, snapping her fingers at the handsome waiter.

"Ah, Madame Gaby," he says, and they share a secret wink.

"Bring us both espressos," Gabrielle says. "This is Linda. A little milkmaid just arrived from the fields."

Tonio nods at her and hurries off.

"You know so many people," Linda observes.

"Life is short," Gabrielle says. "You must meet as many people as you can, and do as many things as possible, in the little time you have."

"Why do you think life is short?"

Gabrielle sighs. "It is just something I have always known."

Tonio returns, setting steaming espressos in front of both of them.

"Thank you so much, Gabrielle," Linda says, taking a sip. "What a tour!"

"Never let it be said that I am completely heartless, that I can't take pity on a waif." She takes a sip of her espresso and eyes Linda over the brim. "Though, of course, people say it all the time."

"That you are heartless? Oh, I can't imagine."

"Well, they do." Gabrielle settles her espresso

back into its tiny saucer. "Can I help it that I must live fast, do as much as I can, see it all?"

"If I may ask, why must you live so fast? You're a young woman. Why do you think there isn't time to see it all?"

Gabrielle's watching the sun beginning to set over the brownstone spires of the city. "No," she says quietly. "No time."

"I don't understand," Linda says.

"Neither do I," Gabrielle says, still focused on the setting sun. "All I know is that I've always felt this way. That there is no time. That it all will end before I'm ready for it to end. I've always felt this way, ever since I can remember."

"Ever since you were a little girl?"

Gabrielle smiles, moving her eyes away from the sunset to focus on Linda. "Do you know I cannot remember anything about my childhood? Nothing. Not a single blessed memory."

"Certainly you remember your parents."

"No. Their faces are just vague masks to me. It is an ache in my heart."

Suddenly it is just as it was before, with Edwin. Linda can see into Gabrielle's mind. She sees a burst of flame, and then there is only smoke.

It is as if time is frozen. Linda stares into Gabrielle's mind and sees only smoke, dark and gray, thick and billowing. But gradually it begins to fade away, and from the smoke emerges the silhouette of a figure. A solitary figure walking across a deserted landscape.

Linda gasps. The figure—it is a woman, and she is naked. Naked as a newborn babe.

The figure walks closer into view. Linda recognizes her.

It is Gabrielle.

She walks as if hypnotized. She walks from the barren landscape into a field, and then into deep, dark woods. She walks without any hesitation to a tall fir tree, kneels down, and begins to dig with her hands. They are strong hands, scooping out hardened earth with the greatest of ease. Finally she uncovers a golden box with a lid, which she opens. She withdraws a long white sheath and some silver coins. Linda watches as Gabrielle slips the sheath on over her head and slips the coins into a pocket. Then she walks off into the woods, and the vision fades.

"My earliest memory," Gabrielle is telling her over their espressos, "is walking in a woods. Alone."

"And then?" Linda asks.

"I'm not sure. Faces come and go, until I met my husband." She looks away. "I never loved him, Linda. Never."

"So why did you marry, then?"

Gabrielle turns to face her. "Because I knew I had to."

"Why did you have to?"

"I wanted a child."

Linda smiles. "And you had a son, yes?"

Gabrielle looks down at the table. "Yes, I had a son. A bright-eyed child we named Arthur." She sighs. "I know what you're thinking. That, to him, I too will someday be but a vague mask, if I keep up this pace, this reckless abandon. . . ."

She's started to cry. Gabrielle is actually *crying*. Linda is staggered by the sight. "But I cannot help myself. Oh, Linda, do you know what joy this is, sitting here with you? Two ladies talking about fashion and style . . . I have never had this before. That is why I tell you these things. Because this is so . . . so . . . unknown to me. Such simple pleasures . . . such ordinary moments . . . but these are not meant to be part of my life. My destiny."

Linda leans in toward her. "What is your destiny, Gabrielle?"

"I wish I knew." She pushes away her espresso and waves Tonio off when he tries to bring her another. "All I know is that whatever it is, I cannot change it. I can't help what I am, Linda. It is just the way it is."

Her tears are gone now. She's hardened her face, steeled her back.

"So there you have it. A personal instruction in style from Gabrielle Deschamps." She laughs with some irony. "Use it well."

She stands. Linda makes a gesture to offer the last of the coins Edwin had given her, but Gabrielle refuses. "Allow me," she says.

With that, she sweeps away into the gathering dusk, a few yellow feathers fluttering free of her dress and tumbling in the breeze.

Linda sits there at the table, not sure what to make of the encounter. What did it mean? She watches as Tonio comes by the table to light a small citronella candle now that it's getting dark. Linda focuses on the tiny flame, watching it flicker. What did she learn from talking with Gabrielle? How did it fit into what she already knows? She lets her mind float into the flame. . . .

"Linda," Kip is calling. "Linda."

She blinks. She's no longer sitting at the table at the outdoor café. She's in the middle of a terrifying inferno. The blaze is so hot, so fierce, that Linda feels she will die instantly. She screams.

This is what it feels like to burn to death, a voice tells her. *Give in to the flames, Linda! Surrender to their passion!*

"No!" she screams.

My power is too great to resist, the voice assures her. It is a male voice. It is not Gabrielle.

Who then?

"I've got to get back to Kip," Linda says, over and over, like a mantra, refusing to go into the flames.

There is an explosion. Fire and debris rain around her, but Linda is not touched, is not burned. In the aftermath, everything grows still. She cannot make out where she is, but she knows she is not back with Kip.

She looks up. She can see the sky. It is a blazingly bright day, the sun shining overhead.

And there are strange voices coming from somewhere. Chanting voices. In a language Linda doesn't understand.

She realizes she is lying on a stone slab, facing the sky. She also realizes it is she who is naked now. And when she moves to cover herself she finds that her wrists and ankles are shackled and secured to bolts in the stone.

She screams.

The chanting becomes louder. She is aware of people approaching. She screams again, struggling against her shackles.

Suddenly above her is a group of dark-skinned people, cloaked in black hoods and robes. They look down at her with black eyes.

"Let me go!" Linda screams.

"Ra!" they chant. "Ra! Ra!"

One of them lifts a burning torch high over Linda's head.

"No!" Linda screams.

My power will live again, comes the male voice in her head once again. *My power will triumph!*

The torch is lowered into Linda's face. She can feel the intense heat against her cheeks and nose. She feels the first sting of pain as the flames begin to sear her flesh.

Linda screams.

CHAPTER 13

"I will not go into the flames!" Linda shouts as loudly and as determinedly as she can.

The horrifying torch disappears. She is left in a cool darkness.

"Linda?"

It's Kip's voice.

"Linda? Are you okay? Can you hear me, Linda?"

"I can hear you," she says, but even as she does she knows he cannot hear her. She is floating—trapped in this netherworld between past and present, dream and reality, life and death.

Is this Gabrielle's plan? Is this how she meant to get rid of her? To leave her endlessly adrift in this world of shadows and nightmares?

"I've got to keep my sanity," Linda says out loud, and the sound of her voice seems to ground her. She looks around. She is in a dark forest—the same, she thinks, she witnessed earlier, where Gabrielle dug up the golden box. The box where she leaves a few trinkets to be reclaimed from life to life, she realizes now. Enough to clothe her, to pay for passage back into the world.

But what then? What drives her to live again, to cause the deaths of her children? She isn't entirely evil, Linda has come to understand. There is remorse. There is regret. There is a sadness at what her destiny compels to her to do.

Yet still she goes on. Her feelings do not keep her from enacting her terrible duty.

"I must try to see," Linda says, and again her voice strengthens her. "I must concentrate on seeing the next phase of Gabrielle's existence."

There is a force that doesn't want her to. It is the voice she has heard, proclaiming that his power will return in triumph.

But she must resist it.

"Concentrate," she tells herself. "See what you need to see."

The woods around her begin to disappear.

All at once something zings past her face. She gasps.

She sees it was a dart. A dart, as in a game.

The dart lands square in the center of a target hung on a wall.

"Bull's eye!"

A cheer erupts from a group of burly men with beer steins in their hands.

"Almost pegged the dame," a man crows, "but I still got the bull's eye."

She's in a saloon. A smoke-filled, beer-stinking saloon. Dozens of men, raucous and drunken.

Where is this place? Linda thinks, almost in a panic. *Why am I here?*

The answer comes to her when she looks across

the crowded floor to spy Patra, Gabrielle's maid, walking up a set of stairs to a second floor.

What part of Gabrielle's life am I seeing now?

Linda pushes through the mob of men, following Patra at a distance. She elbows her way through the crowd, her eyes stinging from their cigar smoke. The place reeks of stale beer and fried foods.

Is Gabrielle here? Linda wonders. *Is this something else I'm supposed to witness?*

Up the same set of stairs that Patra had taken, Linda makes her way, spotting the maid in the hallway above the saloon. She's using a key to unlock a door.

"Patra!" Linda calls.

The young woman turns to look at her with dark eyes blazing.

"How do you know my name?" she asks, standing back, the key still in the lock.

Linda approaches her. "We met at the Sinclairs' house. I'm Linda Leigh."

Patra studies her. "Yes. I remember you now."

"When was that, Patra? When did you see me last?"

The dark-eyed woman studies her. "It was two years ago."

Two years. So now it *is* 1923. *But where are they? What does this saloon have to do with Gabrielle's story?*

"Is Mrs. Sinclair here?" Linda asks.

"You must go away. You must leave us alone."

"Who is there, Patra?" comes a voice from inside the room.

The door opens.

Linda gasps.

It is Gabrielle in the doorframe, but a Gabrielle who is a pale shadow of the flamboyant, beautiful woman Linda had seen last, sipping espresso and staring at the sunset. Now she is haggard and care-worn, with dark circles under her bloodshot eyes. Her skin is pallid and dry, and her lips are cracked.

"It is no one, madam," Patra says, "please go back inside."

But Gabrielle looks at Linda with tired eyes.

"Linda," she says softly.

Gabrielle has recognized her. She extends a bony hand to Linda.

"Why have you come here, Linda?" Gabrielle asks as the two women clasp hands. "Did Edwin send you? How is he? And the boy?"

Linda follows Gabrielle into the Spartan room. From downstairs the music and drunken laughter of the men rises to fill the small space. Linda looks around the room and realizes that Gabrielle has been gone from her husband and son for some time. Just as the Gabrielle of her time would leave Geoff and Josh.

"What are you doing in this place, Gabrielle?" Linda asks, facing her. "Why have you come here?"

She smiles sadly. "My destiny, Linda."

"I don't understand," Linda says.

"You do not need to," Patra says, angry now, gripping her by the shoulders. "You must leave."

That's when Linda notices the urn on the small table. An urn just like the one Geoff had, that he said he and Gabrielle had found on their honeymoon. It burns with a tiny blue flame. Beside it stands a small black onyx figure of a deity. It is a human form but with the head of a falcon, crowned with a sun and what appears to be a cobra.

"I want to know more," Linda says. "You taught me so much in our one day together, Gabrielle. Teach me more."

She lifts the small onyx figure from the table.

"Tell me about this," Linda implores Gabrielle.

"No!" Patra shouts, trying to take the figure from Linda's hand. But Linda is taller, stronger. She avoids her attempt and holds the falcon deity out toward Gabrielle.

"That is Ra," Gabrielle tells her dreamily, taking the figure carefully from Linda. "The sun god. Patra taught me all about him."

"Madam, *please,*" Patra says, urging her mistress be quiet. But Gabrielle ignores her, so the maid simply sighs. She turns and walks away.

Gabrielle has lifted the figure above her in reverence. "Behold the cobra," she says. "It is the sacred uraeus, the sign of Ra's divinity. Ra the great. Ra the Sun God. Ra the Life Giver."

Linda looks from the figure to Gabrielle's eyes. She seems enthralled with the object.

"The sun is the eye of Ra," she says, turning her eyes now to Linda. "Ra created all of humankind with his own tears."

"What does Ra mean to you, Gabrielle?"

The woman with the bleary, bloodshot eyes isn't sure how to answer. But then she smiles slowly, replacing the figure of Ra on the table. She reaches into her ragged blouse and lifts out a pendant that hangs around her neck. It is the same that Gabrielle has worn in Linda's own time. The pendant of a strange bird, its wings lifted upward.

"This is the phoenix," she tells Linda. "The symbol of Ra's eternal life—"

"Madam, *please,*" Patra interrupts, "there is no time."

Gabrielle turns to her with a terrible sadness. "No time. No time. That has always been the way.

No time." She turns back to Linda. "But I remember a day . . . sitting with you . . . an ordinary day . . . there was time then."

She takes Linda's hands. Gabrielle's grip is ice cold.

"An ordinary day with simple pleasures . . . But now, there is no more time."

"Mrs. Sinclair needs to rest," Patra tells Linda.

"Of course." Linda moves away, watching Gabrielle stagger weakly to the plain bed pushed up against the wall. She lies down and closes her eyes.

"I cannot help what I am," she says, to herself as much as to Linda, "or what I must do."

"She will sleep now," Patra says. "And you must leave."

Gabrielle is still upon her bed.

Linda realizes she will learn nothing more here. Something is beginning to happen. It is time for her to go.

But she will not go far.

She heads back down into the saloon, batting away a lecherous drunk who tries to paw her breasts. Standing off in a corner, she keeps her eyes on the stairwell. In moments she notices Patra slink down the stairs. She hurries out of the saloon, out into the night.

Linda considers going back up to Gabrielle's room, but she knows the door will be locked. Rather, she figures, she might learn more by following Patra, so she pursues the maid, keeping to the shadows. She watches Patra cross the street and then stand in place, staring up at the second floor of the saloon. Her eyes are riveted on the window behind which Gabrielle rests.

Where she lies, awaiting her destiny.

As the Gabrielle of my own time will await her destiny in that apartment in Hudson, New York.

Linda glances around the quiet, dark street where she stands. *Where is this place?* she wonders briefly. *Am I even still in Boston? Massachusetts? New England? I might be anywhere. Anywhere at all.*

And then the glass blows out of the window of the room where Gabrielle sleeps, flames bursting forth into the night.

"Dear God!" Linda gasps.

Across the street, Patra falls down onto her knees, a look of ecstasy on her face revealed by the glow of the fire.

No, more than ecstasy.

Rapture.

The saloon patrons come streaming out of the front door, shouting and stumbling over each other as the fire upstairs spreads quickly, lapping up the wooden beams, popping through the shingles of the roof. It snaps and crackles and roars, devouring the old wood like so much paper, destroying everything in a matter of minutes.

And then Linda sees it, almost as if she's been waiting for it.

The phoenix.

The bird of flames, rising up from the ruins of the saloon toward the sky. Its great wings flap majestically as it rides the furious tongues of the conflagration. A long, triumphant shriek sounds above the roar of the fire, and in the shiny black eyes of the phoenix, Linda can see the reflection of the dancing flames. And more.

She can see Gabrielle.

* * *

"You!"

She feels someone grip her arm.

The flames are all around her, but she's not at the saloon. Not anymore.

"You said you'd help my wife."

She turns. The man holding her arm is Edwin Sinclair. And it's his house on fire, not the saloon.

"Help her now! She's trapped inside!"

Linda stands in the doorframe of Edwin's house at 444 Chauncey Street. His neighbors have gathered around, and in the distance Linda can hear the wail of the fire engine on its way.

"The boy!" the neighbors are calling. "The boy's still in the house!"

Edwin is shaking, crying uncontrollably, talking to himself.

Linda remembers the newspaper account. *Mr. Sinclair has been distraught for several weeks, neighbors said, claiming all sorts of delusions, and it was thought that this latest tragedy would only add to the disturbances of his mind.*

"Save him, save my son," Edwin Sinclair mumbles.

Linda forges on into the house. Is this what she was sent back in time to accomplish? Might she actually be able to save the boy?

And might she then prevent the same tragedy from happening in the future, too?

Will saving Arthur Sinclair mean saving Josh, too?

"Arthur!" Linda calls. "Arthur!"

A frantic line of flame sears through the wall to her right. An oil portrait of a man melts in front of her eyes. A spark drops onto an armchair, and suddenly it is a raging inferno. Linda pulls back from the heat.

She pushes on through the parlor.

"Arthur! Where are you?"

The roar above her is getting louder. The second floor of the house must be engulfed in flames. In any minute the ceiling could collapse, killing her, dooming her to die here in the past, never to return to her own time.

To Geoff. To Josh.

Linda heads into the smoky corridor beyond the living room.

"Arthur! Arthur!"

And there, cowering in the kitchen, she spots a boy.

"Arthur!" Linda calls. "Arthur, come to me!"

But then, behind him, suddenly appears another figure, manifesting in the darkness.

A woman in white.

Gabrielle.

"Do not listen to her," Gabrielle tells her son, her voice sharp and cool, not the least fearful, in such horrible contrast to the cataclysm around them. "That is not the way to safety. Come with me, Arthur."

She reaches out her hand to the boy.

Flames burst through the floorboards, erecting a wall of fire between Linda and the boy. Little Arthur, a towhead the same size and coloring as Josh, reacts in terror.

"You can still make it, Arthur!" Linda calls. "Don't listen to her! Come to me!"

"I am your mother, Arthur!" Gabrielle shrieks. "Don't listen to her! Only I know the way!"

Arthur looks at Linda, then back at his mother.

"You can trust me, Arthur!" Linda cries. "I've come to save you—"

But even as she says it, Linda remembers the newspaper article.

An unidentified woman on the scene attempted to lure back the boy, witnesses said, but to no avail.

"Come with me, Arthur!" Gabrielle calls. "Come with your mother! I will show you a way through the flames! Do not fear them! They will not hurt you, my son! Come to me!"

"No, Arthur, you mustn't—"

But the boy turns away from Linda and runs into his mother's arms. She flings open a door and hurries him through it.

"She's taking him into the basement!" a neighbor shouts, having come through the front door. "Why would she do such a thing? There's no escape down there!"

Firefighters are now rushing inside, dragging their long snakelike hoses behind them. "Make way!" they shout. "Everyone evacuate! The place could come down any second."

Linda staggers back into the street. Behind her the sun is rising, its pink and golden rays creeping low across the city.

"Did you see him?" Edwin implores her. "Did you see my son?"

"I'm so sorry," Linda says.

"She wanted him to die," he rants. "Gabrielle—his own mother—she wanted him to die!"

Just then a huge cannonball of flame shoots up through the center of the house, exploding into the brightening sky of morning. The crowd gathered around screams. The house collapses in on itself.

Linda knows Arthur Sinclair is dead.

And that Josh Manwaring will die the same way.

She can see him, there in the flames, burning in agony.

She has come into the past only to have a glimpse of the future.

"No," she cries, crumbling to her knees on the sidewalk, her hands in her hair, utterly defeated. "Noooo!"

CHAPTER 14

"No! No! He mustn't die!"

"Linda!"

She opens her eyes. It's Kip's face looking down at her.

"Kip," she says, and begins to sob.

"It's okay, Linda. You're safe. You're here with us."

Indeed she is. Stretched out on Megan's familiar, frayed, comforting sofa, she allows herself to be embraced by Kip. Megan and Randy look down at her with sympathy in their eyes.

"What time is it?" Linda asks. "How did I get back here? How long was I gone?"

"Gone? You didn't go anywhere, Linda." Kip looks at her strangely. "But your clothes changed. All at once you were wearing the clothes of the 1920s."

Linda looks down at herself. She is indeed still wearing the dress Edwin Sinclair had supplied for her. It is charred and sooty.

"Smell this dress," Linda says. "Go ahead. Smell it."

"Smoke," Kip says.

"I was in the burning house of Gabrielle Sinclair," Linda says.

Kip seems puzzled. "But you never left this room."

"Yes, she did," Megan says, her face pale. "I tell you, I saw her disappear. Just for, like, a microsecond, but I swear she disappeared. I was holding her hand! I felt her go and then come back!"

"That must have been when her clothes changed," Kip says.

"You were very agitated," Randy tells her, "so we carried you over here from the table." He looks over at Kip. "So what happened? Was the séance a success or a failure?"

Kip's eyes are on Linda. "Only you can tell us that, Linda."

She sits up, rubbing her temples. "I did disappear. I was gone for weeks . . . years."

"Such is the paradox of time travel," Kip says, nodding as if he suddenly understands. "You can be gone for any length of time but then return a split second after you left, and it's as if no time has passed at all." He leans in toward her. "Tell us what you experienced."

"Edwin Sinclair somehow showed me a panorama of Gabrielle's life." Linda tries to remember, to keep all the images and experiences straight in her mind. "I saw several stages. The first, she was restless and running around on her husband. The second, she was tired and ready to meet her destiny. And then I saw her as we know her now: determined to take her child with her into the flames."

After she's finished giving them the full account, Kip sits down, nodding as he considers all of it.

"You say she showed you the pendant of a phoenix," he says. "And then you say the phoenix itself rose out of the flames at the saloon."

"Yes. The Gabrielle of this era has the same pendant."

"Can someone explain to me what a phoenix is?" Megan asks.

"The phoenix is a bird of legend that every thousand years burns itself to death, only to rise from its own ashes and live anew," Kip says. "Apparently, some human beings have acquired the same power." He taps the papers he'd been reading earlier. "I've been going through the journals left by my mentor, Dr. Stokes. He writes of such a creature, a woman in Maine, who was reported to have returned various times, always in the same incarnation, marrying into the same family and taking their children with her into the flames."

"But that's what I don't understand," Linda says. "Why would these creatures—these phoenixes— want to sacrifice their own children?"

"For that we need an expert on mythology and ancient religions," Kip says, shaking his head. "Someone who could tell us more about the cult of Ra."

"Geoff." Linda stands, walking across the room to gaze out at the gathering dusk. "Geoff is just such an expert. But he's under her spell."

"Maybe not for much longer." Kip's gathering his papers, shutting down his laptop computer. "Are you ready for a ride back out to western Mass? I think we're going to be needed out there, and soon."

"Of course." Linda's still puzzling over something. "I have to say the most surprising part of my experience of the past was seeing a more human

side of Gabrielle. There was a sadness, a wistfulness . . . maybe even some regret for what she must
do."

"So you're saying that she can't help herself?"
Randy asks. "That she can't stop burning these
children alive?"

Linda nods.

"Well," Kip says, heading for the door, "if she
can't stop herself, we'll have to do it for her."

Linda changes into some of Megan's clothes,
happy to shed the smoky, dirty remnants of her
trip into the past. Heading out along the Mass Pike
toward Sunderland, Linda and Kip say very little to
each other. What's there to say? They can't plan
for what they don't know. Will Gabrielle be there
to confront them? Will the information they now
know about her assist them in defeating her? They
just can't predict what they will find when they arrive in Sunderland.

Megan and Randy had both embraced her before she left, pleading with her to be careful. How
she longed just to stay there on their safe, familiar
couch, to hide in the warmth of their friendship
from the raging flames awaiting her. Even if she
and Kip were able to defeat Gabrielle, what did the
future hold? Could it ever be the same between
her and Geoff again?

"I know what you're thinking," Kip tells her kindly.
"And I don't have to read your mind."

She smiles over at him. "What about you, Kip? Is
there anyone special? Who's got the hold on your
heart?"

He sighs, staring at the road ahead of him. "It's
not easy when your life is like mine. Not many peo-

ple are ready to deal with the kinds of situations I find myself in."

"That woman who was killed?"

A smile stretches across his face. "A dear friend. Perhaps the closest person to me in my life. And a comrade-in-arms, fallen in the line of duty." He looks over at her. "But we weren't lovers. It's been a long time since I've had a lover. Maybe I'm scared. Maybe I look at what happened to Alexis and fear that such a horror could happen to someone else who I love."

"Are you that committed to this work? To this fighting of the supernatural?"

"I don't look at what I do in that way, Linda. I'm not *fighting* the supernatural. I'm trying to understand it. It's the dark side of the supernatural that I fight. The evil. I suppose I'm no different really than a political activist working to run corruption out of government. Or a muckraking journalist trying to root out abuses in the system. My arena is just a little different." He looks over at her. "But, yes. I'm that committed to it."

Linda smiles at him. "It's lonely work."

He nods. "Don't give up on him. Geoff. Not yet."

She looks out the window at the highway signs rushing past them.

"He still loves you," Kip assures her. "There's still time for us to reach him."

"It's the next exit," she reminds him.

He flicks on his turn signal.

Linda prays Kip is right. That there's still time to reach Geoff. To cut through the haze of Gabrielle's seductive powers.

To bring him back.

To me, Linda prays.

* * *

They find him sitting alone on the front porch of the house, staring into the dark.

"Geoff?"

He doesn't budge, doesn't respond to her call.

"Geoff, please listen to me. I've brought some-one with me. Someone who can help us. Someone who can help Josh—because Josh is in danger. You've got to believe that."

She's walking up the front steps, Kip following discreetly a few steps behind. The moon is full and bright overhead. The crickets are chirping in the woods behind them. Geoff still doesn't move or make a sound.

"Geoff?" Linda touches his hand.

His eyes move slowly to meet hers.

"She's gone," he croaks.

"Gabrielle?"

"She's gone. She left me, once again." He seems shattered, utterly devastated. "She said I couldn't come with her and Josh, that I no longer mattered to them."

Linda sits down beside him. "You know that's not true about Josh. You will always matter to Josh. He loves you."

"She's gone," Geoff repeats, staring again mind-lessly into the night.

"*Where* has she gone, Geoff? Where has she taken Josh?"

He doesn't answer.

"Geoff," Linda says, standing to take Kip's arm. "This is Dr. Kip Hobart. He can help us. He can help us bring Josh back home safely."

Kip stoops so that he can place himself in line with Geoff's vision. "I'm sorry I had to deceive you last night, with the whole bit of my car and all. But I needed to see what we were up against."

"It's no use," Geoff tells him. "She's gone."

"I want to ask you a question, Professor Manwaring," Kip says, and Linda notices the slightest perk of Geoff's ears at the use of his academic title. "In your studies of ancient religions, have you ever come across a particular sect devoted to the ancient Egyptian sun god?"

Geoff says nothing at first. He just continues staring straight ahead.

"I believe it may involve the legend of the phoenix," Kip continues. "The mythical bird that would rise out of its own ashes to live again."

"Ra," Geoff mumbles.

"Yes," Linda echoes. "The sun god Ra."

Geoff covers his face with his hands. Linda sees he's crying. She stoops down beside him, taking him into her arms.

"She took my son," Geoff sobs. "She took Josh!"

"There may still be time," Linda says, but whether that's true or not she has no idea.

"Your wife is a follower of Ra," Kip says. "Tell us what you know, and maybe we can still help your son."

Geoff looks into Linda's eyes. She thinks his eyes seem clearer. She thinks they may be the old eyes she had loved so much.

"There was a sect that grew after Egypt came under Roman rule in the last decades before Christ," Geoff says slowly, drawing himself with obvious effort out of the funk Gabrielle had left him in, a funk that was supposed to keep him impotent in any fight against her. "They wanted desperately to keep the old religion alive, and particularly the devotion to Ra."

"The old gods didn't surrender their power without a fight," Kip says. "I've seen it with others. Zeus, Hera, the gods of the pagans."

"But aren't they all myths?" Linda asks. "Isn't Ra just an invention of the ancient Egyptians?"

"Is the Judeo-Christian god an invention? Is Allah? Is Buddha?" Kip laughs. "These deities . . . They gain their power through the devotion of their followers. Gods, demons, it doesn't matter ultimately what they are. They are creatures that crave power. They need allegiance, devotion, to sustain themselves, or else they cease to exist."

"Ra was the life-giver in ancient Egypt," Geoff adds.

"Yes," Linda says, remembering. "Humankind was created through his tears."

"So the story went," Kip explains. "But a life-giver can become a destroyer when his power declines, when his hegemony is threatened." He looks over at Geoff. "Tell us more about the cult that grew around Ra. What was its members' mission?"

"To bring more into their ranks, for only then could they restore Ra's glory."

"And how did they do this?"

Geoff stands suddenly, fully alert now and animated.

"What is it, Geoff?" Linda asks.

He glares at her. "They did it through human sacrifice."

"Dear God," Linda cries.

Kip presses for details. "Gabrielle has succeeded in the past because no one understood. No one had all the information. To win, we must grasp as much as we can about her history, her motives, and her power. Tell us about the legend of the phoenix, Geoff, and how it fits into the story of the followers of Ra."

Geoff sighs, clearly torn between standing there on the porch talking history and rushing out to find his son. But it's clear none of them would know where to start searching. There must be some clue that will tell them where Gabrielle took the boy.

"The phoenix was a bird of red and gold, the size of an eagle," Geoff says. "Its Egyptian origin comes from the Book of the Dead, where it was originally called a bennu. In many ways, the bennu is a prototype for the concept of the individual soul and its eternal, essential life. Because the sun had also been perceived as a bird who flew daily across the sky, the bennu became identified with the rising sun."

He looks out into the darkness of the night.

"It will be dawn when she tries to claim him," Geoff realizes. "That's when Gabrielle will take Josh into the fire."

"Yes," Linda agrees. "It was dawn when Arthur Sinclair died."

Kip's getting anxious. "But how did this legend become associated with the cult of Ra that grew up after Egypt fell under Roman control?"

Geoff turns his attention to him. "Some of the followers of Ra claimed to be incarnations of the old priests—" He pauses. "Or in many cases, *priestesses*—who once led the worship in the temples. They claimed Ra had bestowed upon them the power of the phoenix, to live again and again, to rise through the generations to continue claiming souls for Ra."

"Gabrielle," Linda says. "That's what she is."

"A phoenix," Geoff mutters, the idea clearly staggering him. "Then my son . . . in his blood . . ."

"But these phoenixes began their existences as human beings," Kip says, "and if Linda's account of Gabrielle's wistful regret is true, then some trace of humanity remains." He rests his hand on Geoff's shoulder. "You needn't worry. Josh is every bit as human as we are."

"So now we have a good sense of why, how, and when," Linda says. "For the glory of Ra, in the flames, and at dawn. Now all we need to know is where."

She hears a door slam shut from inside the house. Her eyes dart over to Geoff.

"It must be Julia," he says. "She stayed behind. She didn't go with them."

Linda turns and looks back at the house.

Julia . . .

She doesn't need Geoff's history lesson or Kip's metaphysical philosophy to explain Julia to her. Some of the followers of Ra may well be incarnations of the old priestesses, but priestesses need followers, devotees, servants. These eternal creatures couldn't rise and fall through all these centuries without a little help. In 1923, Gabrielle Sinclair had had Patra, who'd revealed her destiny to her, who'd taught her the worship of Ra, who'd fallen into a final supplicant rapture before the glorious flames of her master.

Gabrielle Manwaring had Julia.

"But will she reveal what she knows?" Kip whispers as they head into the house.

"She damn well better," Geoff growls. "Or I'll throttle her scrawny neck."

"She hasn't spent the last eight years of her life

planning for this night to give in to threats very easily," Linda reasons. "She'd rather die first."

"All this time?" Geoff asks in disbelief. "All this time, she knew Gabrielle would come back and try to kill Josh."

"What I determined from my visit to the past," Linda explains, "is that when the phoenix is first reborn, she is unaware of her destiny beyond a vague sense of being different. In 1923, Gabrielle was stymied that she couldn't remember any of her childhood. She needed Patra to explain to her, bit by bit, why she was there and what she ultimately must do. That's when the wistfulness grew, a sense of powerlessness, and a desire sometimes to act out, to live recklessly."

Geoff grunts. He remembered that stage of Gabrielle's life all too well.

"It would seem that would be the vestiges of humanity," Kip observes, "still in conflict with her mystical nature. But it's always a losing battle."

Linda nods. "And when the last of her human shell is burned away—for this Gabrielle, it was in that apartment in Hudson, New York—she is reborn again as a fully aware, and completely amoral, phoenix, ready to pull the offspring of her human body into the flames as a way of glorifying Ra."

"But the child must be willing," Kip points out. "That's true in any religious tradition. Any convert must come of his own accord, of his own free will—"

"Free will," Geoff snorts. "That's a laugh. Josh is eight years old."

"Ra uses the strongest bond of human love, that between a mother and child, to keep his power alive," Linda says, shuddering.

"Shh," Kip says. "She's moving about upstairs."

Indeed they can hear drawers opening and closing, and footsteps back and forth.

"Let me try her first," Linda says. "You two stand outside the door."

She doesn't knock. When Linda opens the door to Julia's room, she finds the old woman removing her clothes from the dresser and placing them into an open suitcase on the bed.

"Packing to go back to Boston? The summer hasn't even started."

Julia gives her a cold glare. "There's no point in staying now."

Linda smirks. "And if she succeeds? Where you will go then? Is there a master list somewhere, a schedule of when the next phoenix is due to arrive?"

Julia doesn't react. She simply places the last of her sweaters into the suitcase and slams it shut.

"What would keep Geoff or me from calling the police and turning you in as an accomplice to murder?"

"I have no idea what you're talking about."

"Where did they go, Julia?" Linda approaches her, holding eye contact with the old woman. "You're not like she is. You still have a heart, a soul, a conscience. You *know* that little boy. You've cooked for him, played with him, taken him for walks in the park, and given him baths. Are you really going to let her kill him?"

"You must be mad," Julia tells her evenly.

"How many children have you watched die, Julia? How many little lives have you allowed to be snuffed out? And for what? What reward does Ra give you in the end?"

The old nanny stands mute. Her face is serene.

"I was wrong," Linda tells her. "You have no heart, no soul, no conscience. You are even worse in some ways than she is."

"If you'll excuse me," she says, lifting her suitcase from the bed and stepping around Linda. She opens the door to her room, only to see Geoff and Kip standing there.

"Dr. Manwaring, sir," Julia says, still calm and measured. "I hope you'll understand that I've made arrangements to return to Boston now that Joshua has agreed to go away with his mother." She smiles. "Now that the child is gone, my services will no longer be needed."

"I don't recall Josh agreeing to go away," Geoff replies.

"Oh, but he did, sir. You were standing right there when they decided to go."

"He told me he was coming back," Geoff says, remembering it all now. "I said goodbye to him, but he said he was coming back."

"I'm sure you misheard him, sir."

From below, a car's horn honks in the driveway.

"That would be my cab, sir," Julia says.

Geoff looks at her. "It's after midnight, Julia. Why not leave in the morning?"

Linda notices the old woman's steely façade threatens to break. "Thank you, sir," she tells him, "but I need to go now."

"So you can witness whatever is going to happen at dawn?" Kip asks.

"I have no idea who you are or what you're talking about," Julia tells him.

Geoff nods his head toward the stairs. "Go down and tell the cab driver the lady isn't going anywhere," he tells Kip. "And find out where she was having him take her." He returns his gaze to Julia. "I'll venture it wasn't back to Boston."

Julia remains mute. She sits in a rocking chair in her room, her suitcase at her side. Neither was the cabdriver much of a help: he had been told by his dispatcher that Julia's instructions were to take her only a short stretch down the street and then await further directions. Was Gabrielle planning to meet her? Kip promises to keep one eye on Julia and another on the street, in case Gabrielle and Josh show up looking for her.

Meanwhile, Geoff and Linda head into town. Gabrielle and Josh were on foot, so they couldn't have gotten very far. Unless, of course, she used some kind of power. But Linda thinks not. She wouldn't do anything to frighten Josh or make him wary. Not if she plans, at dawn, to reach out her hand to him, as she had done to poor little Arthur Sinclair, and convince him to join her in the flames.

The face of the little boy from eighty years ago is seared into Linda's mind. *I looked into his eyes. I tried to save him, tried to keep him from joining his mother in that burning basement. But I was a stranger to Arthur Sinclair.*

I'm not to Josh.

But was the boy's newfound affection and friendship for Linda enough to win out over the power of his mother? She looks across the seat at Geoff, driving his Range Rover with an intensity she'd never seen before. She realizes Josh has something else going for him that Arthur Sinclair did not.

His father has broken free of Gabrielle's madness.

"Geoff," Linda says.

He turns to look at her.

"We're going to win."

He pulls into a parking space outside the now-closed general store in the deserted downtown. He turns off the ignition. "Linda," he says, and his voice is hoarse. "I'm so sorry."

"I know, darling," she tells him. "It wasn't your fault."

"Why wasn't I stronger? Why wasn't I able to see through her?"

"You did, darling. That's why you've been able to snap out of it. Others before you, fathers who faced similar situations, have been unable to do so."

He smiles. "They didn't have you."

They kiss.

That's when they feel the heat.

"Get out of the car," Geoff shouts, suddenly grabbing Linda hard by the shoulders and pulling her toward him. With his left elbow, he bangs open his car door and they fall into the street—just before the Range Rover explodes into a display of red and yellow fireworks.

Linda screams.

They tumble backward, Geoff deliberately rolling them over and over in case their clothes have caught fire. They come to rest against the wall of the store and lie there stunned, watching the car twist and melt under the flames.

"We've got to run," Geoff says. "Otherwise the fire department and the police will detain us."

She agrees. Standing hurts; she thinks she may fractured her ankle in the fall. But she manages to follow Geoff down an alley behind the general store and into the woods. Behind them the blue night sky is aglow with flames.

"Maybe we *should* get the police involved," she says. "They can put out a dragnet to find Gabrielle and Josh. We can say we think he's in danger."

They're running through the woods back toward the main road, Linda limping on her hurt ankle. It sends shooting pain up her leg every time she lands on it.

"And Julia would say we're holding her against her will." Geoff stops running, a little out of breath as he faces her. "And oh, yeah, another thing. Some cop was by earlier today wanting to ask what you knew about Jim Oleson's death."

"Jim," she mutters. "Poor Jim. . . . How did they connect me?"

"An anonymous phone call," Geoff tells her, and Linda nods, understanding. "No, it's better not to get the police involved. Not yet."

"Okay. Then we've got to think. Where would Gabrielle take Josh? Is there someplace that means something?"

Geoff sighs, running a hand through his hair. "Does the place really matter?"

"I don't know." She starts to feel panicked. "Maybe it can be anywhere that's convenient. What if right now they're on a bus somewhere?"

"What time is it?" Geoff asks as they hear the sirens off in the distance, attracted by the flames rising out of the center of town.

Linda looks at her watch. "A few minutes after two."

"The cops will figure out that's my car and they'll be by the house. We need to go back to be there when they arrive. I'll pretend to be asleep. You'll be nowhere in sight, keeping Julia quiet."

She nods. What else can they do?

"Maybe Kip's been able to get more information out of her," Geoff says as they begin trudging back to the house. "Are you going to be okay on that ankle?"

"I think a sprained ankle is the least thing to worry about now," Linda tells him. "Let's go."

Kip's had no luck with Julia. She remains as tight lipped as ever, sitting in the rocking chair. But now her brow is beginning to bead ever so slightly with perspiration—as if she's becoming frightened, more so as the night goes on.

The police do come and ring the bell, and Geoff makes a great show of putting on the lights and stumbling to the door as if they'd just woken him up. He feigns surprise that his car is gone from the driveway, and even greater shock to hear that it's now a twisted hulk of smoldering metal towed over to Floyd's scrapyard. When asked if anyone was in the house who might have taken it, he tells them the only ones there are himself, his eight-year-old son and his nanny, and his good buddy, Kip, who Geoff swears hasn't left the house all night.

The policeman looks a little suspicious, especially at Kip, and Linda, eavesdropping, knows if Gabrielle anonymously tipped them off about her in conjunction with Jim's death, then she probably threw in Kip's name as well. Linda just hopes this officer doesn't make the connection, at least not right away.

"Why did you even have to say Kip was here?"

Linda says after the cop is gone. She presses an ice pack to her ankle.

"His car's in the driveway," Geoff tells her.

"Oh. Duh." She sighs. "I'm just so tired."

"It's getting closer to dawn," Kip says, peering out the window.

"I'd advise you all to leave," comes a voice.

They turn. Julia is coming down the stairs.

"Not until we know where Josh is," Geoff tells her.

"You're lucky I didn't come down here when that policeman was here and turn you all in for unlawful restraint." The old woman holds her chin high. "It was only because of the longtime respect I've held for you, Dr. Manwaring, that I—"

"Cut the bullshit," Geoff snarls, "and tell me where I can find my son."

"And while you're at it," Linda adds, "tell us the *real* reason you stayed out of sight when the police were here."

Julia says nothing.

"Because if they started hanging around, it would interfere with her plans, wouldn't it?"

Linda has moved up close to stare into the old woman's eyes.

"Why would you advise us all to leave?" she asks. "What's going to happen?"

The first tiny speckle of light begins to filter through the windows, barely noticeable, but there.

"It's going to happen *here*, isn't it?" Linda realizes. "This is where she's planning on doing it. Here, in his home. Home is where she took Arthur Sinclair into the fire."

"And where she took all the others, as near as I can determine," Kip adds, his line of thought following Linda's. "All of Gabrielle's children died in fires *in their own homes!*"

They hear the squeak of the back door opening.

"Daddy! Daddy! I'm home!"

* * *

At first it would appear that all is well, that they no longer have anything to fear. Josh comes bounding through the kitchen and runs straight into his father's arms.

But then Gabrielle walks in behind him.

"My, my," she observes. "Everyone up so early on this fine morning."

"I'm sorry, madam," Julia starts, "I tried—"

Gabrielle shoots her a look that shuts her up.

"Daddy, I was out in the woods, and Mommy showed me so many wonderful things!" Josh is exclaiming. "She showed me magic tricks! She can make stars appear right in her hands!"

"I'm not going to let you take him," Geoff says to Gabrielle.

"Tell your father what you've decided, Joshua," Gabrielle says calmly.

The boy looks up at his father, then turns to search out Linda. He smiles. "I did like you asked, Linda," he tells her. "I said I had to come back here to say goodbye to you."

"Oh, Josh," Linda is near tears.

Already she can smell the smoke. Already she can hear the fire snapping from somewhere in the house.

"Go ahead," Gabrielle urges, the slightest tremor of apprehension now apparent in her voice. "Tell them what you've decided, Joshua!"

"But I haven't!" he protests. "I haven't decided yet!"

Linda hears an explosion from upstairs. The windows blow out from the second floor. The stench of burning wood reaches their nostrils.

"We've got to get out of here!" Kip shouts.

The power goes off then, and they are left in the dark.

"Mommy!" Josh screams.

Linda tries to see, but all is blackness.

"I'm here, darling." Gabrielle's voice is clear. "I'll always be by your side!"

"No, Josh!" Geoff is screaming from somewhere across the room. "Don't go with her!"

"But she promised to show me so many wonderful things!" Josh's voice is close by. Linda desperately tries to see. "She said she'd take me to a beautiful, magical, shining place!"

Without warning, a beam from the ceiling suddenly buckles, opening a long rift above them, revealing the second floor is already engulfed in flames. From the burning beam, the fire leaps onto the floor like an army of mischievous imps, creating a blaze that separates Linda from Kip and Geoff. She shields her face from the scalding heat. But the glow of the fire allows her to see Josh, standing not four feet away.

"Josh!" she calls. "Listen to me!"

His terrified little eyes turn to her.

"No!" shrieks Gabrielle, coming up from behind him and grabbing his arm. "That is not the way to safety! Follow me, Joshua!"

Linda prepares to lunge for the boy, but suddenly there is someone on her, someone stopping her. Hands clutch at her face, fingers try to scratch out her eyes. Linda struggles, feeling as if she might lose her balance, her ankle remains so weak. But then she thrusts her arms back and finds it relatively easy to knock her assailant onto the floor. Whoever it is, it's weak. Old.

It's Julia—who stumbles right into the fire.

"Dear God!" Linda shouts, looking for something to throw on her to put out the flames.

But Julia, writhing in pain, is rapturous as the fire creeps up her dress. "Ra be praised!" she shouts. "I die for the glory of Ra!"

The old woman's face melts under the ravenous flames.

"Dear God," Linda says again, covering her mouth with her hands.

The conflagration is now out of control. In seconds the drapes are on fire. The flames whoosh into a huge wall running between her and Josh. She hears the boy scream. He is frightened out of his mind.

"Josh! I'm still here! We can get out! We can get out alive!"

Behind her the flames have gotten so high that anything Geoff or Kip may be trying to say is drowned out by the powerful roar. Linda can feel the heat bearing down on her from both sides. She knows she's moments away from burning to death.

This is the dream, she thinks. *This is how it began. Is this how it will end?*

She keeps her eyes on Josh. He must be her only focus now. He is her only chance, and she his.

"Listen to me, Josh! Don't go with her! You'll die!"

"Only *I* know the way to safety, Joshua!" Gabrielle

shouts, gripping the boy by the arm and tugging him, pulling him toward the heart of the flames the way she had once done with little Arthur—the way she had done with countless other children through the ages. "I am your mother! Listen to me! Come with me!"

"Gabrielle," Linda says, "if there is any humanity left in you, any soul, let him live!"

The flames jump higher.

Linda can feel her face ready to melt. "I know you have had regrets. I know you have doubts. You told me once that the simple joys of ordinary moments meant something to you. Listen to me now. You can end this horrible destiny of yours forever! Let him go, Gabrielle!"

Gabrielle meets her gaze, her face hideously distorted by the glow of the flames, her beauty completely gone. "I also told you that I cannot help what I am," she says, "or what I must do."

The flames roar up once more, obliterating Linda's view of both of them. She hears Josh scream.

"Josh!" Linda shouts. "I'm still here!"

There's nothing. No sound but the howl of the flames.

"Josh, do you remember the fish we caught? The fish you let live? I told you that you did that because you had a good heart! Because you loved life!"

Through the twisting, writhing blaze she can make out his silhouette.

"Don't go with her, Josh! That way is death! She does not love life like you do. Come to me, Josh! Just run! Run as fast as you can!"

She looks into the flames. She catches a glimpse

of the boy as he turns and looks up at his mother. She stands behind him with her arms outstretched, the flames already hopping at her feet, and she waits for him to join her. But he turns yet again, away from her, and he runs—runs through the flames, safely, into Linda's arms.

"Nooooooo!" Gabrielle screams in agony.

And then the flames rush up her body, claiming her once more into the phoenix fire.

CHAPTER 15

"He's convinced she wasn't his mother, that he'd been right in the beginning," Randy tells them after coming out of Josh's room, back in Boston. "And maybe for now that's a good thing."

Geoff sighs, tightening his grip around Linda's shoulder. "Thanks for seeing him," he says. "Thanks for everything, in fact."

Randy winks. "Hey, what's a little bump on the head between friends?"

"How is that doing?" Linda asks, touching the still tender spot on the back of Randy's head.

"This I can live with." He raises his eyebrows and smirks over at her. "I'm just glad we were both able to convince the police we were nowhere near that cemetery."

Linda smiles. "Megan makes up a great alibi, doesn't she?" She looks up at Geoff. "She swears we were all in a meditation room chanting mantras the whole time, and Kip was our instructor."

"So what's not to believe?" Geoff laughs. "So where *is* the great voodoo doctor anyway?"

"Yeah," Linda says, turning to Randy. "I thought he was coming with you."

Randy shakes his head. "He sent his regards and all sorts of good energy. But he's moved on. I'm not even sure where. Something new. Yet another black magic villain to track down, I suppose."

Linda recalls the conversation they'd had. How committed Kip was. But how lonely he must be, too. She reaches up and pats Geoff's hand on her shoulder.

"Thank him again," Geoff tells Randy, his voice thick with emotion, "the next time you see him."

"I will. And tell Josh I'll be back next week, same time, same channel."

They all embrace goodbye.

When they're alone, Geoff takes Linda in his arms.

"Do you know how much I love you?" he asks her.

"Remind me," she says.

He kisses her.

The wedding date has been set. Her mother has made the plans to come. Even Karen and her husband the chicken-feed salesman will be here.

"Linda, I am so happy for you," her sister Karen had said on the phone. "I really, really I am."

"I know you are," Linda said.

"Mom and I are already packing for the wedding. I simply can't wait to meet Geoffrey!"

Linda smiled. "Oh, yes," she said, looking over into Geoff's beautiful, dark eyes. "I can't wait for you to meet him too."

And Josh is very excited to be ring bearer.

Josh comes out of his room now. He's rebounded well from the ordeal, although he doesn't talk about it much. Randy's working on that. He says he's going to need to talk about it, but he's giving the boy time.

"How you doin', buddy?" Geoff asks his son. "You like talking with Randy?"

Josh nods. "He's nice. He said I can talk all I want—or I can say nothing at all."

Geoff tousles the boy's hair.

Linda watches the two of them. She has a flash of memory: holding Josh close to her body, covering him with her sweater and rushing around the wall of flames. She had stumbled out into the cool night air that had felt like such a salve against her face after the terrible heat of the fire. Her ankle gave out then, and Geoff had to catch his son as Linda fell against the earth, grateful for it. She held onto the cold wet grass as a kind of salvation.

Behind them, the old Manwaring homestead burned to the ground, taking with it all its antique furniture, its family heirlooms, its chart of the generations on the wall. Linda didn't turn around to see, but later Kip would tell her he saw a bird of red and gold rise from the burning house and disappear into the sky.

The phoenix.

Gabrielle, cheating death once more.

"Dad," Josh says, interrupting her thoughts, "I've been thinking. And I've decided something."

"What's that, buddy?" Geoff asks.

The boy looks up at him with a solemn gaze. "Linda and I are going to have to teach you how to fish. You can't be scared of worm guts all your life."

They laugh.

"But you can't keep them," Josh adds, looking over at Linda. "You catch them, then you throw them back in."

Linda smiles.

"You gotta let them live."

Geoff places his arm around Linda as they watch the boy head into the living room to play his video games.

There's part of you that lives on in him, Gabrielle, Linda thinks. *The human part of you. The part I saw so briefly that day, sitting in the café, watching the sun go down . . .*

As for the other part of her, Kip told them she'd be back. Somewhere, sometime, the phoenix will be reborn. Maybe she'll be smart and change her name this time. After all, she must have to do so periodically. Fashions in names change, and sooner or later someone might catch on.

As they did.

Thank God.

"Thank you," Geoff whispers in her ear.

"For what?" Linda asks, looking up at him.

"For being so strong. For being the most amazing woman I've ever known."

She smiles.

Geoff takes her hand. He kisses the top of her head, and together they walk into the living room, following their son.

EPILOGUE

In the woods, a naked woman digs a small box from the dirt beneath a tree.

From the box she lifts a white sheath. She pulls it over her head, concealing her nakedness. Six silver coins are dropped into her pocket, and then she replaces the box in the dirt.

On the road a man in a pickup truck slows down to pick her up. She is beautiful, he thinks as she slides in beside him.

The most beautiful woman he has ever seen.

"Dangerous for a pretty little thing like you to be out walking all alone here in these woods," he tells her.

"Dangerous?" Her hand goes to her head as if it hadn't occurred to her. "Yes, I suppose it is." She smiles over at the man, her eyes dazzling him. "So thank you. Thank you for picking me up."

"Where are you headin' to?"

"Oh, whatever town is up ahead. I just need some place to rest. To buy a few clothes . . ."

"No place in particular?"

"No," the woman says. "Just some place to settle down. To meet some kind people. To find a place to call my own, even if it's just for a little while."

The man scratches his head. "You're a bit of a strange one. Pretty, but a bit strange."

"Strange?" The woman smiles. "Yes, I suppose so."

"What's your name?"

"Ga—" she starts to say, but stops, not quite knowing why. What had she been going to say? What had she thought her name was?

Come to think of it, what *is* her name? She's not sure at first. But then—

"Linda," she tells the man. "My name is Linda."

AUTHOR'S NOTE

When I was a boy, my favorite television show was Dan Curtis's classic daytime gothic soap opera, *Dark Shadows*. For me, one of its most intriguing storylines involved the phoenix, Laura Collins. It was written by Malcolm Marmorstein, Ron Sproat, Gordon Russell, Sam Hall, and Violet Welles, with Laura herself being brilliantly brought to life by Diana Millay. This novel is my tribute to them— the creative team who first ignited my young imagination (pun intended) and have kept me staring into the fire ever since.

To my readers: Let me know what you think about this novel, as well as my others, *Where Darkness Lives* and *Don't Close Your Eyes*. I love hearing from you. Contact me at RobertRossAuthor@aol.com.

Please turn the page for an exciting sneak peek of

Robert Ross's next chilling thriller,

coming in May 2005 from Pinnacle Books!

The girl was going to kill her.

Stop it, Karen Donovan scolded herself. It was just this old house that was making her nervous and edgy. This creepy, smelly, musty old house, and the storm blowing off the sea. Karen had never experienced a storm quite like this, sitting in a one-hundred-year-old house built on a sand spit, with waves crashing at the back door. She half expected the house's foundation—just wooden pilings, after all—to crumble, and the sea to flow in at them, carrying them out into the surf.

"It's not what you expected, is it, Karen?" the girl asked her.

They had lost power and sat facing each other in the dark. Only a flicker of candlelight played over the girl's thin, bony face.

"I'd say it's quite romantic, quite the adventure." Karen stood, leaving the girl to glower in the dark. "Your father told me that when storms hit the Cape, it's like being on a ship. You feel every surge of the wind, every rocking of the sea."

Lightning crashed, filling the room with a terrible white light.

"My father loved being here with my mother," the girl said, once the room had returned to darkness. "Why do you think he has been here so infrequently this summer?"

"He's had a lot of commitments," Karen said, but she said it without any conviction behind her words.

She reached the wall of glass that looked out from the house onto the roiling whitecapped sea. The rain battered against the windows; the waves pounded the casements below. She really did feel as if she were on a ship—trapped—lost at sea. Karen wanted to get out of this house. No, it wasn't what she expected. Not at all.

"You'll love it on the Cape, darling," Philip had promised. "We'll be there, out on the deck, admiring the uncanny light. You and me and Jessie . . ."

She is going to kill me.

Just like Lettie Hatch killed her stepmother, ninety-nine years ago this fall.

In this very house.

This very room.

And Lettie had been Jessie's age, too. Just sixteen, going on eighty-seven. And just as withdrawn and moody and eccentric. The villagers had called Lettie Hatch "Ghost Girl" because she rarely ever left this house. The kids around town called Jessie "Spook" for precisely the same reason.

Even on the most glorious day this summer,

Jessie had stayed indoors, sitting at the old rolltop desk overlooking the bay, writing in her leather-bound journal with her small, cramped penmanship. Her fingers and the sides of her hands were permanently stained with blue ink.

"Are you hungry?" Karen asked, turning around now to look at the girl. "I can make us some sandwiches—"

But Jessie was gone.

Up to her room. Karen could hear her footsteps now, above her head, across the ceiling.

She's getting the axe.

"Stop it," Karen scolded herself again.

She's getting the axe and will be back here soon.

"Stop!" she nearly shouted.

But she couldn't deny the terror. She'd felt it ever since she'd found Lettie Hatch's journal sealed up in the wall of the old house, forever solving the nearly century-old mystery of who had killed Congressman Horace Hatch and his lovely young newlywed wife, Sarah Jane. They had been hacked to death right here, in this very room. Blood was everywhere, the newspapers had reported. Whoever had done such a vile deed had evidently enjoyed their task, smearing the blood all over the walls, drawing flowers and stars and happy faces with it.

It was Lettie Hatch who did it. The daughter. And I have the evidence of it. The proof.

The girl had confessed it all to her journal, then hidden the book inside the wall of the house, where it sat untouched for nearly one hundred years—until Karen discovered it, quite by accident, earlier this summer. Speculation had always centered around Lettie Hatch, with the villagers certain that the "Ghost Girl" had done in her father and his new bride in a fit of jealous pique. Lettie's guilt had seemed assured when, in the middle of that following winter, she jumped off the pier and drowned herself in the cold green waters of Provincetown Harbor, the pockets of her dress filled with rocks.

But no one had never known for sure.

Until now.

Lettie Hatch really did do it—and right here, in her own handwriting, she told the whole story, with all her twisted, perverse thoughts and dreams, and atrocious adolescent poetry filled with images of rage and death.

> *The moonlight beckons*
> *And blood is spilled*
> *As the sea keeps time*
> *With unceasing fury*

"That's quite the find you've got there," her friend Bobbie had told her, indicating the old journal. "What are you going to do with it?"

She had sworn Bobbie to secrecy. She could trust Bobbie—one of the few people in town that Karen had met during these last few months whom she felt she could really trust. She couldn't even trust her husband with her discovery. Philip would take it from her. It would be his find. She could see the headlines now:

BEST-SELLING SUSPENSE AUTHOR
SOLVES MYSTERY OF LIZZIE HATCH

"I'm going to write a book about it," Karen replied. "It's going to be my big breakout. My chance to make it big on my own."

"I agree with you, honeybunches," Bobbie had told her. They were sitting out on the deck a few days before, when the sun was shining and the sea was as calm and still as a sheet of shiny green glass. "You're a writer, too, after all. And if you don't do something to break out on your own, you're always going to live in the shadow of Mr. Famous. Always be Mrs. Philip Kaye instead of Karen Donovan. Why give Philip what you found so that he can make the big noise with it? It's *your* story, not his."

Karen smiled wanly. Already she could feel some of the bold determination fading away. Was it the right thing to do, keeping the journal to herself? He was her husband after all—even if she'd barely seen him since they walked down the aisle six months ago.

"It's his house, Bobbie," Karen said. "I found it in his house. Philip has owned this place for twenty years. He bought it when no one else would touch it, when everyone said it was either haunted or cursed."

Maybe they weren't so far off the mark, Karen thought now.

Bobbie had scowled over at her, squinting into the sun. "When are you going to get with the program, little lady? It's your house, too. Haven't you heard of communal property laws? When you said, 'I do,' you got one-half of this place." Bobbie smirked. "And let's just assume that you found that journal in your half of the house."

"It really will get a lot of attention," Karen admitted with a shrug.

"Attention? Girl, you are going to go mano-a-mano with Katie and Matt over this. I mean, everybody grew up with the story of Lettie Hatch—or Lettie Hatchet, as we call her here in New England." Bobbie laughed, starting to sing the familiar jingle: "Little Lettie and her Hatchet, she swung it hard and let 'em have it!"

Karen laughed, finishing the rhyme. "She looked around and there she saw, the heads of both her maw and paw."

Except Sarah Jane Hatch hadn't been Lettie's maw.

She'd been her stepmother, just seven years older than Lettie.

The exact same age difference that existed between Karen and Jessie.

"You have to admit the parallels are pretty creepy," Karen said to Bobbie.

Her friend was pouring them margaritas straight out of the blender. "Yeah, and the creepiest of them all is that little Spook you got in that house."

Karen had looked up then to see Bobbie gaze off toward the house. Behind the glass, Jessie was inside, hunched up over the rolltop desk, writing furiously in her journal. One more parallel between their story and Lettie Hatch's. Karen already knew the twisted thoughts Lettie had written. What might her strange stepdaughter be recording in *her* journal?

"I thought it was going to be such a lovely summer," Karen said wistfully. "Philip and I sitting out here, admiring the sea—"

"And instead you got me, a drag queen from Chicago," Bobbie said, laughing, settling down with his margarita. "I just don't get that husband of yours. Here you are, still practically on your honeymoon, and he's left you alone almost all summer with that repressed homicidal maniac of a daughter—"

"Oh, don't say that, Bobbie," Karen said, shuddering. "I've had such dreams—nightmares—ever since finding Lettie Hatch's journal."

"You've got to get yourself an agent, sweetheart," Bobbie counseled. "You are sitting on a gold mine. You can tell Lettie's story while setting it against your own. 'Is it happening again? Is the past about to repeat itself?' It will be brilliant!"

"You are freaking me out," Karen said, holding out her glass for a refill. Bobbie complied. "But you're right. I do need to find an agent."

Another crash of lightning lit up the house.

Where was Jessie? Had she come back downstairs?

I surprised her in the dark, Lettie Hatch had written. The words from her musty old journal had burned themselves into Karen's brain. *It was a stormy night and the sea was wild. She was wandering in the dark, alone and scared. She turned just in time to see me approach with the axe. Just then lightning flashed, and I'm certain that the glint of the axe coming at her was the last thing she ever saw. How thrilling it was to hear her scream! How delicious to feel the axe swing down and cut into her soft, mealy flesh!*

Not far from her, Karen heard the distinct creak of a floorboard.

"Jessie?" she called.

No answer.

"Jessie, where are you?"

Another creak. Karen was sure she heard another creak, even beneath the hard, driving rain upon the glass and the incessant crash of the sea against the wooden foundation of the house.

"Jessie!" she called. "Answer me!"

"Why do you call me by such a name?"

The voice was so plain, so real, so terrible, coming out of the darkness. Karen stood in utter stillness, unable to move, frozen by her terror.

The meager candlelight from the table picked out the vague shape of a girl in a long dress, with hair falling past her shoulders, moving toward her through the shadows.

"Jessie?" Karen rasped.

"Come now, Sarah Jane. You know my name. You know who I am."

"No," Karen said, shaking horribly now.

"Say my name, Sarah Jane. Tell me who I am!"

"No!" Karen screamed, falling to her knees.

Lightning flashed. She saw the glint of the axe in the girl's hands, raised up over her head.

"No!" she screamed again. "No!"

More light. But not lightning this time. Harsh, blinding white light shone directly into her eyes.

"What's wrong with you?" came another voice.

She recognized it as Jessie's. Beyond the brilliant glare, Karen could see the girl approaching, a flashlight in her hand. She wore her usual blue jeans and her hair was tied back in a ponytail.

"What are you screaming about?" Jessie asked her contemptuously, standing over her now.

Karen got to her feet, her heart still shuddering in her chest and her ears. "I thought I . . . I . . ."

"Saw a ghost?" Jessie laughed, a brittle little sound. "Lettie Hatch, maybe?"

Karen glared at the girl.

"Really, Karen, I thought you weren't frightened of such things," Jessie said. "Didn't Daddy tell you not to listen to the legends that the locals will tell you? Or has that transvestite you've been hanging around with been filling your head with ghost stories? Really, now. My big brave stepmother, cowering on the floor."

Karen had to grip the edge of a table to balance herself. She counted her breaths, willing herself calm. She leveled her eyes with her stepdaughter's.

"First of all," she managed to say, "Bobbie isn't a transvestite. He's a performer. Second—" Her voice trailed off. What was her second point? *No, I haven't been listening to the tales of the locals. I've read it all, firsthand. In Lettie Hatch's very own journal!*

No, she couldn't tell Jessie that.

"Second," Karen said, finding her voice, "I had a momentary hallucination. That's all. I'm over it now."

Jessie was shaking her head, smirking. "Won't Daddy find it amusing?"

"He'll think it a silly trick of the lightning, which is all it was." Karen was fumbling in the dark at the cupboard, trying to pull out a drawer. She finally managed, withdrawing a candle. "We just need more light around here until the power comes back."

She struck a match and lit the candle. Holding

it up in her hand, she observed Jessie in the glow. The girl's face was pinched and bitter, an old woman despite her mere sixteen years. She was small but strong, with big hands, like a man's. When they'd moved into this house for the summer, Jessie had lifted heavy suitcases and boxes without any effort. Karen tried to tell herself she was being absurd to harbor any fear of the girl, but her hostility, her secretiveness, and most of all her strength left Karen plainly unnerved.

She's to be pitied, not feared, Karen thought, looking at her now. Jessie had no friends, no hobbies, no interests other than writing in her journal. When Karen first married Philip six months ago, she had tried to befriend the girl, actively tried to win her stepdaughter over, but she'd had no luck. Philip lavished the girl with gifts and she seemed, for her part, to adore him, but father and daughter spent precious little time together.

Not that Karen had had much time with her husband, either. Since moving into this house in late May, she had seen Philip a total of three times, each visit lasting less than four days. "They've extended my book tour," was all he said by way of explanation. "But you'll have a chance to get to know Jessie better."

Karen's heart was still racing from the hallucination. Finding Lettie Hatch's journal had been both a blessing and a curse. A blessing because, as Bobbie pointed, it could be her ticket to success. A curse because it made her jump at every sound, see things that really weren't there, and suspect all sorts of crazy things about Jessie.

There once was another lonely, unhappy girl in this

house, Karen thought. *A girl who hated a new young stepmother who dared to take her father away . . .*

A girl who wrote strange poetry in her journal . . .

Poetry of death and rage . . .

Karen walked up behind Jessie, carrying the candle. The girl was staring out into the storm, watching as if mesmerized the waves crashing against the house.

"Jessie, let's have something to eat," Karen suggested. "Maybe we can even pull on our raincoats, brave the storm, venture into town . . ."

The girl turned slowly to look at her. Something in her eyes made Karen pull back. There was a darkness there, darker than usual. Jessie looked straight at her, but they weren't really looking at her. It was as if she were looking at something else . . .

"Brave . . . the storm?" the girl asked dreamily.

"Yes," Karen offered. "What do you say?"

Jessie moved her eyes back to the ferocious sea. "An unceasing fury," she whispered.

Karen felt the fear rise again in her throat. "What did you say?"

"The sea keeps time," the girl replied, her voice far away, "with unceasing fury."

It wasn't possible. Lettie Hatch's journal hadn't left Karen's possession since she found it. Even now it was locked in her bureau upstairs, and Karen held the only key. There was no way Jessie could have read it.

So how would she know the words to Lettie's poem?

Dear God!

Karen stared over at her stepdaughter.

They call it possession, don't they?

The spirit of the dead taking hold of the living . . .

"No," Karen murmured, moving away from the strange, silent girl staring out into the storm.

It's not possible. It's all just a coincidence . . . Or else it's not Lettie's poem at all, it's a poem I'm not familiar with, a poem they teach in schools, so that Jessie would know it and this silly stupid idea about possession would be—

The lights suddenly flickered back into life.

"Oh!" Karen shouted, startled.

Bright yellow light filled the room. Voices boomed out of the television set, which came on in the middle of some inane sitcom, the laugh-track cackling loudly and absurdly.

But Jessie didn't move from her position staring out the window at the roiling sea.

"Finally," Karen said, aware of how much her voice is trembling. "Let's just hope the power doesn't go out again . . ."

Her eyes were drawn by something across the room. Something on the floor. She took a few steps toward it, blinking, her eyesight still unaccustomed to the light. It was the very spot on the floor where moments before she had cowered, convinced the ghost of Lettie Hatch stood over her, holding her axe over her head.

The spot where she had looked up, only to see it was really Jessie.

Karen gasped.

On the place were she had fallen, the place

where she had braced herself against the dead girl's upraised axe, there was blood.

A puddle of bright red blood.

And with it, drawn with a hasty finger, were flowers and happy faces.

Karen Donovan screamed.

BOOK YOUR PLACE ON OUR WEBSITE AND MAKE THE READING CONNECTION!

We've created a customized website just for our very special readers, where you can get the inside scoop on everything that's going on with Zebra, Pinnacle and Kensington books.

When you come online, you'll have the exciting opportunity to:

- View covers of upcoming books
- Read sample chapters
- Learn about our future publishing schedule (listed by publication month *and author*)
- Find out when your favorite authors will be visiting a city near you
- Search for and order backlist books from our online catalog
- Check out author bios and background information
- Send e-mail to your favorite authors
- Meet the Kensington staff online
- Join us in weekly chats with authors, readers and other guests
- Get writing guidelines
- AND MUCH MORE!

Visit our website at
http://www.kensingtonbooks.com

More Books From Your Favorite Thriller Authors

More Nail-Biting Suspense From Your Favorite Thriller Authors

More Thrilling Suspense From
Your Favorite Thriller Authors